mike whicker

Dancing for the Gestapo

◊ ◊ ◊

Dancing for the Gestapo

Dancing for the Gestapo

a novel

by
mike whicker

a Walküre imprint

This is a work of historical fiction

ISBN: 978-1735609829

printed in the United States of America

For

Karen Alderton

Shield Maidens

In Norse lore, female warriors so fierce and skilled with weapons that they were welcomed to accompany the Viking men into battle. The Shield Maidens were revered by the Northmen for their savagery.

—Merriam Webster's Collegiate Dictionary

Part 1

Chapter 1

A singular lunch

Berlin—March 1942

Admiral Wilhelm Canaris, the head of German Military Intelligence—the *Abwehr*—where Erika Lehmann currently worked, ordered her to report for a briefing at 1330 hours about an assignment in America.

Erika was an operative of Abwehr making her a spy for Nazi Germany.

Before reporting to Canaris that afternoon, she decided to find a quick noon meal and remembered the government cafeteria in the building that housed the Geheime Staatspolizei—the state police—a few blocks away. She distractedly walked down the Tirpitz-Ufer, not noticing the cold. What assignment had they for her in the United States? *Probably something in Washington,* she thought, flirting with congressmen or Pentagon officials. Getting them drunk and keeping an open ear. Letting them have their way with her if it fit the needs of the assignment, asking them innocent, well-phrased questions during the heat of the moment, then moving on to someone else. Or picking a target after she had been on the scene awhile and then latching on for an extended period, as she had done on her last assignment with Henry Wiltshire of the British secret service in London. She was always a little apprehensive until she knew the details.

The street where she walked was ornate with posters. *Germans love posters,* Erika thought. She ignored most, glanced at some. One pictured a wholesome farm girl nursing a baby. It extolled the virtues of motherhood and large families. Another poster promoted the Hitler Youth with a drawing of a sturdy, blond boy in a brown uniform. A ghost-like image of Hitler hovered over the boy's shoulder. *Jugend dient dem Führer* the poster preached—Youth serve their Leader. Still another poster had an image of a creature half man and half rat with the words *Die Juden sind unser Unglück*—The Jews are our Bad Luck.

Her thoughts changed as she passed by the building of the Seehaus. The Seehaus monitored foreign radio broadcasts. Not long after she and her father returned to Germany from the United States two years before the war, Dr. Goebbels suggested to Karl Lehmann that his daughter's fluency in English and French could be of service to the Fatherland translating BBC broadcasts, which were transmitted in both languages. It was her first paying job.

Erika's time at the Seehaus and an extraordinary gift for languages enabled her to learn Russian proficiently, along with some Danish and Slovak. She enjoyed her time at the Seehaus, especially the time spent with a handsome young man who had studied at the Sorbonne and who listened in on French broadcasts. It was a busy time for Erika, but she somehow successfully juggled university studies during the day, work at the Seehaus four evenings a week, and rendezvous with her fun-loving Seehaus co-worker.

Soon she came upon the building at 8 Prinz Albrechtstrasse that housed the offices of the Geheime Staatspolizei. Erika had often joked to friends that Germans have a born need to abbreviate. The Schutzstaffel was commonly shortened to SS, and the Abwehrabteilung where she was an agent was commonly just Abwehr. As far as the Geheime Staatspolizei was concerned, it was more commonly referred to as the Gestapo.

Erika referred to the Gestapo as *Himmler's beady-eyed perverts,* and she had her reasons for hating them. Hated but not feared. Erika Lehmann, daughter of a friend of Adolf Hitler and a valued Nazi spy, had no reason to fear the Gestapo. She passed through the door and showed her identification to a pair of solemn men stationed just inside. The men recorded her name and identification number in a notebook. Both men wore business suits. Unlike most of the organizations along the Tirpitz-Ufer and Bendlerstrasse, the Gestapo was not a branch of the military, so much of the time civilian clothing was the norm for Gestapo personnel.

The cafeteria that served the building was located toward the rear of the first floor. The room was crowded but the food line short; most of the diners were already seated. Erika found the stack of trays and followed a short man with a limp down the food line. From an obese, perspiring woman behind the counter Erika accepted a thick slice of ham, boiled potatoes and cabbage, strudel, and a large chunk of heavy rye bread torn from a loaf, not sliced. At the end of the counter another woman handed her a large glass stein of beer. The man in front of her was Gestapo, and not required to pay. The female cashier looked quizzically at Erika, wondering if she should ask for payment. Erika relieved her anxiety by asking how much, then paying her.

All tables were occupied. In Germany, if there are no empty tables in a public place of eating or drinking, etiquette requires those already seated to allow others to join them if their table has empty seats. Erika spotted a table with four chairs, only three of which were occupied. She walked over to that table where sat three men.

"Gestatten Sie?" *(Would you allow?)* she said politely with a smile. The men looked up and stared at her for a long moment saying nothing. Finally one spoke.

"Natürlich, bitte," *(Of course, please)* said the one who looked to be the oldest. He opened his hand toward the empty chair. She thanked the man and sat down.

Erika guessed the man who had offered her a seat to be around forty years old. The other two looked somewhat younger, perhaps early to mid-30s. Both of the younger men wore eyeglasses—one with heavy wire rims, the other pince-nez. Erika knew that many members of the Gestapo had various physical flaws (poor eyesight being a common one) that kept them from military service. The older man, despite a mangled left ear that looked like someone had dealt severely with in the past, had no obvious physical defects that could be observed across a lunchroom table.

The three men made no effort to introduce themselves or to disguise their gawking as she began to eat. She was unconcerned and ate in silence, occasionally looking up and smiling politely. *Keep your enemies close, and never let them know what you're thinking,* her father had told her. She took a drink of beer to wash down a bite of potato and decided to break the silence herself.

"They say a light snow is due us tomorrow," she said, scanning the face of each man.

The two younger men continued to stare at her and did nothing to acknowledge her attempt at table chat. Finally, the older man nodded slightly and said, "Ja, that is what they are saying." He gruffly introduced the other men. "Fräulein, this is Herr Schroetter and Herr Pagel. My name is Kerling. And your name Fräulein?"

"Erika Lehmann." She offered her hand to each man and exchanged a short handshake. Although her father was well known in the Reich, the name Lehmann was not uncommon in Germany. There was no reason for people to make the connection to her father.

"Are you new in this building, Fräulein?" Kerling asked, forcing a smile that revealed a colorful assortment of teeth. One was silver, the rest various shades of rotting brown and yellow.

"No, I am afraid I am not lucky enough to work among such handsome men as I now sit with." As an Abwehr spy, Erika Lehmann was by necessity an expert actress and the ridiculous compliment sounded sincere. "I am a secretary at the OKW." The OKW stood for Oberkomando der Wehrmacht, the High Command of the German Army. The OKW was headquartered a few blocks away, down the Bendlerstrasse. In a roundabout way she did work for the OKW, the only branch of the German military bureaucracy to which Abwehr was answerable. In fact, like many Abwehr agents, her identification card showed the seal of the OKW, not the Abwehr, so the secretary ruse was a common one used when someone inquired of her employment.

"Ah, and how long have you worked there?"

Erika did not have to answer these questions, but she did not mind; her answers would of course be lies anyway, and she even considered this questioning at the hands of the dreaded Gestapo a bit of comedy that took her mind off the meeting with Canaris. She did not hold back a slight smile as she looked down and stabbed a bite of ham.

"Oh, let me see . . . a couple of years or so."

Kerling glanced at the man named Schroetter, the one with the pince-nez glasses. The glance from Kerling was an obvious signal and Schroetter promptly excused himself. Erika knew why he was leaving.

"And what is it you do there exactly?" Kerling continued.

She looked him directly in the eyes and, leaning over the table, answered sotto voce, "It is my job to give the generals oral sex, but please don't tell anyone. They are all married you know, and you wouldn't believe the complaining that goes on among their wives about my job."

The younger man's face grew dark and he started a sentence, "I suggest . . ." Kerling cut him off with a quick glare then turned to Erika. He searched her face for a moment then a slight smile appeared on his lips.

"Tell me, Fräulein, do you enjoy your work?"

She smiled. Perhaps she had underestimated this one. "The hours and the pay are not bad Herr Kerling, but the job requirements are so rigid."

Kerling stared blankly at her for another moment, then he burst out laughing so loudly that it drew glances from people at surrounding tables. He looked at the other man who remained somber. Kerling leaned over and slapped the man on the back.

"Ha, a good one. Hey, Pagel?" Kerling shouted, extorting the man to enjoy the young woman's humor. Pagel's expression remained unchanged. "The Gestapo loves a good joke, right Pagel? Tell the Fräulein a joke, Pagel," Kerling coaxed.

The morose Pagel said none came to mind.

"No?" Kerling was still loud. "Let us see . . . yes, I have one." He turned to Erika. "What are the four shortest books ever written?" Erika patronized him with a smile and shook her head. The man answered his own question, *"A History of Scotch Charities, Virginity in France, The Morals of the American Negro,* and the shortest book ever written, *A Study of Jewish Business Ethics."*

Kerling roared at his own joke and even the stone-faced Pagel grinned. Erika smiled politely. She thought it humor that fit the Gestapo.

Kerling continued to laugh loudly as Schroetter returned to the table and handed Kerling a small piece of paper. Schroetter had first checked with the men at the front entrance who had recorded the information from Erika's identification card when she entered the building. Schroetter then took an elevator to an office on the fifth floor. One of the Gestapo section agents on duty punched the woman's identification number into a teletype connected to the OKW clearance office. The piece of paper he now handed Kerling had come spitting back out a few moments later.

Kerling glanced at the note:

Anfang.
Es ist verboten, diese Person zu befragen.
Im Falle der Verhaftung, sofort freilassen.
Wenn sie im Ausland Hilfe verlangt, ist den Befehlen dieser Person unbedingt folgezuleisten.
Weiter Fragen ans OKW weiterleiten. Ende.

Start.
Questioning this person is forbidden.
If detained, release immediately.
On foreign soil follow orders of this person if your help is requested.
Further questions - contact OKW. End.

Kerling gazed at the young woman who ignored his stares while she finished what she wanted of her meal. This note told Kerling only one thing: this was no secretary. Further questions were forbidden and he knew the importance of following orders in the Third Reich.

The young woman rose from her seat, thanked the three men for their courtesy, and left them for her meeting with Wilhelm Canaris.

Chapter 2

A Job for Zhanna

8½ years later
Arlington, Virginia, USA
Thanksgiving Day—Thursday, 23 November 1950

The Shields Maidens met for Thanksgiving dinner at the Lili Marlene Café in Arlington, just across the river from Washington, D.C. The 'Shield Maidens' was the codename for an elite group of female Central Intelligence Agency operatives whose normal field of operations was Europe, and especially Germany. Three of the Maidens were born in Germany and worked as spies for Abwehr—the Reich's German Military Intelligence—during the war. Those women were Erika Lehmann (the team leader), and the Fischer sisters, Kathryn and Stephanie. The fourth member of the group was Zhanna Rogova, a Russian who had served during the war as a sniper for the Red Army and later an assassin for SMERSH. Finally, there was the most recent member of the team, Amy Radu, a Gypsy who was half Jewish and had been trained as an assassin by Kidron, a sub-agency of the Israeli Mossad.

Technically, Erika owned the Lili Marlene, as it was her money that bought it for her friend Angelika Egermann. Angelika had lived in East Berlin and helped Erika and Zhanna escape back to the Western sector of that divided city during a recent mission. Angelika was forced to flee with them, and Erika brought her to the States where her friend would be safe.

The café was closed today so the women had the place to themselves. Angelika, who spoke little English, knew nothing about Thanksgiving as there was no such holiday in Germany. Yet, her café cook was a German American who was born in the U.S. Her cook prepared the meal.

So now all the Shield Maidens and Angelika sat around a table in the empty bar/restaurant enjoying turkey, stuffing, mashed potatoes and gravy, freshly made rolls, yams, and green beans. Pumpkin pie awaited them. All the Shield Maidens were in their late-20s or early 30s. Angelika was 44 years old.

The Maidens latest mission in Berlin where they escaped the Soviet sector with Angelika ended only last month. Erika asked the group if their CIA boss, Leroy Carr, had contacted them since their debriefings ended.

"Yes," Kathryn answered. "I'm returning to my teaching job at the Naval War College in Rhode Island. I leave Monday."

Carr tried to keep his agents busy between assignments.

"I return to the Farm that same day," Stephanie said. The 'Farm' was a secret CIA training facility located deep inside Camp Peary, Virginia. Stephanie served as an instructor for plebe CIA wannabe agents.

"Amy, how about you?" Erika asked.

"Mr. Carr mentioned something about the CIA could use me translating documents in Romanian and Hebrew. I suppose that's what I'll be doing eventually but first he's sending me to an Army fort in Georgia for some classes."

All the Maidens were bi-lingual; some were polyglots. Erika spoke four languages fluently: German (her native tongue), English, Russian, and French. Zhanna Rogova spoke English, German, and native tongue, Russian. Both on the Fischer sisters spoke English and German. Amy was the only Shield Maiden who didn't speak German, but like Erika, she was fluent in four languages: English, Romanian, Polish, and Hebrew.

"Zhanna, has Leroy talked to you about what you'll be doing?"

"No."

The volatile Russian couldn't hold a job. Leroy Carr had gotten her menial jobs such as washing dishes in greasy-spoon diners around the Washington area, but none had worked out for more than a few days because Zhanna would lose her temper and get fired.

Erika thought for a moment, then addressed Angelika in German, "Angelika, until you learn English, you need a bartender who can translate English to German for you. What do you think about hiring Zhanna?"

Angelika had watched her friend Erika and the Russian kill four men during their escape from East Berlin and was apprehensive. Nevertheless, she trusted Erika and owed her life to both women. She also badly needed a bartender that spoke both languages.

"Wunderbar, Erika."

"Okay, I'll clear it with Leroy the next time I see him."

Chapter 3

In Carr's office

Washington, D.C
Four days later—Monday, 27 November 1950

It wouldn't take long for Erika to see Leroy Carr. The Monday after Thanksgiving weekend, he called her into his office at CIA headquarters on E Street in Washington. Carr was the Deputy Director of the CIA, second in command at the agency to only the Director who was appointed by the president.

"How was your Thanksgiving?" Carr asked her as she sat down.

"It was nice, Leroy. We ate at the Lili Marlene. It was closed so we had the place all to ourselves."

"That seems like a good place," Carr said. He and his wife, Kay, had attended the grand opening the week before.

"The grand opening you attended went well," Erika said. "The place was full that night. Of course, many people were there that night out of curiosity. The trick will be to keep them coming back."

Carr nodded. "I called you in to let you know the next steps for your Shield Maiden team. Kathryn is leaving today for Newport and her job at the war college. Stephanie also leaves today to resume her job as an instructor at the Farm. I'm sending Amy to Fort Benning for some classes. When she completes that duty, she'll work here in this building translating intercepts from Israel and Romania."

"I know all that, Leroy. They told me. What about Zhanna?"

"With Zhanna my options are limited. I cannot trust her with an important job like the others. She can't even hold down a job as a dishwasher. Last spring, I tried to place her at our sniper training facility at Fort Huachuca, but she screwed that up."

"Leroy, that was more her commanding officer's fault. He hates Russians, thinks all of them are fanatical communists, and overruled everything Zhanna wanted to do."

"Nevertheless, it's a pattern with her."

"I've found Zhanna a job," Erika said. "She can work as a bartender at the Lili Marlene, my café in Arlington. Until Angelika Egermann learns English, she needs a bartender who can translate for her."

Carr didn't have to think about it long. "Fine. Maybe working at your place will keep Rogova out of trouble. Tell her the CIA can't continue to put her up at the Mayflower. It's the most expensive hotel in D.C. If she's gainfully employed she has to find her own place."

"She can stay with me and my daughter until she finds something."

"Alright, then that's settled."

"Leroy, you didn't order me here this morning just to discuss everyone's work situation. What's up?"

"There's a mole somewhere inside the Pentagon working for the Soviets."

"Are you sure?" Erika asked.

"We wouldn't be talking about this if I weren't sure, Erika. Report back here at 0900 tomorrow for a briefing. Sheila will join us."

Chapter 4

An old flame

Washington, D.C.
Next day—Tuesday, 28 November 1950

When Erika Lehmann reported to Leroy Carr's E Street office this morning, the red-haired Sheila Reid was already there. The two women hugged. Sheila was a member of the U.S Army and was a former Shield Maiden before being promoted to lieutenant colonel and transferred to the Pentagon where she now headed her own department that oversaw Russian intrigue in Poland.

"How's your restaurant doing, Erika?" Sheila asked. She had attended the grand opening last week.

"Slow since the grand opening. Keep encouraging your Pentagon pals to try it. It's so close to the Pentagon it would be handy for lunch. Angelika's cook makes some fine German dishes, and we've added hamburgers, cheeseburgers, and other sandwiches."

Carr interrupted. "Ladies, if you're finished discussing Erika's entrepreneur skills, may we get down to business?

"As I've told both of you, it's apparent there is someone inside the Pentagon disclosing classified G-2 (Army military intelligence) information to the Soviets. Within the past two months, the Russians have arrested three G-2 assets working behind the Iron Curtain—one in the Soviet sector of Finland, one in Hungary, and one in Czechoslovakia. All three of these men where native to those countries with uncrackable covers. G-2 is headquartered in the Pentagon, as you know. The information has to be coming out of there.

"We don't know how many more names the Soviets have been given. The White House has tasked us with uncovering the mole and given it high-priority status. Right now, we have little to go on. We don't know if this mole is an American traitor or a foreign agent the Russians have somehow managed to imbed at the Pentagon."

Carr now looked at the lieutenant colonel. "Sheila, you work with G-2 in the course of your duties. Any ideas on where to start?"

"I do work with G-2 but only on occasion, Leroy. Mostly I work with the Air Force advising them on aerial reconnaissance of Poland. I give them coordinates of where and what we need aerial photos of, send it up the ladder, and they carry out that assignment. G-2 has offices spread out all over the Pentagon, and I deal with just a select few of them. There are many hundreds of G-2 personnel that work at the Pentagon I have never met."

Carr could understand that happening within the walls of the largest building on earth that employed over 20,000 people and housed myriad organizations.

"Erika, how is your old flame, Max Hodge?" Carr asked.

The question took her by surprise. Max Hodge, the younger brother of Leroy Carr's former righthand man, Al Hodge, worked at the Pentagon. Erika had dated Max briefly last spring.

"I don't know, Leroy. I haven't seen Max since March."

"I want you to get back together with him."

Erika liked Max but see didn't see the point. "Leroy, Max is a civilian and has only a Level 2 clearance. He doesn't see anything top secret. He's basically a paper pusher who relays non-secret memorandums from the higher-ups—generals, colonels, department heads—those sorts of people."

"Yes, but he's in the Pentagon. He might be able to help us in some way."

"By now, Max might have another woman he's seeing," Erika said. "He might even be engaged for all I know."

"He's neither. I had someone check." Carr handed her a piece of paper. "Here's Max's home phone number in case you've forgotten it. Contact him this evening."

[that evening]

Erika and Sheila met that evening for dinner and drinks at the Lili Marlene Café. When they entered, business was slow. Only three men sat at the bar, and only two tables of the twelve available were occupied. Zhanna Rogova tended bar so the two women took stools there, away from the three men where they could not be overheard.

"Hello, Zhanna," Sheila said. The Shield Maiden former colleagues had seen each other last week at the café's grand opening.

"Hello, Sheila," the nearly six-feet tall, jet-haired Russian said.

"How do you like working here?" Sheila asked.

"I like it," the former SMERSH assassin answered.

That was good news to Erika's ears. Leroy Carr was growing impatient with Zhanna's multiple failures at holding on to a cover job.

"Where's Angelika," Erika asked.

"In the back, helping the cook. Those four guys at that one table all ordered cheeseburgers and French fries."

"How has business been the past few days?" Erika asked.

"We have a decent lunch crowd, but those people order sandwiches and no liquor," Zhanna replied. "Angelika makes most of her money from alcohol sales. We need more people in here in the evenings." Zhanna spoke English well, but with a pronounced Russian accent.

A bell rang and the college student Angelika had hired as a waitress went to the back and brought out the cheeseburgers for the men.

Angelika, her help no longer needed in the kitchen, appeared and saw Erika. The two women hugged.

"Who is your friend?" Angelika asked in German.

"Das is Sheila. Sie spricht deutsch (She speaks German)."

Sheila and the former East Berliner exchanged greetings. The rest of the conversation with Angelika was in German, which Zhanna also spoke.

"Zhanna," Angelika said. "Whatever Erika and her friend order tonight is on the house."

Erika broke in. "We insist on paying, Angelika. I will never come here for free food and drinks."

The menu was written on a chalkboard at the end of the bar. Besides the popular American sandwiches, each day had a special-of-the-day German offering.

"Zhanna," Erika said. "I'll have the German special and a glass of Yuengling."

"I'll have the same," Sheila said.

The German special was two bratwursts, sauerkraut, and a potato dumpling that came in a bowl of beef broth.

Angelika vanished into the kitchen to help her elderly cook once again.

Zhanna poured their beers then the three women switched back to English.

"What brings you two together?" Zhanna asked. "Or it just sisterhood?"

"Leroy Carr is convinced there is a undercover mole in the Pentagon and Sheila and I have been asked to work together to bring him to the surface," Erika replied. "Sheila and I are going to request that you be brought into this assignment."

"What can I do?" Zhanna asked.

"I don't know yet, Zhanna, but I have some ideas. The mole has to be either an American traitor or a Russian plant. If he's a Russian plant, there is potentially a lot you can do."

"I like this job, Erika. I feel peaceful here helping Angelika. Will I have to quit?" The former SMERSH assassin asked.

Her statement pulled at Erika's heartstrings. Here stood a woman who had been awarded the highest medal bestowed by her homeland during the war because of her incredible record as a sniper. The Hero of the Soviet Union Medal lanyard had been placed around her neck by Stalin himself. German troops serving on the Eastern Front feared her so much they gave her the sobriquet 'Black Witch' because of her raven hair. Now she worked for peanuts tending bar in America after being fired or quitting every job Leroy Carr had found her, even menial jobs such as a diner dishwasher.

"No, Zhanna. Just the opposite. You working here could be important to the assignment." Erika hesitated but knew she had to tell Zhanna, "Leroy is canceling your reservation at the Mayflower. You'll stay with me and Ada (Erika's 9-year-old daughter) at our apartment until you can afford a place of your own."

◊ ◊ ◊

[later that evening]

Max Hodge relaxed in his favorite chair with a bottle of beer as he listening to the weekly Sam Spade detective capers on the radio. Howard Duff voiced Sam Spade, and his faithful secretary was voiced by actress Lurene Tuttle. Max especially liked Tuttle's character as the effervescent but always confused secretary.

About twenty minutes into the half-hour show, the knock on his door sounded. When he answered, Erika Lehmann stood there."

"Hello, Max," she said.

Chapter 5

The dead drop

Arlington, Virginia
Next day—Wednesday, 29 November 1950

"It was quite a surprise to see you last night, Erika," Max Hodge said. The two sat at a table having lunch in the Lili Marlene. "You disappeared last spring without a word so I assumed that was the end."

"I know, and I'm sorry, Max. As you know, I work for the State Department as a translator and I was sent abroad for several months. I returned just last week. The translators were told to not tell anyone where we were going."

Max Hodge did not know she was CIA, and she couldn't tell him because of his low-level clearance.

"Your visit last night was so brief we didn't really have time to talk," Max said. "You just asked me to meet you for lunch today." He looked around. "I never knew this place was here. How did you find it?"

"A friend of mine owns it. She just opened the place a couple of weeks ago." Erika said this even though she owned the café.

"Is that her behind the bar?"

"No, the bartender's name is Zhanna. The owner is Angelika. Angelika doesn't speak English, only German, so she's works in the back most of the time helping the cook. The cook is American but her mother was German so she speaks that language pretty well."

"That's got to be tough to run a business in the States and not speak English."

"She has help. As I mentioned, the cook can understand German, and Zhanna speaks it, as well."

"How is your daughter doing?" Max had met Ada.

"Fine. She likes her school and is a good student."

Max nodded. "That's important."

There ensued a moment of uncomfortable silence until Max finally said, "So where do we go from here Erika?"

"I'd like to start dating again, Max . . . that is if you want to."

The pleasant looking, 5'10" Max Hodge looked at her for a moment. "How about a movie tomorrow night? That new Hedy Lamarr movie, *Samson and Delilah,* is playing at the Palisade. It's been out a few months but I haven't seen it yet, have you?"

"No, but I'd like to. I love Hedy Lamarr. She's my favorite actress."

"Do you still live in your same apartment?"

"Yes."

"I'll check the playing times and give you a call. I'll pick you up."

After a few more minutes of chat, Max paid the bill. The total for two grilled cheese sandwiches and two RC Colas came to $1.25. He tipped the waitress a quarter.

[late that night]

After dark, a fog rolled into Washington from the Atlantic. Now three hours later the fog had thickened.

Like in a scene from a noir movie, a shadowy figure wearing a fedora and a trench coat with the collar pulled up around his neck walked out of the fog and dropped an envelope into a trash basket near the now deserted Lincoln Memorial.

A few moments later, after the man who made the dead drop had disappeared into the fog, another shadowy figure retrieved the envelope and walked away in the opposite direction.

Chapter 6

An old friend returns

Washington, D.C.
Next day—Thursday, 30 November 1950

Leroy Carr had just hung up his desk telephone on his desk when his secretary buzzed in on his intercom.

Carr pushed the button to answer. "Yes, Effie."

"Mr. Carr. Mr. Al Hodge is here to see you."

"Al?"

"Yes, sir."

Al Hodge for years had been Carr's righthand man, first with the wartime Office of Strategic Services, then until last summer with the CIA. Although Carr was technically Hodge's boss during those years, the two men were great friends and had worked together more like partners.

Hodge had resigned from the agency last year when he was offered a professorship at his alma mater, Brown University.

"Send him in," Carr said into the intercom.

When Hodge entered, Carr got out of his chair and the men exchanged a hearty handshake.

"Al, it's great to see you. What brings you here from the hallowed halls of the Ivy League?"

"Let's have a seat, Leroy."

After the two men were seated, Carr asked, "How are things going with your classes?"

"We began our Christmas break at the university. I'm off until after the New Year. I came down to visit my brother; I arrived here yesterday afternoon. When I called him last night, I told him I wanted to take him to dinner tonight. He said he couldn't because he was taking Erika Lehmann to a movie. What the hell is going on, Leroy? I thought all that was over. That woman will rip out Max's heart, put it in one of those fancy new home blenders and hit puree."

"Al, did you just say you're off for a month?"

"Yeah, why?"

"How would you like your old job back for a month?"

"What are you talking about?"

"You still hold your Level 7 clearance," Carr said. "Say yes then I can tell you all about it. You'll be able to keep an eye on Max. "

[that evening]

Leroy Carr and his wife, Kay, sat at a table in Jocko's Irish Pub in Annapolis. The couple lived in Annapolis and they had been regulars at Jocko's for years.

"Leroy, you seem chipper tonight," Kay said.

Kay Carr had gone on a mission with the Shield Maidens to South America in 1947 where she served as their Spanish interpreter. She held a CIA Level 4 clearance and Leroy could be candid with her on this issue.

"Good news, Kay. Al has agreed to be Erika's and Zhanna's handler on their current mission."

"Is Al back with the agency?"

"Only temporarily. He has a month off at Brown for Christmas break. Those Ivy League schools have long Christmas breaks because all the rich parents take their kids to Europe on skiing vacations in Switzerland or some long journey on their private yachts. That sort of thing."

"What brought Al back in?"

"Erika has taken up again with his brother."

Kay looked at her husband. "You must have had something to do with that, Leroy."

Carr downed a sip of his Guinness. "Guilty as charged."

[same evening]

Erika's eight-year-old daughter, Adelaide Faust, was with her 15-year-old babysitter who lived with her parents just down the hall from Erika's apartment. Erika had used the girl before and Ada (Adelaide's pet nickname) liked her. Erika Lehmann was a widow. He husband (Ada's father) was a German SS commando killed in the line of duty.

Now Ada's mother and Max Hodge sat five rows back from the screen sharing a large paper container of popcorn as the sultry Delilah (Hedy Lamarr) seduced Samson (Victor Mature) for her own gain. Max didn't know it, but he and Samson had a lot in common.

Chapter 7

An expensive dinner

Washington, D.C.
Next day—Friday, 01 December 1950

Erika and Zhanna had been ordered by Leroy Carr to report to his office at 9 a.m.

Zhanna was now living with Erika and Ada, so they took a taxi together. Ada was at school.

When the two women were cleared by Effie to enter Carr's office, they saw Al Hodge sitting in one of the chairs.

"Al!" Erika exclaimed. She approached him and tried to give him a hug.

"Stay away from me Lehmann," he said. "That goes for you, too, Rogova."

"Giving you a hug never entered my mind, asshole," Zhanna retorted.

Carr cut in quickly, "There is coffee and cups on the table in the corner. Help yourselves, ladies, then please take a seat."

The two women filled their paper cups and sat down.

"Al has agreed to a temporary assignment as your handler for your current assignment," Carr told the women. "I've briefed him on everything. He's up to speed."

"Just like old times, right, Al?" Erika said with a smile.

"I agreed to this for one reason, Erika," Hodge said. "I'm looking out for my kid brother."

"Max is a big boy, Al," Erika said before she took a sip of coffee.

"Not big enough for the likes of you. My brother is a good guy."

Zhanna asked, "Does anyone in this damn place have a cigarette?"

Hodge looked at Carr. "See what I mean, Leroy."

Erika, ignoring Al's comment, told Carr, "Leroy, I'll need a car."

"I thought you bought a car. What happened to it?"

"I sold it before the mission in Berlin. I couldn't leave it parked on the street for six weeks. This town has a law about that. Two weeks is all you get without the car being moved then they tow it away."

"You could have parked it in the agency's garage."

"I didn't know that. You never told me."

Carr sighed. "I'll have Effie consign you a car from our motor pool. Make sure you return it intact this time, and not a totaled piece of junk. From now on you and Zhanna will work with Al. Believe it or not, you two are not our only operatives. I have a lot on my plate with Korea and the Middle East. Al's old office in this building is still available and that's where he'll be during business hours. If you have to contact him after hours he'll be staying at the Mayflower. You'll follow Al's orders to the tee. Do we understand each other?"

"Of course, Leroy," Erika answered. "We always followed Al's orders when he was our handler."

Hodge looked at Erika and burst out laughing. "Lehmann, you've missed your calling. You should be doing stand-up comedy in nightclubs."

Carr said, "Al and I will powwow this afternoon, then you two can get together with him this evening and hash everything out."

"I'll meet you for dinner at the Mayflower," Hodge said.

"I have a better idea," Erika said. "Let's meet at the Lili Marlene Café in Arlington. It's on South Nash Street just across the bridge."

"I never heard of the place." Hodge said.

"It's new and has an upstairs storeroom where we can eat and talk privately," Erika said.

"Erika owns the place, Al," Carr added.

"You're telling me Lehmann owns a café?"

Erika said, "It's a German style café with good food and drink. Sort of like what you'd expect of an Irish pub. Zhanna is the bartender."

Hodge looked at both women. "This I have to see."

[that evening]

Hodge told Erika and Zhanna that he'd be at the Lili Marlene at 7 p.m. Erika arrived very early—at 5:30. Zhanna was already behind the bar.

The evening business was again slow. The few customers in the place had not ordered food so there was no need for Angelika to be in the kitchen helping the idle cook who spent her time cleaning. She joined Erika and Zhanna at the bar.

"Business is not good, Erika," Angelika said in German. "What am I going to do?"

"Many new businesses start out slowly, Angelika," Erika said in the same language. "We have to give it time."

"Our lunch crowd is steady, but our evening crowds where most of our liquor is sold is poor, as you can see. I can't pay the bills on the profit from lunchtime sandwiches. I had to send my waitress home early tonight."

Erika's father had left her an inheritance that was now deposited in a Zurich bank account. That's how she bought this place, which was formerly a humble neighborhood tavern.

"Don't worry," Erika said to her longtime German friend. "If necessary, I can withdraw more money to help us through the hard times."

"I set up a table upstairs where we can meet with Al Hodge," Zhanna said.

"Good," Erika said before she looked at Angelika. "I see the German special tonight is Jägerschnitzel. When our friend arrives, we'll eat upstairs. He'll be paying, so we'll have three of the German specials and the most expensive liquor you have. Did you bring in some Asbach?"

Asbach was an expensive German brandy from the Rhine River wine region.

"Yes," Angelika said. "I have one bottle."

"Okay, we'll convince our friend to buy the bottle for the table."

◊ ◊ ◊

Al Hodge arrived at five minutes before seven. He saw Erika sitting on a bar stool. Zhanna was behind the bar talking to her. He sat down on a stool beside Erika.

"Well, well," he said, "I never thought I'd live to see this day—Erika Lehmann and Zhanna Rogova in business together."

"Actually, we're not," Erika corrected him. "A friend of mine runs this place."

"Yeah, but you bought it," Hodge said. "Leroy told me all about it. Your friend was an East German you helped escape."

"Are you hungry, Al?" Erika asked.

"Yes."

"Let's go upstairs. We can eat there in private."

Angelika took over at the bar. If a customer ordered something in English she didn't understand, she had a cheat sheet of all the liquor and menu items Erika translated to German.

The upstairs area consisted of a large storeroom and a small studio apartment where Angelika lived. The table Zhanna referred to earlier was in the storeroom.

When they sat down, Erika said, "Al, I took the liberty of ordering dinner. Today's German special is Jägerschnitzel. I also ordered a bottle of brandy. I hope that's okay."

"That's fine," he said. "Now let's get down to business. Leroy and I had a long talk this afternoon about the apparent mole inside the Pentagon. I still don't know what my brother can do to help, but I agree this mission is top priority. Sheila has a much higher profile at the Pentagon and a much higher clearance level than Max."

"I agree that Sheila is in a better position to help us, Al." Erika said. "Yet, despite his low clearance level, Max is inside the Pentagon. That's why Leroy asked me to call him. You never know what scuttlebutt someone might hear."

"I understand that, Erika. This is not my first rodeo. I'm just asking that you look out for Max."

"I will, Al. I promise."

The gray-haired cook came to the room and told them their meal was ready. Since the waitress had been sent home early, Zhanna said, "Thank you, Bertha. We'll come downstairs and get them."

Erika and Zhanna left Hodge upstairs. They returned with the dinners, the bottle of Asbach, and a three-quarters full bottle of Stolichnaya vodka the Russian Zhanna grabbed off the bar at the last minute.

After a couple of bites, Hodge said, "This is delicious. What did you say this is?"

"It's Jägerschnitzel," Erika answered. "It's like Wienerschitzel but made from pork, not veal."

"Whatever it is, it's damn good."

"Tell your friends about this place, Al. You still have a lot of contacts in Washington."

"I will."

As they ate and drank, Hodge loosened up. The conversation during dinner mostly concentrated on funny stories from past missions when he was the Shield Maiden handler.

When everyone was almost finished, Erika went down to the kitchen and brought back three apple strudels to pad the cost. She handed the bill to Hodge.

"This can't be right," he complained. "Dinner for three people costing $49?" He looked the bill over more closely. "Eleven dollars for the vodka and $21 for a bottle of brandy? We only finished half of the brandy."

"You get what you pay for, Al," Erika said. "You can take the rest of the brandy home."

Zhanna added, "And don't forget a good tip for Bertha."

Hodge looked at the two women. "I should have known."

Chapter 8

Lorelei \ lõr-ê-lī *n* [German] : a siren of Germanic legend whose singing lures
Rhine River boatmen to destruction on a reef
—*Merriam Webster's Collegiate Dictionary: Tenth Edition*

Washington, D.C.
Next day—Saturday, 02 December 1950

Erika had been issued a black 1948 Dodge coupe. As ordered by Al Hodge, she arrived at 11 a.m. at the CIA's E Street Complex. When she entered his office, Sheila Reid was there.

Hodge's face was as bleak as a prison inmate's agenda. "Lehmann, you owe me dinner—more like two or three of them. The people in the bursar's office are going to shit when they see that bill from last night. You and that crazy Russian took me to the cleaners."

"I just wanted you to have a good dinner, Al."

"Bull shit."

Erika and Sheila stifled a grin.

"Here's the latest," Hodge said to Erika. "The Joint Chiefs of Staff are aware of our concerns about a mole at the Pentagon, and the CIA's directive from the White House to help G-2 investigate. General O'Malley of the Joint Chiefs oversees the Army G-2. I spoke with him this morning. He will make sure you are issued a Pentagon pass they call 'Visitor with Special Privileges.' That means you can pass into and out of the Pentagon 24 hours a day. Basically, you can talk to anyone. The only thing off limits is access to meetings of the Joint Chiefs but you can call on General O'Malley when he's in his office. Sheila, as a department head, already has that access."

"If O'Malley oversees G-2, then someone on his staff has to be the mole," Erika said.

"Exactly," Hodge replied. "Why do you think I'm working with him?"

"I'll go there tomorrow," Erika said. "Sheila can give me some pointers about where to start."

"She'll do that," Hodge said, "but you won't go there tomorrow. I've got a better way for you to start. The general and his wife are hosting their annual Christmas party at their home Tuesday night. They always have it on December 5th regardless of the day of the week. Their son, who the general said loved Christmas, was born on that day. The son died in the Pacific Theater during the war. My brother has never been invited, but I cleared it with the general who said he'd make sure Max got an invitation. You'll accompany him as his date for the evening. At the party will be several high-rankings members of G-2 and their wives. You can circulate and get to meet them."

"I'll be there, Erika," Sheila said. "As far as dress, it's a formal affair. Military officers will be in their dress uniforms and easy to spot. Max, as a civilian, will need a tuxedo and you an evening gown."

Hodge added, "You two will not acknowledge one another. Erika, we don't want any of the G-2 officers to know that you're friends with a lieutenant colonel who works at the Pentagon. General O'Malley is the only one who knows Sheila and you two worked together at the CIA. Those records have been sealed to all eyes other than the Joint Chiefs and, of course, the president. Even Hoover doesn't have access to those records."

Erika looked at Hodge. "Al, you know that sooner or later you're going to have to tell Max about me and the mission. If he hears any scuttlebutt he's not going to tell me unless he knows I'm working this assignment."

"Keep your cover as a State Department translator, Erika. If I tell Max about you it will break his heart to know the only reason you got back in touch with him is because you were ordered to. I'm going to meet with Max tomorrow. Leroy gave me the go ahead to tell him about the mission. I'll tell my brother that if he hears anything to let *me* know. I'm not going to mention anything about you. When this is over with, I expect you to leave my brother alone. I know you've heard the term *femme fatale.* That means a woman who brings disaster to any man she gets involved with. That's you. Your codename of *Lorelei* fits you perfectly."

Chapter 9

The Christmas party

Washington, D.C.
Three days later—Tuesday, 05 December 1950

It was mid-afternoon and Erika was getting her hair done at a salon in preparation for tonight's Christmas party.

She had seen Max Hodge twice since her meeting with his brother on Saturday. Sunday, Max and Erika took Ada to a park to play. Last night, he took Erika and Ada to dinner at a popular steak house not far from Capitol Hill.

Al had not told Max anything about Erika.

[that evening]
General O'Malley and his wife lived in a large, elegant lakeside home in an upscale area of Bethesda, Maryland, a 45-minute drive from downtown Washington. His salary as a four-star general and member of the Joint Chiefs of Staff allowed him to afford such a home located on two acres of ground with a private country club and golf course just a half mile away.

The Christmas party was set to begin at 7 p.m. Max, wearing his rented tuxedo, picked up Erika at her apartment at six. She wore a cranberry-red velvet evening gown with her blonde hair piled high on her head and a diamond choker on her neck. (The jewelry came from a CIA vault of confiscated valuables. She would have to return it to Al Hodge tomorrow.)

Max knew he had to be careful tonight. His brother had told him to keep an open ear, especially among the G-2 officers that would be attending, but he couldn't let Erika know. She was a government translator, and he knew she didn't have the proper clearance.

◊ ◊ ◊

When they arrived, at least twenty other cars and three limousines were already parked along the red-bricked circular driveway, or on the grass. A doorman took their coats and Max's hat as they entered the large main room already festooned with holiday garland. A 12-foot-tall Christmas tree ablaze with stringed blue lights stood at attention in one corner. Numerous flowered wreaths hung on the stone walls rising up from a Tennessee marble floor. A string quartet quietly played Christmas music not far from the open bar at the back of the room. Waiters and waitresses circulated among the guests carrying platters of either champagne or hors d'oeuvres.

"Geez," Max said to Erika. "It's not seven o'clock yet. I thought we were getting here early."

"You know the military, Max. They aren't going to be fashionably late to a four-star general's party."

Indeed, most of the men wore military uniforms. Erika spotted the uniform of a Navy admiral, a couple of rear admirals, and a Navy captain. One Marine general stood talking to an Air Force general. The Army contingent was the largest, made up of generals, full-bird colonels, and a couple of lieutenant colonels. Sheila Reid was one of the latter. Erika saw her and her husband, Ricky, talking to an Army brigadier general and his wife. Erika and Sheila locked eyes for a brief moment then both turned their heads away.

As far as civilian men in tuxedos, Max was one of only seven which included a senator and two congressmen.

Al Hodge had supplied Erika with a list of the names and photos of the officers affiliated with G-2. Five had been invited to the party. Those are the men she would seek out. Erika had noticed that Sheila had already corralled one of the G-2 officers.

A waiter approached and Erika and Max each took a flute of champagne from his silver platter. "I guess we should mingle, Max," she said.

"Right." He didn't know she was on basically the same assignment as he—keep an open ear. The problem was he had never done it before. Conversely, she was very experienced at sly but purposeful socializing. She had been doing it for years, dating back to her time as a German spy for Abwehr during the war.

Erika spotted a colonel whose face she recognized from the photos Al gave her. He was talking to a woman. She took Max's arm and subtly navigated him in that direction. "There's a couple, Max."

"That full-bird colonel? I don't know him."

"That's what mingling is all about," she said. "Introduce yourself first, then me as your date for the evening. Don't put on airs to impress anyone. Just be honest. That's all there is to it. And don't be nervous, Max. It's a party. The goal is to have a good time."

"Okay. Got it. As a translator for the State Department, I know you must have attended many of these things oversees."

As they approached, the colonel turned and looked at them. His military name plate read "Grainger."

"Colonel Grainger," Max said. "I'm Max Hodge. I work in procurement at the Pentagon. This is my date, Erika."

The colonel stuck out his hand and Max shook it. "It's nice to meet you Mr. Hodge, and you too, Erika. This is my wife, Agatha."

The colonel's wife smiled and shook both of their hands. "You look lovely, my dear. I love your gown."

"Thank you, Mrs. Grainger."

"And your necklace is exquisite."

"I'm afraid I don't own it. A friend loaned it to me for the evening."

"Regardless, it looks stunning on you."

A waitress came by with a tray of crab stuffed mushrooms. They all used toothpicks to stab one.

"So, Mr. Hodge," the colonel said, "I don't have any direct dealings with your department, but the procurement people have a fine reputation."

"Thank you, Colonel. I'm not the head of the department. That's Major Everett, but we have a lot of good people who work hard."

Erika said, "Mrs. Grainger. It must be exciting to have a husband assigned to the Pentagon."

"Yes, it is Erika. We have traveled so much overseas throughout the years it's nice to be back home in the States. And I've met so many interesting people. Tell me, what is it you do, my dear?"

"I'm a French, German, and Russian translator for the Department of State. I travel to Europe quite often with State Department representatives."

"Three languages besides English," the colonel said. "That's impressive."

"Thank you, Colonel. But I'm nothing special. We have several translators who can speak two or three foreign languages fluently."

"I understand," he said. "We have quite a group of talented translators we access at the Pentagon." Then he made a joke. "Most of them are spoiled Ivy League kids whose rich parents took them around the world when they were teenagers. They've never had to work a day in their lives, so they spent their college days learning languages."

Everyone smiled.

"I'm afraid I wasn't that lucky, Colonel," Erika said.

"No? How did you learn to speak those languages?" he asked.

Now was the time to give the G-2 officer something to think about, but she had to avoid anything Max didn't already know about her.

"Actually, I was born in Germany to a German father. English is my second language. I learned it from my British mother. During my childhood before the war, we often visited Paris. That's where I slowly picked up French—my mother also spoke that language (which was true). I studied Russian at the Charité in Berlin. I am an American citizen now."

It was true she had studied Russian at the famous university in Berlin, but she honed her Russian language skills with Zhanna Rogova. If Grainger was the traitor, he'd have the Russians check her story. If he wasn't, he'd have G-2 investigate her.

"That's fascinating," the colonel's wife said.

The G-2 colonel just looked at her.

The rest of the evening was spent talking to other couples but concentrating on the G-2 officers from Al's list. With each one, Erika delicately supplied them something to think about. Max never picked up on any of it.

Sheila did the same.

Chapter 10

An invitation from Zhanna

Washington, D.C.
Next day—Wednesday, 06 December 1950

Erika and Sheila had just sat down in Al Hodge's E Street office.

"Here's the necklace back, Al," Erika said as she handed him the long, purple velvet jewelry box. He opened it to check.

"Don't you trust me, Al?"

"I've dealt with you a long time, Lehmann. You're damn right I'm going to check. Knowing you, you might have put a dog turd in the box just to get my goat."

Once he was assured the diamond choker was in the box, he laid it down on his desk.

"Alright," he said. "Have you two compared notes on last night?"

Sheila said, "Yes, Erika and I got here about an hour ago."

"Then let me have it. How did it go?"

"Good," Sheila answered. "At least as far as I know. We both spent some conversation time with all five of the G-2 officers that General O'Malley invited. I told them the truth, that I worked for the OSS during the war. The natural curiosity of a G-2 man should propel him to check out my story."

"Erika. How about you?" Hodge asked.

"I had to be careful because your brother was with me so I couldn't mention anything about me Max doesn't already know. I told them I was born in Germany and a few other details but nothing about my time during the war. Like Sheila said, a G-2 officer should want to check us out. What we have to look for is one that doesn't."

Al nodded and replied, "Nick Stark, who works with us at the State Department, called me. He told me Colonel Grainger contacted the Assistant Secretary of State this morning about a background check on you, Erika. The assistant secretary funneled the request to Stark because he's in charge of State Department intelligence."

"Well, at least we know Colonel Grainger is not the traitor." Erika was glad. She liked the colonel and his wife.

"Before you leave, write down the facts you told Grainger and I'll relay them to Stark so he can confirm your story to the colonel."

[that evening]

CIA business about General O'Malley's Christmas party had been taken care of with Al Hodge that afternoon. With that behind them, Erika and Sheila met for a drink at the Lili Marlene. Zhanna was behind the bar.

"What is 'pro wrestling'?" Zhanna asked.

Erika asked in return. "Why do you ask about that?"

"A man was in here this afternoon with a friend," Zhanna replied. "They had a couple of beers at the bar and started talking to me. One of them said he was a pro wrestling manager."

"Pro wrestling is an entertainment," Sheila said. "Most people think it's all rehearsed, not real like boxing."

"He gave me three tickets to a match Friday night," Zhanna told them. "One of the wrestlers is Russian. I want you both to go with me."

"I'll go," Erika said. "How about you, Sheila?"

"Sure. Why not?"

Erika smiled. Even though she and Zhanna were now friends, her introduction to the Russian sniper/assassin was anything but friendly.

Chapter 11

A Russian Senior Lieutenant

Flashback
Moscow
Late August 1945

For two hours, six people had sat crowded onto a wooden bench deep in the bowels of a brown brick building on the banks of the Moskva River. Three miles west of the Kremlin, the building had been a library before the war but was now one of three buildings in Moscow used by SMERSH, an acronym meaning "Death to Spies." SMERSH had served as the Soviet counter-intelligence arm of the Red Army since 1941.

Among the waiting group were four Germans, a Czech, and a Hungarian. Dressed alike in gray fatigues, all looked to be in their twenties or thirties and all were men except one of the Germans. A door opened and two SMERSH officers entered. One, a bearded major, walked a step ahead of a female senior lieutenant who held a clipboard. The major ignored the sitting group; the female lieutenant glanced at them with a look of satisfaction. All of the foreigners spoke Russian, but neither of the officers addressed them as they passed through another door.

"Did anyone recognize those two?" one of the German men asked in Russian.

Most in the group began shaking their heads until the Hungarian spoke up. "I don't know who the major is but the woman they call the Black Witch. This is our bad luck."

"What makes you say that?" asked the German.

"She is not right in the head. They say she kills for pleasure."

After a few minutes, the door the two officers had disappeared behind opened and the one referred to as the Black Witch smiled sweetly and politely asked the group to enter. They passed into a spartan room that had no windows, no furniture (not even a chair), no posters, and no photos or trimmings on the wall. The dim light came from a single, naked bulb hanging from a wire in the center of the ceiling. Here, underground, the walls were stone and the floor concrete. Only tic-tac-toe arrangements of steam and cast iron plumbing pipes crossing the ceiling kept the room from giving the impression that they had just entered an oversized sepulcher.

The female SMERSH agent directed the group to line up and face the major then took her place beside him. The major spoke.

"My name is Major Nikoleav. This is Senior Lieutenant Zhanna Rogova. We are both with SMERSH, an organization all of you have worked for or been affiliated with in various capacities since before the war ended. Now that the Japanese have surrendered to the Americans and the war is over, our national objectives have changed. The senior lieutenant and I have been assigned the duty to decide what capacity foreign nationals, like you, who have aided us during the war, can best serve the Union of the Soviet Socialist Republics in the future. We have held meetings with others like you for several days." The major turned to Zhanna Rogova. "Senior Lieutenant, conduct your roll call and briefing."

Her smile now gone, Rogova stepped up to the first man in line, one of the Germans. "Name and nationality!" she barked.

"Alrich Kranz, German," the man said nervously.

Rogova looked at her clipboard, found the name, and read the information to the major. "Kranz, Alrich. 32 years of age. A German Army prisoner of war who served in German Army Supply Group C during the invasion of our country. After his capture in Kiev, he gave us information about German Army supply routes and modus operandi."

Rogova continued down the line. The Czech and Hungarian were both Jews and anti-Nazi former university professors who had served as interpreters for the Russians after the take-over of their respective countries. The second German Rogova came to was a Luftwaffe radio operator on a Dornier Do-17Z bomber when the plane was shot-down over Belorussia. He had supplied the Red Army with German Luftwaffe radio code information. The next German was a captured SD officer who had given SMERSH names of German spies in Warsaw, all of whom were apprehended and shot after the Russians forced the Germans from that city.

Finally, Rogova stood in front of the lone woman in the group. "Name and nationality!"

"Erika Tanzer. German." Tanzer was Erika Lehmann's alias. She now worked for the American OSS and Leroy Carr had given her the task of infiltrating SMERSH with a phony backstory.

Rogova read to Nikoleav. "Tanzer, Erika. 27 years of age. Not a Jew, but a German dissident who was incarcerated with her parents at the German concentration camp Sobibór in Poland for their anti-Nazi political views. Parents were exterminated; Tanzer escaped the camp during the mass escape in October of 1943. She was hidden from the Germans by Polish resistance until the spring of this year when she made her way to Red Army lines and surrendered. Because of her hate of the Nazis and what they did to her parents, she offered to work against the Germans. For the duration of the war and since the war ended SMERSH has used her to translate interrogations of captured German soldiers. This report says this woman is multi-lingual – speaks German, Russian, English and French."

Rogova scanned the fit and pretty German with a look of delight. "You have many talents, don't you, Fräulein? You're one of the very few to ever escape from a Nazi concentration camp. You're beautiful and a blonde. Hitler would have promoted you as one of his perfect Aryan whores. And how is it you speak four languages?"

"That should be in my report, Senior Lieutenant."

Rogova laughed and then moved to stand menacingly close. Erika could feel the Russian's breath. Rogova was not unattractive. Jet hair as black as a raven's eye and her fit appearance could bring appreciation from both men and women. High cheek bones, sculpted nose, and dark brown eyes could lead one to consider her Greek. All this made her look younger than someone who had circled the sun thirty times. However, belying her sultry beauty was a scar impossible to overlook. A 1½-inch-wide scar fully circled her neck just above her uniform collar; a scar that looked less like it was applied by a knife and more like a severe rope burn. The hideous scar helped to heighten the menacing aura of Zhanna Rogova.

"I admire your spirit," Rogova stated in a pleasant voice. "However, that's not odd. It's been my experience that German sluts have fortitude.

But we break them all sooner or later. Yes, the information is in the report; still, I want to hear it from you."

Erika repeated her false background that she knew was in Rogova's folder. "My father was a professor of languages at university. He taught me Russian and French. For three of my Gymnasium years and for one of my university years my parents and I lived in the United States. Of course I had to learn English. My father taught at a college there on a fellowship for four years . . . ."

"Enough!" Rogova exclaimed when she tired of hearing information she already knew. The Soviet major, who had said very little and given the impression he deferred to the lesser-ranked Rogova, moved to the side as Rogova circled around behind the group, walked back to the first man in line, pulled her pistol and shot him in the back of the head. The deafening roar of the gun in the closed room made the other foreigners jerk in surprise, duck down, and cringe at the ear-splitting noise as the man fell heavily to the floor. Instead of falling forward, the force of the bullet exiting from his forehead made him reel backwards and brush against Rogova on his way to the floor, leaving blood on her pant leg. This seemed to amuse her. She looked down and smiled at the dead body, "Thank you for your service to Mother Russia, but we no longer need information about German Army supply routes."

Rogova looked at the major, thinking he might be amused at her joke, but his face remained as one seen in a waxworks. She walked back to stand behind the German woman and remained silent for a sadistic long pause. Erika expected death until she finally heard Rogova say, "I'll take this one, Comrade Major."

Zhanna Rogova's hotel—Moscow
Same evening—late August 1945

Erika had been ordered to report to Zhanna Rogova's hotel room. As soon as she entered the hotel lobby a bald man with shaggy, frosted eyebrows and a gray goatee approached. He was a scarecrow of a man—thin, like a beggar's wallet. He wore a dark brown, three-piece suit made of houndstooth tweed. If his garb would have instead been a long robe and peaked hat, anyone would have been convinced he was a wizard. Perhaps he served as a Russian version of a concierge but more likely he was security, Erika thought, if people like Zhanna Rogova lived here. The man politely offered his help and asked for her name.

"Erika Tanzer."

"Ah yes, Comrade Tanzer. Comrade Rogova is expecting you. If you don't mind, please sign in and I'll show you the way."

Erika followed him through the aesthetically unimpressive lobby to the main desk where she signed her name on a 2"x 4" card that already had her name typed at the top.

"Please follow me," said the wizard. He led Erika to the rickety lift and when they reached the fifth floor he walked her down the hall to a suite. He gently used the brass doorknocker. There was a delay and just as he lifted his hand to try again, the door opened. Answering the door was not Rogova, but a beautiful, extremely tall, red-haired, green-eyed woman wearing a dressing gown tied with a sash—the short gown revealing long and shapely legs.

"Comrade Rogova's appointment has arrived," the man announced.

The woman scrutinized Erika like a sultry witch sizing up Gretl for that evening's stew, then gave a hand motion for her to enter. The man left as the door closed. The room included a foyer, and without speaking the red-haired woman led Erika down a short hallway to a large living room area that included two sofas with four matching, cushioned chairs and a large, pentagon-shaped, oak coffee table. The windowed wall was covered with elegantly embroidered burgundy drapes; several lamp tables with expensive-looking vases and figurines sat underneath posh paintings and sculpted artwork hanging on the adjacent, light-brown plastered walls. The lavish suite failed to fit in with the simplicity of the hotel's exterior and lobby. Erika concluded this was intentional. It would be bad form to let the Russian public know their communist/everyone-is-equal government supplied such luxury to its henchmen, or henchwoman in this case. Erika could not stop herself from thinking she had just penetrated the jackal's lair.

Zhanna sat on one of the sofas thumbing through the American magazine *Life.* When Erika and the red-haired woman entered, Rogova abandoned the magazine to the coffee table in front of her.

"There you are," said Rogova as she stood up. Unlike the barefoot, red-haired Amazon, Rogova wore slippers with her jade-colored, knee-length, silk kimono with peacocks and yellow orchids that looked hand-painted. In the absence of her uniform collar, the ugly scar around her neck was even more demanding of the eye's attention.

"Thank you for coming, Fräulein Tanzer," Rogova said pleasantly. "Or may I call you Erika?"

Erika was slightly taken aback by Rogova's informality and the implication that reporting here was anything but mandatory. Being a pleasant hostess was not something the German expected from Zhanna Rogova. Erika answered, "If you prefer, that would be fine, Senior Lieutenant."

The Russian smiled. "Please, for tonight, call me Zhanna. And let me introduce my friend. This is Riika. She tells me her name is Finnish for 'peaceful ruler.' I like that." Zhanna then referred to the woman as if she were a travel souvenir. "I got Riika in Finland during the Lapland War in '44 and brought her home before I returned to the front. Riika, would you be so kind as to get our guest a sherry? And perhaps some caviar would be nice."

Rogova sat back down. "Have a seat, Erika . . . please. Make yourself comfortable."

Erika sat down on the opposite sofa. Riika returned with a silver platter. On it was the caviar and unleavened bread, a carafe of sherry and two small sherry glasses. She filled both glasses and handed one to Erika and one to Rogova. The Finn had yet to say a word. Erika emptied the small sherry with one gulp, an act that seemed to please Zhanna. Riika was quick to refill.

"Brava, Erika. Unfortunately, Riika does not drink. I'm afraid she is quite the . . . what is the term in America? –'stick-in-mud.' I know you must be familiar with the term, as you spent so much time in that country."

Erika replied, "'Stick-in-*the*-mud.' Yes, I've heard that expression." Erika suddenly got the impression she was being tested.

"Of course I know you're wondering about my scar. How can I put it . . . courtesy of your SS. Bestowed on me just one year ago during fighting in the Korsun pocket. My unit was surrounded and captured.

The SS shot or hanged all my male comrades immediately. As the only woman, I was lucky. The SS men kept me alive for a few days to satisfy their needs. By the time they got around to hanging me our forces to retake the village were almost upon them. I could hear shooting as they placed the noose around my neck. The SS enjoyed hanging people slowly and watching them jiggle on the rope. This turned out to also be to my luck. I'm sure they thought I was dead, and I was close to being so. The Germans were forced to flee, and our troops arrived in time to cut me down."

The unflinching German looked Rogova in the eyes. "So you consider being raped repeatedly for days and hanged slowly to be lucky?"

"I'm alive today because of it."

"I'd rather be dead."

Rogova ignored Erika's remark. "I speak English, by the way," said Rogova. "Not as well as you and not without an accent, but I can get by. Riika also speaks a bit of English. She's not fluent, but she can understand simple conversations if the speaker doesn't talk too fast."

Erika had no clue where any of this was going. The only reply that came to mind was, "That's good, Senior Lieutenant. About the English, I mean."

"I asked you to call me Zhanna for tonight."

"Pardon me . . . Zhanna."

"Wonderful. Have some caviar. It's Siberian, the best in my opinion. It goes nicely with the sherry."

Erika broke off a cracker-sized piece of the thin, unsalted hard-bread and used the silver knife to spread the delicacy. Zhanna did the same. Riika, now ignored by her mistress, stood aside like a butler, joining them in neither food nor drink.

"Don't hesitate to drink, Erika," Zhanna said as she finished off her glass. "It's good for you." Riika topped off both glasses. "Tell me more about your time in America."

"As I've told you . . . Zhanna, everything is in my file. But to say it again, I spent most of my teenage years in America when my father was offered a fellowship at an American university."

"You speak Russian with a German accent, but your file says you can speak English with an American accent. So I assume you credit that to living for some years in American?"

"Exactly. I didn't grow up in Russia. But because I spent many of my formative years in America I picked up on the American accent."

"And you learned much about American life and customs."

"Yes."

There were a few more questions about America and then Zhanna said, "So you want to volunteer to be a field agent. Can you fight or shoot a gun?" Erika told her no but that she would be willing to learn. Suddenly the Russian said, "Stand up and take your clothes off."

The German, who prided herself on being unshakable, nevertheless was surprised. "What?"

Rogova's warmth immediately vanished. "I believe I was clear with my request," she sneered. "Stand up and take off your clothes. The number of Russian women sent to your concentration camps and forced to undress and whore for your SS if they wanted to live another day is uncountable. So you have no right to be shocked or offended." Riika smiled seductively, sat down by Erika, and attempted to begin undressing the German. Erika jerked away and said, "I'll do it."

Doing her best to not give the Russian the satisfaction of knowing she was uncomfortable, Erika stood and began undressing, stopping at her undergarments. Rogova grew impatient and sensing this Riika stood behind the German and undid Erika's bra and pulled down her underpants.

"I can see that you are a natural blonde. At least that is one thing truthful about you. But I know you are deceiving us, and I will uncover your secrets." Rogova looked at the Finn, "Riika, it's time you appraise our guest."

On Zhanna's orders to "appraise" Erika Tanzer, Riika walked over to stand behind the German. The beautiful but imposing Finn stood at least six feet tall. From behind, Riika felt Erika's arms and back. The Finn kissed the German's neck and shoulders while caressing her buttocks. Riika walked back in front of Erika and felt her stomach and thighs. Zhanna watched intently.

"You're not blushing, Erika," the Russian commented. "Have you had women before?"

"Maybe I'm just frightened," Erika replied.

Zhanna laughed. "Somehow I doubt that. Of course if you really are afraid, you can stop Riika by telling me who you really are."

Rogova was right. Erika wasn't scared. "You already know everything about me."

"Really? I'm happy to hear that. You can't fight—that's what you claim."

"That's right. At least, I have never been trained. I can learn with the right teacher."

"Riika, what do you think?"

For the first time the Finn spoke. "This is not the body of a salesgirl," Riika spoke in Russian but with a heavy Finnish accent. "Her muscles are hard, like a tennis player. I've had tennis players."

"I competed in swimming and have been trained in gymnastics," Erika interjected. This time she was telling the truth. In fact, she had won awards in swimming, and many thought she was good enough to have competed for Germany in the 1936 Olympics, but at the time she and her parents lived in America.

"Thank you, Riika," said Zhanna. The Russian rose from the sofa, walked over and gave Erika a long, passionate kiss on the mouth. Erika did not respond, but with little choice she stood and waited for it to end. Suddenly, the German was sent reeling when Zhanna crashed a fist into her jaw. Erika flew backwards, fell to the floor and was immediately pounced on by Riika, who straddled her and began delivering blows of her own. Zhanna laughed as the Finn sent punch after punch to Erika's face.

Suddenly, Erika returned the barrage with a crashing blow of her own—one hard enough to send the Finn backwards and off of her. Erika quickly scampered to place Riika's left arm in a bone-breaking hold. "Fucking bitch!" Erika shouted. She increased the pressure until the Finn roared in what more resembled a wounded animal's growl than a woman's cry of pain.

Erika was more than willing, and intent, on breaking Riika's arm when Zhanna quickly moved in and kicked Erika in the ribs—the power of the kick worthy of any man. It forced Erika to gasp and relinquish her hold on the Finn. Erika avoided a second kick and flew at Zhanna. The two women fought for an exhausting time, knocking over lamp tables and breaking expensive figurines and a Grecian vase in the process.

Riika finally recovered use of her arm, came up from behind Erika and applied a choke hold. The women fell to the floor as Erika tried at the same time to breathe and break the woman's grasp. Riika bit Erika's shoulder, drawing blood. Zhanna moved in and crashed her knee into Erika's jaw, leaving her dazed and semi-conscious.

"That will do, Riika. Thank you." Both Zhanna and Riika stood up. Zhanna placed her foot on the half-conscious German's throat and stepped down, again choking her. "So you can't fight?" Zhanna jeered, breathing heavily. "I dare say it would be unwise to steal something from a German store if German salesgirls *can't* fight like you. I knew you were lying about who you really are."

Just before Erika was about to pass out, Zhanna removed her foot from her throat. As the German lie gasping, she coughed out, "Fight me . . . one at a time. I'll kick both . . . of your asses." Zhanna, bleeding from her nose and with a cut over her eye said, "Riika, you may continue."

The Finnish Amazon, whose swelling left jaw showed scrapes and already was turning blue, undid her sash and let her dressing gown fall to the floor. She wore nothing underneath. The Finn knelt down and began caressing the barely conscious German. Zhanna Rogova wiped her bloody face with a napkin from the caviar tray then returned to the sofa to watch.

Chapter 12

Sonderführer

Back to present
Washington, D.C.
Thursday, 07 December 1950

Two days after the soiree at the General O'Malley's home was Pearl Harbor Day. Leroy Carr had been summoned to a morning meeting at O'Malley's Pentagon office. Normally, if someone in government wanted to talk to Carr (the second man in command at the CIA), they would have to report to his E Street office. The only exceptions were if he was summoned by the White House, the Joint Chiefs of Staff, or a Senate or Congressional committee.

When Carr was escorted into O'Malley's large office by a major, the four-star general sat behind his desk. Another man, a colonel, sat in a nearby chair. Carr recognized Howard Grainger. They had never met, but it was the CIA's business to know everyone involved in any type of intelligence gathering for the United States. Carr knew Grainger was G-2 and he had been briefed by Al Hodge on the reports from Erika and Sheila Reid.

"Thank you for coming, Mr. Carr," O'Malley said. "This is Colonel Grainger. I'm sure you know what service he supplies us here at the Pentagon."

"Yes, General. How do you do, Colonel Grainger?"

The two men shook hands then Carr sat down.

"Colonel," O'Malley said, "go ahead."

"Mr. Carr," Grainger said. "I met a woman named Erika at the general's party Saturday night. I ran a check on her with the State Department and they confirmed her story, but we know who she really is. The G-2 recently had dealings with her in Berlin. She is one of your operatives—Erika Lehmann, with the codename *Lorelei.*"

"That's right, Colonel," Carr responded.

O'Malley cut in. "Both the CIA and G-2 share the concern about certain G-2 operatives with airtight covers overseas being arrested in the past few months. The CIA is not the only one who knows there must be a traitor or Russian agent who has infiltrated G-2."

"I spoke with the president yesterday," O'Malley continued. "Your CIA and our G-2 will work together on this. By the time you return to your office, you'll have the official orders from the White House on your desk."

Carr said, "To be honest, this is best for the mission, General."

O'Malley ended the meeting with, "Colonel Grainger wants Miss Lehmann to report to his office at three o'clock this afternoon."

[3:00 p.m.]

"Please take a seat, Miss Lehmann."

Erika sat down.

"It was very clever of you at General O'Malley's party to give me just enough information that would force me to request a background check on you. You have had dealings with G-2 before."

Leroy Carr had ordered her to cooperate. "That's right, General. This past autumn in Berlin."

"What does your escort at the party know about you?" Grainger asked.

"Max Hodge knows what I told you at the party. Nothing more. He doesn't know that I'm CIA. He thinks I do translation work for the Department of State. He's a civilian, Colonel Grainger. We shouldn't involve Max. I used him only to gain access to the General's affair."

"I see."

"Colonel. May I ask how many of the five G-2 officers at the Christmas party Tuesday night asked for background checks on me or Lieutenant Colonel Sheila Reid? It would be shirking one's duty if one of the five didn't and it might give us a lead."

"All five did," Grainger replied.

"Well," she said softly, almost as if she were talking to herself, "then we're starting from scratch."

"Perhaps not, Miss Lehmann. There is a man on my staff I have some concerns about."

"Really? Who is he?"

"We're running checks on his bank accounts to see if he's made any substantial deposits that might raise an eyebrow. That said, I will not throw a Pentagon officer under the CIA's bus until we have finished our own investigation. If after the inquiries we are making reveal something of concern, then we will inform the CIA. Not before."

Erika came back with, "Leroy Carr told me the White House has ordered G-2 and the CIA to work together. Is that not true?"

Grainger looked at her, displeased with her comment. He wasn't used to being cross-examined. "And that is what we're doing. Since you brought it up, keeping in mind the spirit of total cooperation you mentioned, tell me what you did during the war, Sonderführer Lehmann."

Sonderführer was Erika's Abwehr rank as a Nazi spy during the war. She had to give him credit.

"It's obvious you already know, Colonel. Very well, I'm sure Mr. Carr or my handler will notify me after you call them to express your reservations about me."

"You're dismissed, Miss Lehmann."

Erika rose from her chair. Before she left his office, she said, "Please tell your gracious wife, Agatha, that I said hello."

Chapter 13

Grumpy Sausage and the Russian Bear

Washington, D.C
Next day—Friday, 08 December 1950

Tonight, Erika and Sheila Reid had a date with Zhanna. The wrestling match would be held at the Uline Arena on 3rd Street NE in downtown D.C. with the first bout scheduled to begin at 7 p.m.

At six o'clock, Erika drove the '48 Dodge she had been issued by the CIA and picked up Sheila at her brownstone. From there it was to the Lili Marlene Café to pick up Zhanna.

Zhanna was behind the bar. Erika and Sheila picked bar stools. Business was still not good—the place looked as hollow as a chocolate Easter bunny. One man sat alone at the other end of the bar. Only two of twelve tables were occupied, both by couples.

Erika and Sheila ordered a Yuengling beer from Zhanna.

The 6-foot-tall Russian delivered them along with a double shot of vodka for herself.

"Angelika told me my drinks were on the house," Zhanna said. "But she can't afford that. I run myself a tab and pay up at the end of the week—on pay day."

"Is Angelika in the back?" Erika asked.

"Yes," Zhanna said.

A moment later, Angelika walked out to the bar. She was happy to see both Erika and Sheila.

Erika asked in German, "Angelika, are you going to be alright tonight without Zhanna?"

"Yes. Business is slow, and I'm not going to learn English working in the kitchen and talking in German to Bertha. I need to be out here. I have learned a few English phrases and I now have the food menu printed in English, with German just below it. The customer just has to point to what they want. With your help, Erika, I also have such a sheet for cocktails. Bier and Wein are not a problem as those words in English are 'beer' and 'wine', pronounced much the same. Rot Wein is 'red wine' and weiß Wein is 'white wine'. That's easy enough. I also now have learned the American coin and paper money values. It is good for Zhanna to have a night off and for me to start dealing more with customers."

"You're learning fast, Angelika," Sheila said.

"And I know business will increase," Erika added. "As I said before, it takes time. This is a good place with good food and drink at reasonable prices. Word will get around eventually."

Everyone had one more drink. Zhanna put hers on her tab and Erika and Sheila paid.

As the three women walked out of the café, Zhanna said, "I have cigars."

◊ ◊ ◊

They arrived at the arena about ten minutes before bell time for the first bout. They had tickets so they didn't have to wait in line. Inside the venue, the cigar and cigarette smoke were heavier than a tart's makeup.

They bought beers at the concession stand before finding their reserved seats in the fourth row, ringside. Sheila sat between Erika and Zhanna.

"These are good seats, Zhanna," Sheila commented.

Zhanna was still distracted by the price they had paid for the beers. "Three dollars for three beers?" Zhanna said. "That's crazy."

"It's not any different than baseball or football games in this country," Erika responded. "They know you have to pay their prices if you want it."

The crowd was mostly men, although there were more women than might be expected. However, all of them except Erika, Zhanna, and Sheila were accompanied by men.

The main event on the card tonight would come after a warm-up bout. That first battle was between two lady wrestlers—Big Mama Mickie and The Vixen. Big Mama weighed 235 pounds. The shapely, big-bosomed Vixen weighed in at 140.

"Where can we place a bet?" Zhanna said. "There's no way The Vixen will beat Big Mama Mickie."

"Zhanna," Sheila said. "I wouldn't be so quick to place my bet on Big Mama. Remember that this is entertainment. The Vixen is attractive and the men will be cheering for her. The promoters usually want to please the crowd. But not all the time. Once in a while they have the more popular wrestler lose to set up a rematch. Anything is possible. It's your bet. I'm just saying keep that in mind."

None of Sheila's advice registered with the Russian. She had no concept of professional wrestling being rehearse and outcomes decided on ahead of time. This wasn't the case with Russian wrestlers competing in the Olympics. "I want to bet."

"Let's find out what the odds are," Erika said. "That might give us a clue."

Erika was a steadfast gambler. It was her vice and she was good at it. In the course of her CIA assignments, she had played the tables at the highbrow casinos of Monaco as well as high stakes poker games with organized crime families. She had already spotted several illegal bookies shrewdly making their way through the crowd and noticed that men in attendance who wished to place bets would take off their hats to summon one of them. She took off her floppy, wide-brimmed ladies' Panama hat. A bookie spotted her and sprinted up the steps.

"What are the odds?" she asked the middle-aged man with a pockmarked face. He was thin, like a watery pancake. An inch-long ash on the tip of his cigarette threatened to drop at any second.

"Vixen is a 5/2 favorite, sister."

That told her that the odds had been set to tempt suckers to bet on the attractive Vixen, the crowd favorite. This way the bookies would clean up if The Vixen lost.

"How much do you want to bet on Big Mama, Zhanna?" Erika asked.

"I'll bet $5."

Erika and Sheila placed the same bet. The bookie took their money but didn't look happy, which assured Erika even more that they placed the right bets. He gave them each a green stub of paper with the amount of their wager, who they bet on to win, and their seat numbers. If Big Mama won, each of them would collect $12.50—$7.50 profit for their $5 investment.

When the bell rang, the faster Vixen rushed Big Mama Mickie and took her to the mat. The men cheered. As Sheila had assumed, most of the men had placed their bets on the attractive wrestler. The women rolled around for some time, often changing who had the upper hand. When Vixen held the better position, the crowd cheered. Boos sounded loudly when Big Mama was on top.

The bout lasted for 2½-rounds with Big Mama finally pinning Vixen. Boos and cursing erupted from the raucous crowd as beer cans and miscellaneous objects began pelting the ring, directed at the referee.

Order was finally restored when the referee was hustled into the locker room by security.

"Girls," Erika said. "We just won $7.50 each."

The bookies began circulating to pay off the few who had bet on Big Mama.

Zhanna handed out cigars and they all three lit up.

"I like this pro-wrestling," Zhanna said. "I knew that the weight difference was too much. That Vixen should wrestle smaller women."

Erika and Sheila smiled at each other.

"You were right, Zhanna," Sheila said. "But I feel Vixen might win her next match." She then turned and whispered to Erika, "The promoters will make sure of that."

Erika got the attention of a beer hawker walking the steps and used some of her winnings to order them all another round.

After a 15-minute intermission where the ring was cleared of debris, it was time for the main event. A new referee entered the ring. Two giant men appeared, walking to the ring from opposite tunnels. One wore black wrestling trunks and a gold cowl that covered all but his mouth and chin, the other red togs with a hammer and sickle image on his trunks.

Jeers from the crowd erupted immediately when the Russian appeared. Zhanna stood and cheered.

A man sitting behind her yelled, "Sit down, you dumb broad! That's a Russian commie."

Zhanna turned, hopped over her seat and began pummeling the man. The woman sitting beside the man screamed, "Leave my husband alone, you crazy bitch!"

Zhanna then went after the wife but Erika and Sheila swooped in quickly, restrained Zhanna, and convinced her to sit back down.

The man's nose was bleeding. He and his wife got up and left but not before the wife again cursed Zhanna. "You're a fucking lunatic."

Zhanna looked ready to again leave her seat, but Sheila, sitting next to her, put her hand on the Russian's forearm, "Let it go, Zhanna. We'll get kicked out of here and you won't get to see the main event. Because of the other fights going on in the crowd, it looks like security missed us. Let's settle for that."

A horn sounded, drawing the crowd's attention back to the ring where a tuxedoed announcer stepped up to a microphone lowered from the rafters. Lights were dimmed over the crowd to focus on the well-lit ring of battle.

"Ladies and Gentlemen!" the announcer thundered bombastically. "Now to the main event of the evening! In the black corner wearing the black trunks and weighing in at 310 pounds, a wrestler whose records stands at 42 wins with only 5 losses, I give you Howard 'Grumpy Sausage' Bergwitz."

Cheers erupted.

"His opponent in the red corner, from Leningrad, Russia, weighing in at 285 pounds with a record of 31 wins against only 7 loses, please welcome the Terror of the Caucasus, Ivan the 'Russian Bear' Popov!"

Nothing but loud boos.

"Did you hear that, Erika?" Zhanna said. "He is from Leningrad, like me! Where's that bookie man?"

"Let's check the odds first, Zhanna," Erika replied.

"Fuck that. I'm placing $15 on the Russian Bear."

Erika looked at Sheila. They knew they had to support their fellow Shield Maiden. Erika again removed her hat. All three women placed $15 on the man in the red corner. The same bookie took their bets. He seemed pleased this time. Erika knew they each had just lost $15.

Both wrestlers stepped to the center of the ring for the stare down while the referee gave them final instructions. After returning to their respective corners, the bell rang. Both mammoth-sized men began circling around the ring looking for an opportunity. Grumpy Sausage was the first to move in for a hold, but the Russian Bear quickly reversed out of it and placed Grumpy Sausage in a half-nelson. The crown showed its displeasure with boos and vulgar diatribes directed at the Russian. Zhanna got onto her chair and cheered.

"Nothing good is going to come of this, you know that Erika," Sheila said.

After four more rounds where it was clear that the Russian was getting the best of the American wrestler, the fifth and final round was about to begin. Zhanna was still standing on her chair. Some of her cheering had been spoken in Russian, which drew derisive glares from those within earshot.

"We win this round and we win!" Zhanna exclaimed to Sheila and Erika. Then she shouted toward the ring, "Pobeda, russkiy medved, pobeda! (Win, Russian Bear, win.)

Someone a few rows back shouted, "Shut up, commie!" but lucky for him, Zhanna didn't hear him in her exuberance.

The bell rang. Grumpy Sausage knew he was losing on points and would need to pin the Russian. His corner also knew it and supplied him pre-arranged means to do so.

About one minute into the final round, just after the two men had broken apart from a mutual hold, Grumpy Sausage reached into his trunks. The next time the Russian Bear approached, Grumpy Sausage threw pepper into his eyes. This temporarily blinded the Russian and he staggered back. The crowd cheered. They had bet on the American and didn't care what it took for him to win.

"Did you see that!" Zhanna yelled in rage. "The American is cheating."

"Zhanna, it's all part of the act," Sheila said but to no avail. Zhanna rushed past the people in her row and flew down the steps toward the ring.

"Oh, shit," Erika said. "Let's get her, Sheila. Quick."

Grumpy Sausage had the Russian Bear in a pin hold and the ref began counting to three as Zhanna shot through the ropes, jumped onto Grumpy Sausage's back, and applied a choke hold. It surprised him so much, for a moment he didn't know what was happening. The same spelled true for both wrestler's corners. The corner men looked around at each other asking, "Who put this in the act?"

The referee was the first to react. He tried to pry Zhanna off the coughing behemoth's back. In the process, Zhanna's scarf got pulled off revealing her hideous neck scar. The Russian Shield Maiden kicked the ref between the legs and the man slowly crumpled to the ground like a building being demolished by dynamite.

Pandemonium reigned. Erika and Sheila jumped into the ring at the same time the corner men finally figured out this was not part of the plot. The Russian Bear had not been pinned. Zhanna had made sure of that. Grumpy Sausage stood up and began turning in circles trying to shake Zhanna off his back. He attempted to grab her hair, but she held on like a bull rider at the Cheyenne Frontier Days as corner men tried to detach her.

Several security men flooded into the ring, just adding to the chaos. Sheila pushed one of them out of the ring as the man attempted to come through the ropes (once a Shield Maiden, always a Shield Maiden). Erika dove into the back of Grumpy Sausage's legs, crashing him and Zhanna to the floor as boos and beers cans rained down from the crowd.

There were probably forty people in the ring when the announcer finally managed to make his way to the heart of the free-for-all where Zhanna had finally been pried off of Grumpy Sausage like a stubborn barnacle. He remained on the mat, gasping for air. His thick, muscular neck had saved him.

"Get these screwy dames out of here," the announcer/promoter ordered. "Take them to Joey's locker room before someone calls the cops."

Once safely inside the locker room lair of the Russian Bear, Zhanna introduced herself in Russian and asked the wrestler where he served during the war.

"I don't understand a word you're saying," the wrestler said with a New York City accent. "My name is Joey Baccala. I'm from Brooklyn. I've never been to Russia in my life."

Zhanna first looked shocked, and then angry. Erika saw her lean over and start pulling up her pants leg, going for the dagger inside a sheath taped to her lower leg. Erika, the strongest of the Maidens, took Zhanna down. "Sheila, get her dagger." Sheila quickly did so.

Erika then turned to Baccala's trainer who was also in the room. "There was no pin and the match was not completed. That means the match is a draw or ruled unfinished, is that correct?"

"That's right," the bald-headed man replied.

"Then we are entitled to a refund of our bet. We each bet $15. Here are our tickets."

"You dames have to settle that with a bookie."

Erika shoved him against a locker, making a loud bang. Sheila put Zhanna's dagger to the man's throat. The phony 'Russian Bear' started toward Erika and Sheila with thoughts of rescuing his trainer but stopped abruptly when Zhanna pulled a handgun from underneath her jacket and held it to his right temple. Erika dug into the trainer's pocket and withdrew this wallet. She took out $45, left the rest, and dropped the wallet and the three betting vouchers on the floor. "You have the tickets, get your money back from one of your crooked bookies."

"Let's go," Erika said to Zhanna in Russian so the men wouldn't understand. "We have to get Sheila out of here before the police arrive. An Army lieutenant colonel can't get caught up in this mess."

The three Shield Maidens left the arena from an alleyway door and ran into the gloom as police sirens grew louder in the distance.

They had to lie low in alley shadows for over an hour until the arena emptied and the police left. They then calmly walked to Erika's car and headed toward the bridge for a nightcap at the Lili Marlene.

Part 2

Chapter 14

Back to zero

Washington, D.C.
Next day—Saturday, 09 December 1950

Erika, Sheila, and Zhanna sat in Leroy Carr's office. Al Hodge was there.

Carr or Hodge knew nothing about last night. Out of control melees were so common at area pro-wrestling events that the local newspapers quit reporting on them unless someone was stabbed or shot and a suspect was at large.

"This concerns the man on Colonel Grainger's staff that he has concerns about," Carr said. "We still don't have his name. I talked to the colonel yesterday afternoon. He tells me this man has made no suspicious deposits in his bank accounts. The colonel has cleared this man—at least in his own mind—and won't release his name."

"Great," Erika said. "Now we're back to zero."

"It seems so," Carr replied.

Erika said. "This morning, Sheila invited all the G-2 officers and wives we met at General O'Malley's Christmas party to the Lili Marlene tonight for cocktails, along with a few other G-2 men Sheila knows at the Pentagon—ones who were not invited to the General's party. I called Colonel Grainger. He and his wife will be there. Zhanna will be behind the bar. Al, Max will be coming but not until later. I told him I'd be helping out as a waitress so I won't be able to sit with him until the crowd starts thinning out. I need you and Leroy to be there. Leroy, please bring Kay. I'll reserve you and Al a table."

Both Carr and Hodge stared at her for a moment.

"We'll be there," Carr said. "What time?"

"Eight o'clock."

◊ ◊ ◊

[later]

Erika and Sheila arrived at the Lili Marlene three hours early to help Angelika and Bertha in the kitchen preparing German meatballs. Zhanna was already behind the bar. The appetizer would be free to guests. This was Angelika's idea—a way to drum up more business when people found out how delicious Bertha's food tasted.

"This will be a good night for the café, Angelika," Erika said as she and Sheila rolled meatballs. "A lot of liquor will be sold.

"Sheila, what time is Ricky coming?" Erik asked.

"About seven-thirty. He's going to sit at the bar because I'll be working. No sense in him taking up a table."

Erika and Sheila were waitressing tonight for two reasons. First, their help would be needed. The young waitress Angelika employed would not be able to keep up. Secondly, waitressing would allow them to circulate and talk to everyone.

◊ ◊ ◊

At only a few minutes past 8 p.m. the Lili Marlene bustled. Leroy and Kay Carr sat at a table with an unaccompanied Al Hodge. Hodge was a widower whose wife died in the late '30s. Even though he had occasionally dated over the years it never lasted long. He had never been able to move on.

All the other tables were occupied, mostly by Pentagon personnel. Colonel Grainger and his wife occupied a table with another man and woman. Both of the men wore civilian clothes as did all the other men in the café. Every bar stool was taken, keeping Zhanna on her toes.

Grainger's table had already had drinks delivered by Erika when Sheila stopped by with a platter of meatballs, each stabbed by a toothpick. Sheila also wore civilian dress.

"I've never been served meatballs by a lieutenant colonel before," Grainger joked. "Your friend, Erika, brought our drinks. What brings you two here?"

"Erika own this place, Colonel," Sheila said. "I'm just helping them out. Business has been slow. Since the Pentagon is so close, we thought something like this might help increase business."

Grainger had looked around the room and saw that many of the men were G-2. He also saw Leroy Carr and Al Hodge. Grainger suspected Sheila's reason wasn't the only one for this event. He couldn't speak freely. The couple with him and his wife were civilian friends.

"If you have the time, why don't you stop by my office Monday morning," Grainger said. "And bring your friend, Erika."

Sheila knew this was an order.

"I'd be glad to, Colonel."

A few tables away, Al said to Leroy, "I hope something good comes of this."

"I hope so, too, Al. Erika and Sheila should have cleared this with you first."

Hodge shrugged. "It's par for the course with Lehmann."

Kay said, "My goodness, you two. It's still a pleasant night out. You both need to keep that in mind. Not everything in life revolves around cloak-and-dagger."

"You're right, Kay," Hodge replied. "Who would have ever thought that Lehmann would own a tavern." Then to Leroy, "How are things going in Korea?"

Kay rolled her eyes. *Here they go again.*

"Not good."

Suddenly, Erika showed up at their table with another round of drinks.

"We're not done with our first round, Erika," Hodge said.

"That's okay. I'm running you a tab. You can pay when you leave."

Leroy said, "I've watched you and Sheila talking to a lot of people. I know you have to be discreet during any conversations, but do you have anything to report?"

"Not yet, Leroy, but it's early."

Chapter 15

A Ukrainian wife

Arlington, Virginia
Next day—Sunday, 10 December 1950

The Lili Marlene was closed on Sundays. Erika, Sheila, and Zhanna met Leroy Carr and Al Hodge for breakfast at the Hamilton Diner in Arlington, a popular breakfast stop that Carr and Hodge had frequently used over the years if on Sundays Carr didn't want to open his Washington office for a brief meeting.

"Colonel Grainger wants me and Erika to report to his office tomorrow morning," Sheila told the two men.

"That's fine," Carr said. "I imagined he would. Do any of you have anything to tell us about last night?"

"Sheila and I got to know a few more G-2 officers," Erika answered. "That might prove to be helpful in the future, but everything had to be held to idle chat. We can't single anyone out as raising suspicion. However, Zhanna might have something."

Carr and Hodge looked at Zhanna who had just put a big bite of her sunny-side-up eggs and hash browns in her mouth. She chewed and swallowed.

"Toward the end of the night," Zhanna said, "a man at the bar noticed my accent and started talking to me in Russian. All I know is his first name is James. I have no last name."

"Description," Hodge uttered.

"An American," Zhanna replied. "I know this because his Russian was understandable but not good and he spoke it with an American accent. About 5'10" with brown hair and eyes. He wore eyeglasses and a dark gray fedora."

Hodge said, "If this guy is the Pentagon mole, he has to be the dumbest mole in history to start talking Russian amongst a room full of G-2 men."

"He was very drunk," Zhanna said.

"Alright," Carr said. "I agree with Al. If this guy is the mole, he must be stupid, but we have to check it out. Sheila, can you do this at the Pentagon?"

"I don't know," she said. "With only a first name it will be difficult, but I'll try."

"Let's leave Zhanna out of this for now since Grainger doesn't know about her," Carr said. "Tomorrow when you two meet with Grainger, cooperate with him but don't mention this 'James' until Sheila has had time to see what she can do."

"One more thing," Zhanna said matter-of-factly. "James told me he was learning Russian from his wife who was born in the Ukraine."

Chapter 16

Rouladen

Washington, D.C.
Next day—Monday, 11 December 1950

At 10 a.m., Erika and Sheila sat in Colonel Grainger's office. Sheila was in uniform as required by Pentagon protocol for military personnel.

Grainger started with chinwag. "My wife and I had a good time Saturday night. Erika, Sheila told me you own that place."

"I invested in a friend," Erika replied. "She runs it."

"The German meatballs were delicious," he said.

"Thank you, Colonel, but I can't take credit. We have a fine cook."

Grainger now got down to business. "I noticed that Leroy Carr and Al Hodge were there Saturday night. I also noticed that many of the guests were G-2. Fill me in, Lieutenant Colonel Reid."

"Sir, we thought it a good opportunity to mingle with G-2 men," Sheila said.

"Anything to report?" he asked.

"Nothing of importance. Erika and I, in the course of waitressing, got to chat with some of the men, but neither of us came across anything worthy of a report."

"Who is that bartender with the Russian accent?" Grainger asked.

Erika spoke up. "She's just a friend of mine who needed a job."

"It's nice that you could help out a friend, Erika. What's her name?"

It was obvious that the shrewd Grainger was conducting his own investigation.

Erika had no option. She had been ordered by Leroy to cooperate and giving Grainger a phony name would serve no purpose with his G-2 capacity to uncover backgrounds.

"Zhanna Rogova," she told him.

Grainger stared at her for a long moment.

"Thank you, Erika and Lieutenant Colonel Reid. I'll get back to you."

◊ ◊ ◊

As soon as Erika left the Pentagon, she found the nearest pay phone, dropped a nickel in the slot, and called Al Hodge at his E Street office.

"Al, Sheila and I just left the meeting with Colonel Grainger. Sheila had to return to her office. Grainger asked about Zhanna and I had to give him her full name. If Grainger found out I was lying to him, which he would probably do sooner than later, he could cause trouble because of the White House directives. I got the feeling Grainger recognized Zhanna's name."

"Okay, Erika. I'll let Leroy know right away. You better come in so we can talk."

◊ ◊ ◊

"Grainger can't cause us any trouble concerning Zhanna," Carr said. Erika and Al sat in his office. "Rogova is not accused of war crimes by the United States or any Allied nations. The only country that would like to get its hands on Zhanna is the Soviet Union. They consider her a traitor because she now works for us.

"With that said, this mission is starting to shape up into a rivalry between the CIA and G-2. That's got to stop. I'm going to call Grainger and ask him to a dinner meeting tonight with me and Al. Erika, Al told me about the upstairs room at your pub where he met privately with you and Sheila for dinner. If we can use that place, I'll set it up there. It will be a little bit of extra income for your business."

"Thanks, Leroy," she said. "Sure, you can use that room."

"I told you I'd try to help your place," Carr said. "You and Sheila should be at the pub in case we want to talk to you, but the dinner will just be me, Al, and Grainger."

Al ended the conversation with, "By the way, Lehmann, I finagled Max a temporary transfer to a procurement substation at Fort Hood, Texas. He flew out this morning and he doesn't know I was behind it. He thinks it's a promotion. You will not contact him. If he contacts you, tell him you don't think it will work out between you two and it's time for you both to move on. Those are orders. Max has no experience in our line of work and nothing good will come of it from his or the mission's standpoint."

[that evening]

Sheila Reid greeted Howard Grainger when he walked into the Lili Marlene.

"Hello, Colonel Grainger."

"Good evening, Lieutenant Colonel." He didn't see Erika, but Zhanna Rogova stood behind the bar serving up beers for two civilian men wearing construction clothes.

"Mr. Carr and Mr. Hodge are already here," Sheila said. "Please follow me."

Sheila walked Grainger through the kitchen where he saw a woman who looked to be around mid-40s helping an elderly cook. Erika stood washing dishes in the sink. A young blonde-haired girl who looked to be about 8 or 9-years-old stood beside her drying the dishes with a towel.

When Erika spotted him, she grabbed a towel and dried her hands. "Colonel Grainger," Erika said. "Let me introduce you to everyone. This is my daughter, Adelaide. We call her Ada." The little girl looked at him with her mother's hazel eyes. "This is our cook, Bertha, and this is Angelika. She runs the Lili Marlene."

Grainger nodded and briefly addressed them all, then Sheila took him up the wooden stairs. When they entered the private room, Leroy Carr was sitting at the table with a gin and tonic, Hodge with a Scotch on the rocks.

"What would you like to drink, Colonel?" Sheila asked.

"Bourbon neat."

"I'll bring it right up."

Sheila departed and Grainger sat down.

"Interesting bartender they have here," Grainger said.

"Erika told us that she thought you recognized Zhanna's name," Carr replied. "What do you know about her, if I might ask."

"I know of her war record as a Red Army sniper and SMERSH assassin. The reports we got in 1946 was that she was dead. I assume Rogova now works for the CIA."

"That's right," Carr answered.

Sheila knocked on the door and brought in Grainger's drink.

"Thank you, Lieutenant Colonel."

"We'll bring up your dinners as soon as they're ready," Sheila told the men. "I took the liberty of ordering you all one of Bertha's German specialties. I know you'll like it."

"Thank you, Sheila," Hodge said.

After Sheila left, Grainger said, "I have to admit, Mr. Carr and Mr. Hodge, that you have a unique place here. A place were a former Russian sniper and assassin works as a bartender, a CIA agent washes dishes, and a lieutenant colonel assigned to the Pentagon is our waitress. Did the CIA establish this place for a particular reason, or can you not tell me?"

"Colonel, the CIA had nothing to do with establishing this pub—or café as they call it." Carr said truthfully. "Erika Lehmann financed it for a friend. Angelika Egermann is her name. You can check her out and find out she's a civilian. She's from Germany."

"I met this Angelika in the kitchen a few minutes ago. When I spoke to her she didn't seem to understand me."

"She escaped from East Berlin just a couple of months ago. She doesn't speak English. I told you to check her out if you wish. Al and I didn't ask you here tonight so we can be interrogated. We asked you here to discuss the cooperation between the CIA and G-2 on the particular mission we are both working on. Something that was ordered by the White House. I think that cooperation is falling short."

Grainger didn't like being chastised, but as far as influential government positions, his rank of colonel placed him several steps down the ladder from Carr. "I feel the same way, Mr. Carr. What do you suggest?"

"I will give you full disclosure on anything the CIA uncovers that concerns the Pentagon mole. I will admit that we have not done that so far, but neither have you. On your part, as operations head of G-2, you will give me or Al full disclosure from your end. This is not a rivalry between agencies, or at least it shouldn't be. G-2 men are disappearing in Europe. Men who will be tortured during interrogation and either be shot or shipped off to a Siberian gulag."

"Mr. Carr, I personally know the men who have disappeared. They worked for me. I know their families. I want this leak to end faster than anyone. You have my word. From now on I'll fill you in on everything concerning our mutual task."

Carr nodded. "Then I'll start. A man attended the party here Saturday night who had a few too many drinks. He noticed Zhanna Rogova's accent and tried speaking Russian to her at the bar. Zhanna could tell he was an American because of his accent while he spoke his poor Russian. He told Zhanna that he was learning Russian from his wife who is from the Ukraine. This needs to be checked out. We assume he might work at the Pentagon because most everyone present that night works there. Sheila tried to check him out but we have only a first name—James—and Sheila has limited access because of certain Pentagon protocols. She can check out anyone in her Poland unit, or anyone that might be a person of interest to her command. Other than that, she's limited, as I said."

Grainger replied, "A 'James' that has a Ukrainian wife. I can find out who he is if he works at the Pentagon. A file on spouses is recorded in everyone's personnel file. My department can run intel on anyone at the Pentagon. A 'James' with a Ukrainian wife can be uncovered."

Al Hodge asked, "How long might that take, Colonel?"

"It shouldn't take long. I'll tag it as high priority. Give me a day or two. I appreciate this, gentlemen. As I said, no one wants to uncover the mole more than me."

"It might lead to nothing," Carr added. "This 'James' might be totally legitimate and he might not even work at the Pentagon. There were a few neighborhood customers in here Saturday night. The get-together wasn't limited to invited guests."

"I understand," Grainger said. "Still, it's something to work on. G-2 has entered a blind alley. I congratulate the CIA for supplying us a lead, regardless of if it pans out or not."

"And per our agreement," Carr said. "You'll contact me immediately if you uncover this man at the Pentagon."

"Yes, I will."

"Good. Now I'll tell you what you can do for me. If you find such a man, you'll turn over the investigation of him to the CIA. If this man is affiliated with G-2, as the mole has to be, he will recognize any of your men or women who might try to shadow him or approach him in a bar or restaurant. He won't recognize my people."

"Asking me to lay off is asking a lot, Mr. Carr. He would recognize Zhanna Rogova. You said he talked to her at the bar."

"Zhanna will not be the shadow. She wasn't trained in that art. And it won't be Erika or Sheila. He surely would also recognize them. They circulated throughout the crowd Saturday night as waitresses. I have someone else in mind. Please don't make me remind you of our accord we just agreed upon, Colonel."

Grainger knew Carr, as the second in command of the CIA, had strong White House connections.

"Very well, Mr. Carr. It will be as you say."

Just then a knock came at the door. Erika and Sheila entered with the meals. Ada was with them carrying napkins and silverware. The two women sat plates down as Ada meticulously arranged the silverware.

"This is Rouladen with a Spätzle and red cabbage," Erika said. "This was my father's favorite meal and Bertha prepares it wonderfully. We'll bring you another round of drinks. Bon appétit, gentlemen."

Grainger sat there knowing he had been cleverly manipulated by Carr, Hodge, and the women agents.

Chapter 17

Sheila

Flashback
Knoxville, Tennessee
January 1947

Erika watched from the darkness of the warehouse's second tier as one of Grusha's men threw a bucket of cold water on their prisoner. Grusha, a female Soviet assassin, had been sent to America to find and eliminate Zhanna Rogova. Sheila Reid, one of the Shield Maidens, had been beaten and tied to a chair. The cold water ripped her awake and she slowly raised her head. Her left eye and jaw were already swelling and turning purple.

"Now I want the truth!" Grusha shouted in Sheila's face. "Who are you and where is the woman named Zhanna that accompanied you on the train? And who do your work for—the FBI? Tell the truth and I'll make your death painless." The Russian pulled out a stiletto and pressed it to Sheila's throat.

"Okay, okay," Sheila said. "I'll tell you."

"I'm listening," Grusha removed the slim dagger from her throat.

Sheila said, "Untie me from this chair, so I can bend over and you can kiss my ass."

Grusha plunged the stiletto into Sheila's shoulder. The Army major grimaced from the searing pain but refused to scream.

Immediately, Erika jumped from her second storey perch onto one of Grusha's men. The blow to his head delivered by an elbow as she fell on him knocked him unconscious. He fell to the floor with Erika on top of him. It was such a high jump that the impact of landing was tough on Erika and she was slow to stand. When Erika got to her feet, Grusha shouted, "Shoot her!"

The second man raised a gun but just then a shot rang out, striking the man in the knee and shattering his knee cap. It was the best shot Kathryn had as the man's upper body, from her angle, was obscured by warehouse equipment.

The man toppled like a sawed oak tree. Erika quickly limped over and smashed his face with the butt of her Thompson machinegun.

The Russian agent, Grusha, had a handgun tucked in the back off her pants but decided since there was another gunman somewhere in the dark warehouse her best move would be to circle around her prisoner and hold her dagger to Sheila's throat.

Erika raised her Thompson and aimed at Grusha.

"Those American Thompson's are not accurate and spray everything, Erika," Grusha said. "If you pull that trigger you'll kill your comrade." Grusha was crouched behind the still-bound Sheila and tightened her hold.

"You're right," Erika said. "I have another way to free Sheila."

"Sheila! So now I have a name," Grusha smirked.

At that moment, Zhanna Rogova slowly walked out of the darkness so Grusha could see her. The weak yellow lighting made Zhanna's severe sniper makeup look evermore fiendish, like an image from one of Edgar Allan Poe's macabre nightmares.

For a moment Grusha was taken aback by Zhanna's severe manifestation and the smirk disappeared, yet she kept her cool.

"Welcome Zhanna," said Grusha. "This is the moment I have always wished for—the day that I kill you."

Both women spoke in Russian.

"That remains to be seen, doesn't it? Perhaps you have mistakenly looked forward to this day." Zhanna laid her shotgun and handgun on the floor. She brought out her knife, "It's now between just you and me, Grusha."

Just a couple of seconds later, Kathryn emerged from the darkness with her M-1 zeroed in on Grusha.

"How do I know your comrades will not get involved?" Grusha again applied pressure to Sheila's throat with her stiletto.

Erika dropped her weapons to the floor. She put a hand on Kathryn's shoulder as a sign that she should do the same. Kathryn wavered for a moment, but eventually bent over and placed her rifle on the floor.

"Other weapons on the ground!" Grusha barked.

Erika and Kathryn laid their handguns and knives on the floor.

"Step away!" Grusha ordered.

The two women took several steps backwards.

Now Grusha addressed Zhanna. "Kick those weapons over to me or your comrade dies!"

Zhanna did so, then said, "Can we get down to our purpose tonight—you and I? Both of us want the same thing—that one of us dies before the sun rises." Zhanna dropped all her weapons to the floor except her knife, which she held at her side.

"So it is a knife fight you propose," Grusha sneered. "I salute you for not bringing your sniper rifle with which you are famous."

Grusha released her grip on Sheila and with the thin but twelve-inch-long stiletto in hand, walked out into the brighter light to wait for Zhanna.

When Carr, Hodge, and Marienne Schenck heard the gunshot from Kathryn's rifle, they immediately ran across the street toward the warehouse's heavy double doors.

Inside, Zhanna and Grusha stepped into battle. Grusha drew first blood when a swipe with her dagger put a deep slice into Zhanna's left forearm. Zhanna was not a small woman at 5'11½". With most opponents, she would have used the opportunity to rush Grusha, but a trained assassin like Zhanna has to know her mark's strengths and weaknesses. At over six-feet tall and heavier, Grusha was physically stronger than Zhanna, so she avoided rushing Grusha and possibly ending up in close hand-to-hand combat. On the other hand, Zhanna was quicker and more agile than her opponent.

Grusha realized that Zhanna was going to keep her distance, so she tried to rush her. It was a mistake. Although Grusha managed another glancing strike, this one opening a small cut on Zhanna's cheek, Zhanna plunged her Bowie knife into Grusha's right leg. Unfortunately for Zhanna, she missed the femoral artery. Grusha was slowed for a moment but showed no signs of pain. In fact, she smiled and kept trying to close in on Zhanna.

Just then a loud explosion rocked the warehouse. At the other end of the building, Carr and Hodge had set position grenades and blew off the warehouse's heavy steel doors.

Zhanna and Grusha ignored the tumult and kept their attention focused on each other.

Grusha kept stepping toward Zhanna. Zhanna kept up her strategy of keeping her distance.

"What's the matter?" Grusha growled. "Is the great Zhanna Rogova afraid?"

It was the opening Zhanna had waited for. Talking during any kind of fight diverts the talker's attention and slows reaction, if only minutely. Zhanna sprang toward Grusha like a cheetah onto a wildebeest. Zhanna had been fighting with her knife in her right hand. She brought that hand around in a stabbing motion. Grusha blocked the thrust, but the knife was not there. Zhanna brought her left hand around and buried the knife deep into Grusha's chest, under ribs and up into her heart.

Grusha was quickly dying with a look of utter surprise on her face, but in the few seconds she had left she managed one last swipe of her knife. Zhanna was able to deflect this one and Grusha's final act managed to put only a cut in Zhanna's left ring finger.

It was as if Grusha refused to die. Even with her heart penetrated she remained standing. Zhanna kept trying to push the knife deeper. Finally, Grusha dropped to her knees, looked at Zhanna and then fell forward on her face, dead.

Carr and Hodge finally found the women in the expansive building, and with Marienne alongside, they rushed up fully armed and ready for whatever was to come. They were too late. The fight had taken no more than ten minutes.

"What in the hell happened?" Carr asked. His eyes scanned from Grusha's body to the two unconscious men several yards away on the floor.

No one answered. Erika and Kathryn untied Sheila. Erika still limped from the twenty-foot-high leap from the second tier, but she ignored it and removed her shirt. She tore off a sleeve and used it to apply pressure to the profusely bleeding knife wound in Sheila's shoulder. Luckily, the bleeding had been slowed somewhat by the frigid temperature inside the unheated building.

"Leroy, we have to get Sheila to a hospital," Erika said calmly. "Zhanna needs some attention, too."

Carr sent Hodge to the car to radio for an ambulance.

Chapter 18

Marienne

Back to Present
Washington, D.C.
Two days later—Wednesday, 13 December 1950

Both the Pentagon and CIA Headquarters had secure telephones. Both had 24-hours-a-day permanent line tapping technician crews that checked phone lines coming in or out for bugs. This included inside the buildings and at outside telephone poles even if blocks away. All telephone poll lines that could lead to a phone ringing inside one of the two buildings were checked daily and surveilled.

At 9:12 a.m. two days after Colonel Grainger met with Leroy Carr and Al Hodge upstairs at the Lili Marlene Café, Effie buzzed Carr on his desk intercom.

"Mr. Carr," she said. *"Colonel Grainger from the Pentagon is on the line."*

"Patch him through, Effie."

"Good morning, Colonel," Carr said.

"Hello, Mr. Carr. We ran that check on 'James.' A James Brunnell is a civilian who works a low-level G-2 job here at the Pentagon in data sorting. The data that crosses his desk is never high-level stuff. He would never see a list of our foreign agents, so that's not a promising lead from our viewpoint. However, for what it's worth, he does have a Ukrainian wife—Svetlana, maiden surname Urashova. According to Brunnell's file, the two met in Vienna a few months after the war when Brunnell was in the military."

"I commend your men for tracing through over 20,000 personnel files in less than two days," Carr said. "This is at least something we can work on." Then Carr reminded Grainger of their agreement. "Please send me a copy of Brunnell's file. Then the CIA will take this from here, Colonel."

When they hung up, Carr immediately called Al Hodge to his office. Carr filled in his old partner on the call from Grainger concerning Brunnell.

"Al, this Pentagon business is your baby from now on. You have complete authority. I leave for Seoul tomorrow to meet with our South Korea teams. I don't know how long I'll be gone. Call Marienne Schenck. You have to be persuasive and on your best behavior. The last time we needed her two years ago I had to fly to Pittsburgh and still had a helluva time convincing her."

Hodge nodded. "I'll call her this afternoon."

[that afternoon]

Thirty-three-year-old Marienne Schenk and her husband, Harold, owned a lucrative tugboat/barge business in Pittsburgh that moved goods of every kind up and down the city's three famous rivers: the Alleghany, Monongahela, and the Ohio.

During the war, Marienne worked for Carr at the OSS where she gained the reputation as the agency's best shadow. After the war, when Harold returned from fighting in the Pacific, she resigned from her job with the OSS. Since then, she had accepted a couple of CIA assignments when Carr or Hodge needed a shadow for a high-priority mission, but she also had turned down some of their requests. She wanted a normal life and children.

The desk telephone rang in her office.

"Hello," she said. "Three Rivers Cargo Company. Marienne Schenck speaking."

"Marienne, this is Al Hodge."

There came a slight pause before she said, "Hello, Al."

"How is Harold and your daughter?"

"They're fine, thanks. Stephanie will be two next August." Marienne had named her first child after Stephanie Fischer, one of the Shield Maidens.

"That's great. Glad to hear it."

"I know you have a reason for your call, Al, other than asking about my family."

"We have an emergency, Marienne."

"Al, I thought you resigned the agency for a job as a professor at one of the Ivy League schools."

"Brown. I'm back only temporarily. Leroy is leaving for Korea tomorrow. May I fly to Pittsburgh this afternoon and talk with you? Maybe take you and Harold out for dinner."

"Harold is captaining one of our tugs pushing two barges to Louisville. I can't take off right now for Europe or South America or wherever."

"The job is in the Washington area. That's only a little over an hour's flight from Pittsburgh and I'll make sure a plane is at your disposal. Good men are dying, Marienne."

She thought for a moment. "Alright, Al. I'll hear you out but I make no promises, Harold's brother works here and knows the ropes. I'll have him run the company until Harold or I return. I'll send Stephanie to my mother. There's no need for you to come to Pittsburgh. Just send a plane tomorrow morning."

"Thanks, Marienne. I'll have a driver waiting at Andrews to bring you to my office for a full briefing. I'll issue you a car and have Effie reserve you a room at the Mayflower."

[that evening]

When Erika walked into the Lili Marlene, there were five neighborhood locals spaced out along the bar and three tables occupied by couples. *This is better than it has been on most weeknights,* Erika thought. *Perhaps business is picking up.*

Erika walked up to the bar and sat down on a stool. Zhanna saw her and walked over with another woman on her heels.

"Who's this, Zhanna?" Erika asked.

"Her name is Susan. She's an American but speaks German. Angelika hired her to cover the bar when I can't be here. This is her first night. I'm training her."

Susan was a pretty, short-haired blonde who looked to be around 30.

"Hello, Susan. My name is Erika. Welcome to the Lili Marlene."

"Thank you," Susan said. "I appreciate having the job. Even though it's part time, it will help."

"How did you learn German?"

"I studied it in high school, but I learned much more during the war. I spent two years in Morgantown, Kentucky as a kitchen worker at the German POW camp there."

"What do you want to drink?" Zhanna asked Erika.

"Just a beer—Yuengling."

Zhanna looked at Susan and the new employee walked away to pour one from the tap.

"Is Sheila coming?" Zhanna asked.

"No, we're on hold until tomorrow so she and Ricky are spending the night together at home."

"On hold? Why?"

"I got a call from Al Hodge. Marienne Schenk will be here tomorrow."

Chapter 19

Captain Wedeking

The Pentagon
Arlington, Virginia
Next day—Thursday, 14 December 1950

Colonel Grainger expected the cacophony of his office intercom to annoy him at any moment and he wasn't disappointed. To stop the annoying buzz, he pressed a button. The voice of his WAC secretary came through the small box sitting on his desk.

"Colonel, Captain Wedeking is here."

"Send her in."

In a moment, a 5'9" blue-eyed blonde walked into his office and closed the door behind her. She was dressed in her Army uniform.

"Have a seat, Captain."

Captain Susan Wedeking sat down.

"Any progress?" Grainger asked.

"Yes, sir. Yesterday I was hired as a part-time bartender at the café you asked me to surveil."

Grainger was pleased. "Well done, Captain. You understand that you must proceed with the utmost caution. There is no action to be taken on your part. Just keep me informed of what goes on at that bar. I picked you for this assignment for three reasons. First, I want you to try and get close to the women named Erika and Zhanna. Second, you speak German and can understand if the women speak in that language. And lastly, because you are not G-2, if G-2 men visit that bar they will not recognize you. The Pentagon mole has to be G-2."

Susan Wedeking was a military policewoman with an impeccable background who worked out of Fort Dix, New Jersey. Grainger met her during the war, had dealings with her over the years, and trusted her.

"I understand my orders, Colonel Grainger."

"Getting this job at the bar, you used your alias surname, right?"

"Of course, they know me as Susan Lauer."

Grainger had his G-2 forgers produce her a driver's license under that false surname. He knew the always suspicious CIA would run a background check on her so her real name was avoided.

[later that morning]

Erika sat in Al Hodge's office.

"I had the Bone Hunters run the name you called me about last night," Hodge said. "They came up with nothing about a Susan Lauer. The Army kept no permanent records of civilian kitchen workers at State-side POW camps, so nothing can be dug up there."

'Bone Hunters' was the nickname used with in agency for the CIA's Background Research and Location Division.

"Okay, Al, thanks. Nothing about her raised suspicion last night, but no harm in checking. When is Marienne getting here?"

"She should set down at Andrews Air Force Base around noon. I have a man who will pick her up and bring her here to E Street. Don't go anywhere. Be available in your office. I'll brief her then call you in."

[2:40 p.m.]

Erika had been summoned to Hodge's office. We she entered, Marienne Schenk rose from her chair and the two women hugged.

"Marienne, how is your baby?" Erika asked.

"Growing like Jack's beanstalk, Erika. And Ada?"

"She'll be nine next May. She's thriving. Harold is well, I hope."

"He's fine."

Hodge waited patiently until the reunion was over and they took their seats.

"Marienne arrived two hours ago," Hodge told Erika. "I've briefed her about the task on hand. She'll be the in charge of shadowing during this mission."

"You couldn't have gotten a better one, Al," Erika conceded. "Marienne is the best I've ever worked with."

[that evening]

Marienne Schenk and Erika entered the Lili Marlene together. Marienne immediately spotted Zhanna behind the bar wearing one of her various scarves to cover the gruesome rope burn that encircled her neck.

"Zhanna Rogova tending bar," Marienne chuckled. "Al told me that you owned this place, but when he said Zhanna was the bartender I almost didn't believe him."

"It's true," Erika smiled. "And Zhanna likes her job."

"Who's the other woman?" Marienne asked.

"Her name is Susan. She just started yesterday. She'll handle the bar when Zhanna can't be here. She's working with Zhanna until she gets comfortable handling the bar by herself."

"This is a nice little place, Erika. I never pictured you as an entrepreneur."

"Business is not great, but we hope that will change. A German friend of mine runs the place. You're a successful businesswoman. If you have any tips, let me know."

They took seats at the bar. When Zhanna approached, she looked at Marienne but with her usual unfriendliness said nothing.

"It's nice to see you again, Zhanna," Marienne said. "You're looking well."

Susan Wedeking, who stood just behind Zhanna, now knew these two women recognized each other.

Without a return greeting, Zhanna asked coldly, "What would you two like to drink."

Marienne ordered a highball with 7-Up, Erika a shot of Jägermeister with a Yuengling chaser.

Zhanna looked at Susan who then departed to get the drinks.

Erika said sharply, "Zhanna, what's wrong with you? This is Marienne, our friend."

"I didn't know she was coming."

"What are you talking about? I told you last night. Why the attitude?"

"I'm sorry, Marienne," Zhanna apologized. "It's nice to see you again."

"That's okay, Zhanna," Marienne said. She had worked with Zhanna on previous CIA missions and understood the Russian's quirky disposition.

Private conversation was forced to halt when Susan delivered the drinks.

"Thanks, Susan," Erika said.

Two men at the other end of the bar raised their hands to signal they wanted another round of Budweiser. Zhanna sent Susan to pour the beers.

"Marienne," Erika said. "The first person I want you to tail is our new bartender. This afternoon I stopped by the address she listed on her application form. I don't think she lives there."

Chapter 20

Confrontation

Arlington, Virginia
Next day—Friday, 15 December 1950

The Lili Marlene opened at 11 a.m. so the place was deserted at breakfast time. Erika brought some bagels and cheese to the closed café. Zhanna put on a pot of coffee. Sheila was with them as they awaited the arrival of Marienne, who walked in about 20 minutes later.

They gathered at one of the tables.

"You were right, Erika," Marienne started out. "Susan doesn't live at the address on her application. I followed her to a hotel just outside Arlington called the Arbor Inn, which means two things. One she doesn't live in the area permanently, and two, she's not as broke as she makes out. That hotel looks pretty nice from the outside.

"I stayed in my car across the street from the hotel all night. This morning I found out why she's not broke. Susan walked out of the hotel wearing a U.S. Army captain's uniform. I tailed her to the Pentagon where she parked and walked inside."

Everyone looked around at one another.

"I'll take care of it," Zhanna blurted out. "She'll disappear tonight."

"Zhanna," Erika grumbled. "Quit talking crazy."

"It's obvious she's working for Grainger," Sheila said. "He wants someone keeping an eye on us."

"Should I report this to Al?" Marienne asked Erika.

The team leader thought for a moment. "Not yet. Let's find out more about her first. For now, everyone treats Susan as if nothing has changed. Do you understand, Zhanna?"

"Yeah, yeah. I understand. Get off my back, Erika."

Marienne slightly smiled as she thought, *Zhanna hasn't changed. Still a rascal until the chips were down and one of her fellow Maidens was in trouble.*

[about the same time at the Pentagon office of Colonel Howard Grainger]

"Captain," Grainger said. "I'm sure you're being extraordinarily cautious about being followed. These women you're dealing with are very experienced."

"Yes, sir," Susan Wedeking said. "I never drive directly back to my hotel. I weave around blocks that take me out of my way."

"Good. Now give me your report."

"I met a new woman last night. It was obvious that Erika and Zhanna know her. Her name is Marienne. A last name was not mentioned, and I knew it would seem suspicious if I asked. She's a brunette, about 5'5". I'd guess her age to be early 30s. Other than that, I have little to report. When I was within earshot of any of the conversations between them, I heard only small talk."

"Of course," Grainger said. "They're not going to let you hear anything they don't want you to hear. See if you can find out this new woman's last name and I'll have G-2 run a background check. But be careful how you go about it. You're right that asking last night would draw suspicion."

When Susan Wedeking left his office, Grainger sat back in his chair. He hoped he had done the right thing. The captain was smart and tough, but she was an MP, inexperienced in dealing with women like Leroy Carr's Shield Maidens. Women that impressed him as being more like mobsters than field agents. He hoped he wasn't throwing Captain Wedeking to the wolves.

[early that evening—the Lili Marlene Café]

Erika and Sheila entered and approached the bar. It was Friday night so Angelika's part-time waitress, the college coed Patty, was working. Four tables were occupied with customers eating food.

"Where's Marienne?" Sheila asked softly as soon as they sat down. Zhanna and Susan were at the other end of the bar waiting on three men.

"She'll be here," Erika said, also sotto voce. "She had to get some sleep this afternoon. She spent last night awake and freezing her butt off in her car."

After Susan helped Zhanna finish with the three men, Zhanna walked toward her Shield Maiden cohorts with Susan.

"Hi, Susan," Erika said. "How are things going with your new job. I hope you like working here."

"I love it, Erika. I still have a lot to learn about how to mix certain cocktails, but Zhanna is a good teacher."

Erika didn't doubt it. Zhanna didn't have a bartender's license so technically she was breaking the law working behind the bar. Nevertheless, Zhanna knew booze. In the same regard, Susan didn't possess a bartender's license either, which she was upfront about during her interview with Angelika but was hired anyway because she spoke German. Erika and Angelika had two illegal bartenders.

"I'll have a brandy, Susan," Erika said. "Angelika brought in some Asbach."

"I'll have a vodka martini," Sheila said.

Zhanna told Susan, "A vodka martini is one-part vermouth and five parts vodka. Mix in a shaker with ice but not too long. You want the ice to cool it but not dilute it. Then garnish with a lemon slice unless they want olives."

"A lemon slice is fine," Sheila said.

Marienne Schenk suddenly walked in, saw Erika and Sheila at the bar, and joined them.

"Sheila and I just placed drink orders, Marienne," Erika said. "What would you like?"

"A highball with 7-Up. Same as last night."

The women watched Susan walk away to prepare the drinks.

"I got a call from Al this afternoon," Erika told the other women. "He wants us all in his office tomorrow morning at nine o'clock. He said he has more information about the man with the Ukrainian wife. This means we have to confront Susan tonight. We don't want her hanging around and forcing us to hold our tongues around her.

"We'll take care of this after the café closes and she returns to her hotel. Sheila, you'll leave the café with Marienne an hour before closing.

Marienne can take you to Susan's hotel. Enter her room without any signs of forced entry and be there waiting for her. My lock picking tools are in my car. I'll get them for you before you leave. Marienne, when Sheila has Susan secured, return here. When the café closes, you can take Zhanna and me to her hotel. Sheila, do what you have to do but don't mess up her face."

The Shield Maidens and Marienne had a couple more rounds with the conversation held to innocuous chat. At one point, Erika got up and walked into the kitchen. Angelika was there with Bertha. Erika and Angelika hugged.

"It looks like business might be getting better," Erika said in German so her friend would understand.

"I think so, also." Angelika said. "Yet for a Friday night crowd, it still has to improve. We're not making any profit, Erika. We're not breaking even after all the bills and salaries are paid. Perhaps you made a mistake in investing your money in me."

"Angelika, don't say that. You helped save Zhanna and my lives when you gave us a safe overnight haven when we were fugitives behind the Curtain. I will never regret getting you out of East Berlin and bringing you here. We're in this together. Things will work out."

The middle-aged woman looked as if she would cry. She hugged Erika again.

◊ ◊ ◊

The Lili Marlene closed at midnight. Many Arlington bars stayed open until 2 a.m., but business at the café didn't warrant those hours. Susan helped Zhanna clean up. The Army MP captain had seen Sheila Reid and the woman called Marienne leave an hour ago. Erika was still there.

With the cleanup finished, Zhanna told Susan she could leave for the night. Susan, playing her part, gathered her meager tips. She drove back to her hotel, again keeping a close eye out for a tail along her surreptitious route.

When she entered her hotel room, before she had a chance to turn on a light, a heavy blow was delivered to her stomach. Susan dropped to the floor, gasping. The light came on. Standing over her was Sheila

Reid. Sheila grabbed Susan's hair, jerked her to her feet and roughly pulled her past the hotel bed and deposited her in a chair near the window. The window blinds were closed.

Susan suddenly flew from the chair and took a swing at Sheila, but the former Shield Maiden ducked, and the blow barely grazed the top of her head.

Sheila punched Susan's sternum, sending her crashing back into the chair.

"You just proved that you're not who you say you are," Sheila straddled Susan and pinned her arms. "A down-and-out woman willing to work for 45 cents an hour plus tips would be scared if she came home and discovered an intruder."

"Get off of me, you bitch!"

What's your real last name? We know it can't be Lauer."

"Screw you!"

Sheila pulled her handgun from underneath the back of her blouse, got off of Susan while aiming the weapon at the captain's forehead. "You'll sit where you are quietly. Friends of yours will be here soon."

◊ ◊ ◊

After dropping off Sheila at Susan's hotel, Marienne returned to the Lili Marlene to pick up Erika and Zhanna.

All three entered the hotel room. Susan was seated in a chair. Sheila sat on the bed holding her handgun.

"This one has grit, Erika," Sheila said. "She took a swing at me."

"Interesting," Erika replied. She smiled at Susan. "You took a swing at a superior officer. You could be court-martialed and thrown in the brig for that, Captain."

"How did you find out who I am? I know I wasn't tailed."

Erika glanced at Marienne and smiled. "Of course you weren't tailed. A Gypsy fortune teller told us. We know you have to be working for Colonel Grainger. Tell us all about it."

"I'm not telling you shit," Susan said, then flew from her chair at Erika. Erika took her to the ground like a Notre Dame linebacker tackling a running back. Zhanna started to draw her handgun but Sheila stopped her. “Erika doesn’t need any help, Zhanna.”

Erika, still on top of Susan, started laughing. “I’m starting to like you more and more, Captain. We’ll leave you now. Have a good night. Don’t be late for work tomorrow; it’s a weekend night and hopefully business will be good.”

The menacing women departed quietly as Susan laid on the floor exhausted, not sure what had just happened.

Chapter 21

Svetlana Urashova

Washington, D.C.
Next day—Saturday, 16 December 1950

At nine o'clock in the morning, Erika, Sheila, Zhanna, and Marienne sat in Al Hodge's E Street office.

"Okay, here's the latest," Hodge said. "James Brunnell, the man Zhanna told us about who was at the Lili Marlene speaking poor Russian to her has been cleared. His level of clearance prohibits him from seeing any data about G-2 field agents working oversees. That means his Ukrainian wife could not be getting any information of any significant nature from her husband that the Soviets would be interested in."

"What is the wife's background?" Sheila asked.

"She was a peasant girl, raised on a farm outside Vinnytsya. She's now a housewife," Al stated.

Erika asked, "What's her name?"

"Svetlana. Her maiden surname was Urashova."

Zhanna, who had been ignoring most of the conversation as she puffed away on a cigarette, suddenly looked at Hodge. He noticed this.

"What is it, Zhanna? Do you recognize the name?"

Zhanna blew out smoke and said, "Of course not. Why would I recognize the name of a Ukrainian peasant girl?"

Erika looked at Zhanna who briefly glanced back.

Hodge continued. "Now it's time for your report, Erika."

"Colonel Grainger tried to infiltrate the Lili Marlene."

"What are you taking about?"

"Angelika hired a part-time waitress who can speak German to communicate with Angelika when Zhanna's or I can't be there. Thanks to Marienne, we found out that this woman is an Army captain. She has to be working for Grainger. Marienne watched her walking into the Pentagon yesterday.

Hodge fumed and picked up his telephone receiver. "I'm calling that son-of-a-gun right now. Grainger is violating our agreement."

"Please put the phone down, Al," Erika said.

He ignored her and began dialing, looking at a piece of paper with a phone number on it.

"Al, please put down the phone until you hear us out."

Hodge slammed down the receiver, "What is it, Erika?" he exclaimed loudly.

"We want you to call Grainger, but for another reason. Tell him you found out about his plot and you want the captain to partner with us on this assignment. Her name is Susan Lauer, but that's probably an alias. Marienne shadowed her to the Pentagon but of course never got close enough to read the name tag on her uniform so we can't run a background check."

"Why in the world would I say any of that? If her cover is blown, Grainger will have to withdraw her."

"We want to find out this captain's real name and why Grainger tagged her to do this. She must be something other than G-2 and is staying at a hotel so she's apparently from out-of-town. We confronted her last night. She's got spunk and is resilient. She should be working with us on this assignment instead of spying on us. She can still report to Grainger, which will make him happy. He'll jump on this opportunity."

Hodge looked around at them all, then back at Erika. "I'll call Grainger, but I'm not okaying this until I have her real last name and can check her out."

"Fair enough, Al. Thanks."

◊ ◊ ◊

Two hours later, the phone rang at the Lili Marlene. Erika picked up. It was Al Hodge.

"Lehmann, I dialed your home. As usual you weren't there so I figured you'd be at that doggone tavern. It's Saturday, why aren't you home with your daughter?"

"We call it a café, Al. And I'm with my daughter. Ada's here. She likes helping Bertha in the kitchen—cleaning, mopping, that sort of thing. If you're done questioning my maternal fitness, tell me what you found out."

"I talked to Grainger. I read him the riot act, which he didn't appreciate and started cursing. But we both want the same thing—to uncover the mole. The captain's real last name is Wedeking. I had the Bone Hunters check her out. She's a military police supervisor stationed at Fort Dix. The only MP officer there who outranks her is a major who oversees the entire MP contingent at Dix. This Wedeking received several commendations for her work in Europe during the war and was involved in the post-war interrogations of Hermann Göring, Rudolf Hess, and the other Nazi bigwigs because she speaks fluent German. She was present during the entirety of the Nuremberg trials."

"Well, that pretty much says it all," Erika said. "We can use her help."

"As soon as we hang up," Hodge said, "I'll call Grainger back and tell him we want Wedeking to work with your team. Grainger knows this will allow both the CIA and G-2 to claim we are fulfilling White House orders to cooperate on this mission. I'm doing this on your request, Erika. If it doesn't work out, we'll have a big problem on our hands."

"I told Susan we'd see her tonight. Her shift starts at five o'clock. Tell Colonel Grainger to make sure she's there."

"I'll do that," Hodge said. "And Grainger and I will both be there. You can bet your ass on that."

[later same day]

Susan Wedeking walked into the Lili Marlene at 4:40 p.m. wearing civilian clothes. Earlier this afternoon, Colonel Grainger called her into his office and briefed her on the latest developments. Zhanna was behind the bar. Susan approached the Russian and started to sit down on a barstool.

"Keep your ass off that barstool," Zhanna growled. "Pour what you want to drink and I'll take you upstairs. Angelika will cover the bar for us."

Susan poured herself a Jameson on the rocks.

"That Irish whiskey is expensive. Be sure you pay for that," Zhanna said. "None of us expect free drinks here."

"I intend on paying for it, Miss Congeniality." Susan rang up 75¢ on the register and put three quarters in the money tray. She followed Zhanna into the kitchen.

"Angelika," Zhanna said in German. "We're taking that break now that I told you about."

Angelika nodded and went out to tend the bar.

Susan greeted Bertha and Ada. The little girl stood on a box at the sink washing beer glasses.

The two women walked up the stairs. When they entered the storeroom, Grainger was there along with another man Susan had never met. Also around the large table sat Erika, Sheila, and the woman she recently met—Marienne. They all had drinks in front of them.

"Thank you for coming, Captain," Grainger said as if she had a choice in the matter. "You know all the ladies here. I'd like to introduce you to Al Hodge. Mr. Hodge is in charge of this mission from the CIA's end. Please have a seat."

Susan sat down. Zhanna remained standing.

"Captain Wedeking," Grainger said. "As I told you in my office this afternoon, we're taking a different direction concerning your assignment. From now on, you'll work with the CIA team. Mr. Hodge and I will be cooperating closely. You'll report to both me and Mr. Hodge. Erika Lehmann is your team leader, as requested by Mr. Hodge. You'll follow her orders. Any questions?"

Susan paused as she looked around the room. The intimidating Amazon, Zhanna Rogova, stood near her. Erika looked at her with She-Wolf eyes.

"Captain," Grainger frowned. "I asked you if you have any questions concerning your orders."

"Mr. Hodge, may I ask how you found out about me?" Susan asked.

Hodge directed her attention to Marienne. "You've met Marienne Schenk. She's in charge of shadowing on this assignment."

Marienne said, "Susan, your biggest mistake was weaving around too many blocks to avoid a tail on your way back to your hotel Thursday night. That immediately told me you were cautious of being followed. That strategy sometime works during the day, but not at night when all you can see in your rearview mirror is multiple headlights."

Zhanna, who loved her humble job at the café, grew impatient. "Can we get on with this? It's Saturday night. Susan and I are needed at the bar."

◊ ◊ ◊

The briefing by Hodge and Grainger ended at 6:30. Both men had left the café. Erika, Sheila, and Marienne now sat at a table with a drink as Zhanna and Susan manned the bar. The place was about half full.

"Erika," Marienne said. "You asked me if I had any tips that might help you increase business. I don't know anything about running a bar, but a friend of Harold's opened a tavern in Pittsburgh. This man's business was slow starting out, but he drew in new customers by offering competitive dart tournaments and wrist-wrestling competitions. All those guys drink a lot of beer. Maybe bring in a pinball machine. Harold's friend was surprised at how many dimes he collected at the end of each day from just one machine. Some nights it was over $30. Same goes for a jukebox.

"Your food is terrific and Bertha and Ada keep the kitchen immaculate. You just need to get more people in here to try the menu and spread the word. There's no reason this place can't be successful, and not just from Arlington locals. When people get wind of a good new place, they're willing to take a reasonable drive to check it out. Downtown D.C. is only a 30-minute drive."

"Those are all good ideas, Marienne. Thanks."

"If you decide to do any of that," Marienne said. "Be careful who you get the pinball machines and jukebox from. Organized crime families control much of that business. They'll demand half of any revenue from the machines, plus many times they'll demand protection money. Meaning your business won't burn down in the middle of the night if you pay the extra 'insurance' money."

Erika nodded. Marienne's warning about the workings of organized crime was not new information for Erika. Three of her previous missions during the post-war years had dealt in some way with organized crime figures. Either directly or indirectly.

Sheila changed the subject. "So what's our plan for Captain Wedeking?"

"We want to talk to Zhanna first," Erika replied. "I have a strong feeling Zhanna recognized the name Svetlana Urashova—James Brunnell's wife. I haven't had the opportunity to talk to Zhanna about that since we left Al's office. We'll wait until after we close."

"Are you including Wedeking in that conversation?" Sheila asked.

"Yes, if she's going to fulfill her orders to work with us, we have to be able to trust her. This way we'll find out. If she betrays us, we'll have to resolve that matter."

Everyone knew what that meant.

[closing time]

Last call for drinks had passed and all the customers were now gone. Zhanna turned over the 'Closed' sign in the window by the front door. When Zhanna and Susan finished cleaning the bar, Erika approached them and asked both women to join her and the others at their table. Still wearing their short bartender aprons, Zhanna and Susan Wedeking sat down. Angelika, Bertha, and Ada were still cleaning up in the kitchen.

Erika said, "Zhanna, I got the feeling in Al's office today that you recognized the name of the Ukrainian wife of James Brunnell."

"Am I supposed to speak freely?" Zhanna asked Erika as she browsed Susan.

"Yes," Erika said. "Susan is part of our team now. That's the arrangement with G-2."

"For a time during the war, Svetlana Urashova was a friend of mine," Zhanna told the group. "In 1943, I was her supervisor for six weeks at the Red Army sniper school outside Ryazan, which is about 200 miles southeast of Moscow. I know it is the same women because the Svetlana I knew was born outside Vinnytsya in the Ukraine, as Al Hodge's report stated. After training, she followed me back to the front and we worked together as snipers for two months until she was transferred to another unit. I never saw her again after that. I've often wondered if she survived the war."

"What do you think of a reunion with Svetlana?" Erika asked.

"For what purpose?" Zhann asked. "Hodge told us her husband can't be the mole because he has no access to information that is getting G-2 men arrested overseas. Even if he did, Svetlana would not do anything to help the current Russian regime. She hated Stalin as much as I did. We both joined the Red Army to fight against the barbaric Huns who invaded our motherland and killed innocent women and children. We didn't join to fight for Stalin and the Proletariat."

"Still," Erika said to Zhanna. "Keep in mind a reunion with Svetlana. We all know the old protocol we learned at the CIA Farm, 'If you have little to work with then work on that little thing.'"

Susan spoke up. "What's going to be my role in this mission? I assume you told Mr. Hodge you want me for more than what I was hired for—covering the bar when Zhanna is not here."

"Don't underestimate your role as Zhanna's substitute, Susan," Erika said. "You can help the mission by doing that for now. You'll understand why later. But to answer your question, we'll have further directives for you when the time comes."

Chapter 22

Susan asks for a transfer

Arlington, Virginia
Next day—Sunday, 17 December 1950

It was obvious that the Lili Marlene Café had become the unofficial meeting spot for the Shield Maidens. Even though today was Sunday and the café closed, the Maidens, Marienne Schenck, and Susan Wedeking sat around a table in the empty café. Zhanna and Susan had prepared coffee. Erika brought apple strudel for everyone.

"Erika," Marienne asked, "Why do you close on Sundays. This can be a big day for churchgoers who want to stop for breakfast either before or after services. Perhaps consider opening for breakfast."

"It's a German thing, Marienne. On Sunday in Germany everything is closed, restaurants, department stores, grocery stores, things of that sort. The only exceptions are hospitals, police, fire departments—necessary services like that. And hotels. They have to serve food for out-of-town guests.

"I have, however, given thought to your suggestions about dart boards, pinball machines, and a juke box. I'll find out who to contact about those things this week."

"Okay," Marienne said, "just be careful who you go into business with. Remember what I told you, there are a lot of seedy characters running those businesses."

"Got it," Erika said.

As the women drank their coffee and ate the strudel, the conversation shifted to Susan.

"Susan, are you satisfied with your assignment?" Sheila Reid asked.

"I might be if I knew what my assignment was, Lieutenant Colonel. The only thing I've been told so far is that I am to help Zhanna cover the bar, with some vague reference made by Erika that other responsibilities might come along later. I'm in the dark."

"First of all," Sheila said, "never refer to me by my rank unless we're in the Pentagon and I'm in uniform. It's 'Sheila' the rest of the time."

Erika said, "Your main job right now is to be our eyes and ears here at the café when we're not around. Also, to protect Angelika, Bertha, and Patty, our waitress. There might be some unsavory men stopping by the café this week. You'll make sure the ladies are not harassed."

"So I'm a bouncer," Susan quipped.

"Use the name you prefer," Zhanna said sharply. "You'll obey your orders."

[that afternoon]

Even though it was a Sunday afternoon, Susan Wedeking found Colonel Howard Grainger in his Pentagon office. The Colonel had not taken a day off since G-2 European agents had begun disappearing.

"What is it, Captain?" Grainger said to Wedeking.

"Colonel, I respectfully request that I be allowed to apply for a transfer from my current assignment."

Grainger frowned, "Why."

"It's become obvious to me that the CIA team is not going to include me in this assignment in anything other than a trivial role."

Grainger didn't know what she was talking about and didn't care. He never even allowed her to explain. "Your request is denied, Captain. You don't realize what I had to go through just to get you inside that café. Just continue doing what those women expect of you and keep reporting to me."

Part 3

Chapter 23

Egg salad at Woolworth's

Arlington, Virginia
Next day—Monday, 18 December 1950

Svetlana Urashova had just ordered an egg salad sandwich from the Woolworth's diner counter when a tall woman sat down beside her. Svetlana glanced at her briefly and nearly fell off her stool.

"Hello, Svetlana," the woman said.

"Zhanna!"

The two women hugged. "We both survived the war," Zhanna said. "Imagine that."

"I can't believe my eyes," Svetlana was still in shock. "How . . . how did you end up here in America?"

"By strange fortune, Svetlana. How about you?"

"I married an American soldier. He got his discharge in 1947 but now works as a civilian contractor at the Pentagon." Al Hodge had already given Zhanna this information. She was glad her old friend was not covering up.

"Does your husband treat you well?" Zhanna asked.

"He's very loving and kind."

"Good. Svetlana, I can't stay. I have to return to work. I tend bar at a small café on South Nash Street here in Arlington called the Lili Marlene Café. You and your husband should try and stop by for a drink or dinner some night this week."

"We'll do it, Zhanna." The women hugged again. "I can't wait to tell James." When Zhanna left, Svetlana continued to sit there dumbfounded. The great Zhanna Rogova, Hero of the Soviet Union, now working as a bartender in a small café. The woman who had saved her life.

[late that afternoon]

As soon as James Brunnell walked into his house, Svetlana was waiting.

"James, you're not going to believe what happened to me today." She spoke good English but with a strong Russian accent.

"What happened?" he asked.

"You remember me mentioning my Red Army instructor, Zhanna Rogova. The one that later saved my life in fighting outside Kyiv."

"Yes, I remember."

"I ran into her today at Woolworth's."

"You're joking."

"No. Zhanna is now a bartender at a café here in Arlington. She invited us to come in for dinner some night this week. Can we go?"

"Sure, honey. If that's what you want. I've been in that place. How about Friday evening?"

[that evening]

Susan was behind the bar at the Lili Marlene.

Erika, Sheila, and Zhanna sat at one of the tables. Marienne was not there. She hadn't yet returned from shadowing Svetlana. Marienne had tailed Svetlana to Woolworth's that afternoon then posed as a shopper while calling Zhanna. Marienne was still shadowing her.

"I don't think we'll find anything of concern about Svetlana," Zhanna told the group. "I think she's just a happily married housewife."

"I hope so, Zhanna," Erika said. "We all know she's a friend of yours. But you know we have to be sure."

"Al also said her husband doesn't have the clearance level to be in a position to furnish the Soviets with any information about G-2 field agents, so I don't see the point," Zhanna mumbled.

"Zhanna, the sooner we get your friend and her husband cleared the sooner we can move on," Sheila added.

It looked like everyone at the bar had a full drink so Erika flagged Susan to come over.

"Do you still like your job, Susan?" Erika asked as Susan stood at the table.

"It's not a job, Erika. It's an assignment. A boring one at that, but I fulfill my duties."

"I might be able to offer you something more than boring tomorrow, Susan. Tomorrow morning at ten o'clock, I'm having two darts boards, two pinball machines, and a jukebox delivered here to the café."

"What's the big deal about that?" Susan asked.

"I'm getting them from the Russian mob. They will demand a big payment up front and half of our revenue from the machines. We'll make them a counteroffer. I've given Angelika and Bertha the morning off. I don't want them exposed to this. Tomorrow, Sheila has to be behind her desk at her Polish section, and Marienne will shadow James Brunnell tomorrow if he leaves the Pentagon. Here at the café it will be just you, Zhanna, and me. Bring your handgun."

"I thought Marienne warned you not to deal with those people," Susan said.

"And that gave me an idea," Erika said. "They're Russians. As the Americans say, 'Do you get my drift?'"

A few minutes later, Marienne Schenck entered the café and sat down with the women.

"Nothing suspicious so far," Marienne said. "Svetlana made a few shopping stops after she left Woolworth's. One key that negates suspicion is that she didn't stop to make a call from a telephone booth after meeting Zhanna. After shopping she went home. She and her husband live in a bungalow on Pickett Street near an elementary school on the northern edge of Arlington. James Brunnell arrived home at 5:37 p.m. and they had not left nor had anyone call on them at their house when I pulled the plug on the tail—a couple of more indicators that they're legitimate. I'll switch focus to the husband tomorrow."

"Thanks, Marienne," Erika said.

Chapter 24

A delivery

Arlington, Virginia
Next day—Tuesday, 19 December 1950

The Lili Marlene didn't open for business until 11 a.m. At 10 a.m., Erika, Zhanna, and Susan waited alone in the closed café when the heavy knock rattled the door glass.

Erika opened the door.

"We a delivery have," said a gruff Russian in broken English. Russia was America's ally during the war and many Russians had been allowed to immigrate in '46 and '47 before the Cold War heated up. Russian communities could be found in almost any large American city. Most Russian's were hardworking, law-abiding citizens, but not all. A sizable number of Russians who immigrated were wartime black marketers seeking to escape post-war punishment in their motherland.

"Ah, yes," Erika spoke in Russian to better communicate with the man. "We want the dart boards on that wall (Erika pointed). The pinball machines over here and the jukebox over there."

The man signaled his crew who began unloading a truck parked in front.

When everything was in place, the man said in Russian, "That will be $200 for delivery. Your rental will be $50 each week plus 50 percent of the profits from the machines. Also, you need an insurance policy to protect your establishment from accidental fire. That costs $100 a week."

Erika smiled. "Why don't we bargain. I propose that we pay you nothing now or later."

Susan didn't speak Russian so had not understood the conversation, but when she saw Zhanna go for her handgun she did the same, outdrawing the men.

"Now you will leave," Erika told the men. "And don't come back without your boss. I have an offer for him. Tell him to ask for Erika."

"You can trust he will be here tonight," the spokesman sneered. "And trust me when I say you'll regret this."

As the men began stomping out, Erika added, "And tell your boss we want untaxed cigarettes to sell."

[8:00 p.m.—the Lili Marlene]

Only three Russians entered the café. A tall man whose gray hair shined underneath his country gentleman hat and two younger men who looked more like lawyers or accountants and less like the thugs dealt with earlier today.

The hoary-headed man approached the bartender. "I'm here to see the woman Erika," he said in fluent English albeit with a Russian accent.

"She's waiting for you upstairs," Susan said. "Follow me."

"Thank you," he said pleasantly.

When Angelika saw Susan walk through the kitchen, she went out to replace her at the bar.

When Susan and the three men entered the upstairs storage room, Erika and Zhanna sat at the table. Sheila and Marienne were not present for a reason. Erika was protecting Sheila's Pentagon background, and Marienne should not be seen by the men if a tail was required. Ada was home with the babysitter. Not knowing how this might turn out, Erika didn't want her daughter around if trouble ensued.

Two bottles of Stolichnaya vodka sat on the table with several glasses. Erika poured the men a drink.

"Za zdarovie!," Erika said. The men repeated the Russian toast.

"My name is Dima Lukov," the gray-haired man said, still remaining amiable. "Associates of mine who made a delivery here earlier today told me you had a problem with our payment arrangement. Now you must tell me why."

"I have a counteroffer, Mr. Lukov," Erika said. "Zhanna."

Zhanna removed her neck scarf, revealing her shocking wound. It was the first time Susan had seen it.

From the look on Lukov's face, he obviously recognized Zhanna Rogova. He had never met her, but all Russians knew of her exploits during the war from the Russian wartime propaganda newsreels shown in the movie theaters.

"Here is my proposition, Mr. Lukov," Erika said. "Zhanna works undercover for the Soviets. She has information that needs to be relayed to the Soviet embassy in Washington from time to time. She needs a courier. That courier could be a man who works for you. I can offer you a place within the shadow of the Pentagon where you and your men can congregate. That place is here in my café. In return, our debt for the delivery today will be wiped clean along with any future money owed. That money will go to the café. If you accept this offer, I want your word that all your men will be on their best behavior when inside the café. The manager who runs this place and our cook are never to be informed of our accord and those women will be protected and Zhanna's name will not be mention at the Soviet embassy. Those are my terms."

"May I ask who you are?" Lukov queried.

"My name is Erika. I'm just a friend of Zhanna's."

"And this woman," Lukov asked about Susan.

"Susan is one of our bartenders and is in charge of the café's security and the protection of our manager and cook," Erika said.

This was the first time Susan had heard that.

"Oh, and one more thing," Erika added. "We want untaxed cigarettes to sell. What are cigarettes before taxes, about 5¢ a pack?"

Lukov smiled. "Something like that."

"Do we have an agreement, Mr. Lukov?"

Lukov wasn't a Soviet spy, he was a mobster. But he saw the opportunity just offered to him. The astute gangster saw the chance for a generous profit. The gambling equipment and protection money extorted from this tavern was chicken feed compared to what he could earn from the Soviet government for classified information.

Lukov said, "We have an agreement, Miss Erika." Lukov then looked at Zhanna. "Comrade Rogova, it is indeed my pleasure to meet you."

"Yeah, yeah," Zhanna said then switched to Russian. "Pass that bottle, asshole."

Erika knew how mobsters think. Everything was about business and making money. She didn't think it would be hard to strike a deal and she had been right.

◊ ◊ ◊

Two hours later, Lukov and his men had left. Zhanna was now behind the bar. Erika and Susan sat on barstools.

"What's this all about, Erika?" Susan asked.

"It's a trap Al Hodge and I dreamed up. Al says this Lukov character is not a spy, but I know a thing or two about mobsters and Lukov will gladly sell intel to Russian agents. That's why our offer appeals to him. If he wants to uncover information he can hawk to the Soviets, what better place for his people to gather than at a café frequented by Pentagon officials ten blocks from the Pentagon with Zhanna, whom Lukov obviously admires from her wartime exploits, working with them? It's a lead, Susan. We have to pursue it."

"You mentioned to Lukov my duties."

"You're an MP officer with a sterling background. Guarding people is what you've been trained to do. From now on you'll be in charge of the café's security. I'll bring in an assistant for your security team, but you'll be in charge. Our agreement with Lukov is that his men will be on their best behavior. If not, kick them out. You'll have complete control of the café's security. Most of all, protect Angelika, Bertha, Patty, and my daughter if she's here helping in the kitchen."

Susan was glad to be finally brought out of the dark and have a definitive assignment.

The Army captain nodded, "I understand. Who is this assistant you mentioned?"

"His name is Axel Ryker," Erika answered.

Chapter 25

An assistant for Susan

Washington, D.C.
Next day—Wednesday, 20 December 1950

"Have a seat, Lehmann, and fill me in," Hodge said. Erika sat down across from his desk.

"Lukov agreed immediately when I offered him the deal, Al. He didn't even take a moment to think it over."

"He'll sell anything," Hodge agreed. "And he knows there would be big bucks in it for him if he came up with something significant he can sell the Soviet embassy. Our goal is to not put Lukov out of business, that's the FBI's responsibility. The only thing we're focused on is luring the mole out of his burrow. How are you handling things with Angelika and Bertha?"

"I told Lukov that they are not to be bothered or be told anything about what's going on. I placed Susan Wedeking in charge of security."

"And you told Lukov any men he sends in there have to have American accents, right?"

"Right. And they have to be on their best behavior. Whether Lukov sends in his own men or contacts the Soviet embassy and lets them handle it for a finder's fee on his part remains to be seen."

"Our next step is to get some G-2 men to frequent your place. The trap won't hold up if the place doesn't have Pentagon officials coming around like you promised Lukov. I'll contact Grainger and fill him in. He can handle that end of it."

"This was your brainchild, Al. I have to give you credit."

"And yours, as well. But before we start patting each other on the back, let's see how it goes."

"By the way, Al. I promised Susan to give her an assistant for security—Axel Ryker."

Hodge looked surprised. "This is the first time you've ever asked for Ryker. Normally, if Leroy or I send in Ryker we have to quarrel with you."

"Yes, but my daughter occasionally works in the kitchen. I want her protected. Susan will be in charge but she'll need an assistant. She can't be there all the time."

"Ryker's in Philadelphia," Hodge said. "That only an hour's flight away. I'll call him in tomorrow."

[that evening at the Lili Marlene]

Colonel Howard Grainger had done his part. Tonight, a small contingent of Pentagon G-2 officers who he had briefed on the mission were either at tables or sitting at the bar. Angelika, who knew nothing about the circumstances, was ecstatic.

"Erika, this will be a good night," she said in German.

"Ja, Angelika, eine gute Nacht," Erika answered.

Both Zhanna and Susan were busy behind the bar.

"How do you think Susan will feel about Ryker?" Sheila asked.

"He'll be here tomorrow," Erika said. "I told Susan not to be put off by his appearance. It's more his personality that concerns me."

Chapter 26

There is strength in the union of even sorry men.
—*Homer, (ca. 700 B.C)*

Flashback

Berlin, Gestapo headquarters
8 Prinz Albrechtstrasse

July 1942

Axel Ryker sat down heavily in the chair facing Heinrich Himmler's desk. Ryker, a repatriated German from Lithuania, was a man called upon by Himmler from time to time for 'special' tasks. Ryker possessed several qualities that augmented his usefulness to Himmler and the Gestapo. He spoke fluent Russian (his native tongue), acceptable Slovak and Czech (most speakers of Slovak had few problems with the similar Czech), and German. Ryker even managed to stumble his way through English, although his English consisted of a strange mixture of Russian, Czech, and German accents.

He could also snap a man's neck as easily as a chicken bone, which he had proved on more than one occasion. For Axel Ryker, liquidation and torture were job skills honed sharp and sometimes even pleasant diversions.

Ryker was a full six-feet tall but a wide, heavily muscled torso gave him the appearance of being shorter. A shaved head and dark, pitiless eyes under a protruding brow gave him a caveman countenance. On the brow grew thick black eyebrows barely separated in the middle. Adding to his already grisly genetic features was a nose that had been smashed and never repaired. The mashed nose was a souvenir from the early 1930s, courtesy of a pipe-swinging communist who crept up on him during a street brawl. Ryker was a teenager at the time.

To frighten women and intimidate men, Axel Ryker simply had to enter the room.

But Ryker was no mindless automaton dusted off only during the Gestapo's murder and maim hour. In addition to his impressive aforementioned language skills, Ryker possessed an innate craftiness, including an almost supernatural ability to discern when someone was lying to him. These qualities allowed him to ferret information when others failed.

A week ago, Ryker had been in Budapest investigating a break-in at the Romanian embassy. Some sensitive papers detailing Nazi plans to arrest a popular, but pro-resistance, Catholic priest in Oradea had been stolen. Ryker was ordered to Budapest to take over the case. His first task would be the apprehension of the embassy thieves; his second the eventual arrest of the priest.

A suspect in the burglary, under torture, had failed to implicate others. That is until Ryker had the man's wife and four small children brought in. The youngest child was still nursing, the oldest not yet seven years old. As the family stood in front of the bleeding, half-conscious father, Ryker transferred the infant from the mother's arms to the oldest child, took out his Walther and held the muzzle to the mother's temple in front of her husband and children. The man knew Ryker wouldn't hesitate to pull the trigger. The bleeding father gave Ryker the information he sought on condition his family be released. The man's associates were arrested and the papers recovered before they could be circulated. Ryker had the father and all the conspirators shot, of course. The penniless mother and children were released on the streets of Budapest. Axel Ryker kept his promises.

Back to Present

Now, because of his considerable European contacts, Axel Ryker worked for the CIA under the agency's protection. Since the war, his English had improved to the point he could be considered fluent.

He had been summoned to Washington. Now, instead of staring across a desk from Heinrich Himmler, he gazed at Al Hodge. Erika Lehmann was also present.

"What is Lehmann doing here?" Ryker groused. "Why must I continue to work with the Shield Maiden team? I have asked to be transferred to all-male CIA team many times."

"Yes, you have," Hodge said impatiently. "And those requests have been denied. Need I remind you Ryker that the only reason you haven't been hanged for war crimes in Germany is because of our protection? Now sit there and listen. Erika will brief you about why you were called in."

Erika spent about an hour bringing Ryker up to speed about the current mission. "Axel, your job will be to assist Captain Wedeking with security of the Lili Marlene Café. She's your boss, get that straight, but she has daily meetings with the G-2 colonel I told you about and cannot be at the café all the time. Your job is to guard the café, and especially my daughter. Also bodyguard my café manager, Angelika; our waitress; and our cook who know nothing about any of this."

"Any questions, Ryker?" Hodge asked.

"I obey my orders, Mr. Hodge. This I gladly did for the Reich and I'm now forced to do for my current employers."

"Be at the Lili Marlene tonight at seven o'clock," Erika told Ryker as she handed him a piece of paper. "Here's the address. Give this to your cab driver. The café is in Arlington, just across the Potomac River bridge."

If it weren't for her daughter, Angelika, Bertha, and their waitress, Erika would have never requested the horrific Ryker, but she now knew Ada and the café staff would be safe with Susan and her 'assistant.'

[that evening]

Susan poured a glass of wine with her back to the bar. When she turned, a monstrous man with ruthless eyes stood glaring at her. Multiple, deep facial scars and a mashed nose added to his ferocious visage. On his head was a black porkpie hat cocked to one side.

"I was ordered to report to a woman at the bar named Wedeking," Ryker groused in his gravelly voice. "My name is Ryker."

"I'm Susan Wedeking. Erika told me you'd be here tonight."

Erika had described Ryker but seeing him in person made that description seem restrained.

"We'll go upstairs and talk," Susan said. "Zhanna is here. I'll ask her to tend bar."

Upstairs, they took a seat at the table.

Erika had briefed Susan on Ryker's background. Susan had seen some of the Gestapo's handiwork in Europe and hated the prospect of working with Himmler's top henchman. Nevertheless, for the sake of the mission, she had little choice but to attempt to make it work.

"Erika told me you have been briefed about me and our mission here. You'll call me Susan and I'll call you Axel. Two bartenders addressing each other as Mr. or Miss and a last name would seem odd in front of customers. Especially, never refer to me by my Army rank."

Ryker seemed to be ignoring her. He lit a cigar with a Zippo lighter and blew smoke. "Where is Lehmann and the Reid woman?" he asked.

"They're out picking up cartons of cigarettes. Erika got us a special deal. They'll be here later. Now, make sure you understand your duties, Axel. It's our job—yours and mine—to handle security for the café. Part of the deal with Lukov is that his men remain on good behavior when inside the café, but with gangsters one never knows what can happen. We have the establishment to protect and even more importantly innocent civilians—Angelika, the manager; Bertha the cook; and our waitress named Patty. Erika's daughter isn't here tonight but Ada often helps clean in the kitchen. We have to protect them at all costs. I assume you're armed."

"A Walther PPK," Ryker replied.

"Good. Always have it on you but never take it out unless there's no alternative. There is also a baseball bat behind the bar."

"I won't need a bat to eject a drunk, Captain Wedeking."

"I asked you to never refer to me by my rank." Erika had told her it was easy to become impatient with the combative Ryker. Susan now knew why.

A roguish grin appeared on Ryker's hideous face.

"The café opens at eleven in the morning every day and closes at midnight except Sunday when we're closed all day," Susan said. "You'll work those hours. You can eat lunch and dinner here. I will be here during those hours except for times I have to report to my directing officer at the Pentagon. A thirteen-hour day is a long one but we can relieve one another for breaks. Where are you staying?"

"The Mayflower Hotel. Room 511."

"Here is my home phone number in case you ever have to reach me after hours." Susan handed Ryker a piece of paper. "You'll start tomorrow. Report to work at least fifteen minutes early each day. That means 10:45 a.m. at the latest. Any questions or comments?"

"Just one comment," Ryker said. "I hope you are not a weak woman. I hate working with women, especially weak ones."

"I'm not going to justify that with a response."

Ryker let out with a chilling laugh. "Watch your step with Lehmann and Rogova. You might think they are friends, but neither of them will hesitate to open your throat if they think you have disappointed them."

Without being dismissed, Ryker stood up and left.

Susan remained in her chair with stomach churning after her first meeting with Axel Ryker.

Chapter 27

Svetlana visits the Lili Marlene

Arlington, Virginia
Next day—Friday, 22 December 1950

It was mid-afternoon. The lunchtime crowd had thinned at the Lili Marlene. Ryker was behind the bar. Susan had just returned from the Pentagon and she now sat with Erika at a table.

"Colonel Grainger interviewed all the G-2 men he sent in here last night," Susan told Erika. "None of them were approached by strangers. This is not to say Lukov didn't have scouts in here being cautious and checking things out."

Erika nodded. "Yes, that would be smart on his part—proceed with caution. Feel things out first. How did your meeting last night go with Ryker?"

"Under what rock in Hell did you find that man?"

"Susan, I have no control over who the CIA employs. I understand your feelings, believe me. But the USA is not the only country that has offered safe haven to Nazi war criminals who have useful contacts. The list is long in both England and Russia. Ryker has those contacts in Germany and the Eastern bloc countries. The Soviets were eager to have Ryker work for them, but Leroy Carr found him in South America and beat them to the punch. One thing you can count on, Ryker obeys orders. This has been embedded in him since his Gestapo days."

"He told me last night that if I do anything to disappoint you, Zhanna will slit my throat."

Erika didn't answer. The two women stared at each other. The German's absence of denial told Susan a great deal.

"I see," Susan said. "then all there is for me to say is that I won't be intimidated by Ryker or anyone else. He has been ordered to assist me and follow my instructions."

"That's right," Erika affirmed.

"He will do that or I'll demand to Colonel Grainger that Ryker be taken off the project. His and my assignment is to protect the café and civilians who work here. That's what I intend to do because those are my orders. If Ryker doesn't follow suit that will be on the CIA's pillow, not mine."

"Susan, as I said, Ryker will follow orders; still, I'll have a talk with him. I knew you were right for this job. You proved that in your hotel room the night we visited you. That's why I requested you."

"I guess I'll take that as a compliment," Susan said before joking, "At least until Zhanna slices my throat open."

Her nonchalant humor was not lost on Erika. The Shield Maiden leader was even more confident she had picked the right person to be head of security for the café until this assignment was over.

[that evening]

Tonight would be another good night for business at the Lili Marlene. Grainger again sent his small group of G-2 officers, as he would do until the mission was either successful or a flop. A few more locals were also on hand, enticed there by word-of-mouth reports of the good food, dart games, cheap cigarettes, pinball machines, and a juke box with all the latest hits. In fact, the café was almost at full capacity, forcing both Ryker and Zhanna to man the bar, while Susan helped Patty deliver food to the tables.

One of the locals dropped a dime in the juke box and, since Christmas approached, chose Gene Autry's new hit *Rudolf the Red-Nosed Reindeer.*

A group of four men played darts—a pair of men at each of the two boards. Both pinball machines were occupied.

In the kitchen, Angelika and Bertha hustled to fill food orders. Ada again stood on her box washing dishes.

Erika and Sheila sat at one of the tables. Marienne was again not there. If she were assigned to shadow someone in the bar, it would be best if she were not seen there ahead of time.

"I'm sorry I can't be here more often, Erika," Sheila said. "The Soviets have undertaken a build-up in Poland and we're monitoring it closely."

"I understand, Sheila. Your duties at the Pentagon are very important. No one expects you to ask for time off for this CIA mission. I know Al Hodge doesn't and neither do I."

Erika saw a man and woman enter the café. The woman spotted Zhanna, smiled, and guided the man to the bar. Zhanna smiled when she saw the woman, and they leaned over the bar for cheek kisses.

Sheila had her back to the bar. Erika directed her attention. "That must be Svetlana Urashova and her husband. I'll be right back."

Erika rose from her chair and approached the bar, standing beside Svetlana's husband.

"Zhanna, I'll have another Asbach," Erika said.

As pre-arranged, Zhanna introduced her Russian friend. "Erika, this is my friend, Svetlana, and her husband, James."

"How do you do?" Erika asked. "Any friend of Zhanna's is welcome here. I see there's a shortage of tables. Would you two care to join me and my friend?"

Svetlana and James agreed. He said, "That would be nice. Thank you, Erika."

"What would you like to drink?" Sheila asked Svetlana and her husband after the foursome sat down.

Svetlana got me hooked on those vodka martinis," James answered. "We'll each have one of those."

Sheila flagged Patty and placed the orders. Before the drinks even arrived, Erika noticed Svetlana spot someone at another table who caused the look on her face to turn gray.

"I'm sorry, Erika and Sheila. James and I must leave now."

James looked as surprised as anyone. "What's the matter, honey?"

"Please don't ask," Svetlana said. "Let's just go."

Svetlana stood and gathered her purse.

"I'm sorry, ladies," her husband said as he dropped $2 on the table to pay for the drinks that had not yet arrived.

The Ukrainian and her American husband quickly walked out the door.

Erika turned and looked in the direction Svetlana had looked, but most of the tables were full of men—none of whom were any of Lukov's thugs she had previously met.

"Well," Sheila said. "That was certainly interesting."

Chapter 28

Weihnachtskarpfen

Arlington, Virginia
Next day—Saturday, 23 December 1950

It was nine o'clock in the morning. The Lili Marlene would not open for another two hours. Angelika and Bertha were in the kitchen preparing for the lunch crowd. Ada scampered around hanging up Christmas decorations around the bar.

Erika, Sheila, Susan, Zhanna, and Marienne sat at a table drinking coffee.

Erika had informed Zhanna about the bizarre quick exit of Svetlana and her husband last night. "I don't think her husband knew what was going on Zhanna. This man that alarmed Svetlana must be someone from her past. Did you recognize anyone from your days with the Red Army?"

"No one," Zhanna said, "but Svetlana and I spent only a few months together. It was a long war."

"We have to rely on you, Zhanna, to approach Svetlana and find out who this man is who caused her to leave the café so quickly last night. Then Marienne tail him."

Zhanna nodded.

"Okay," Erika said. "The café will be closed for the next two days. Tomorrow is Christmas Eve and a Sunday so we are closed anyway. We will also be closed on Christmas Day on Monday. On Christmas Eve we'll have a private eggnog party with German treats. On Christmas Day on Monday, Angelika and Bertha will be making a traditional German Christmas feast just for us. You are all invited and bring a guest if you like. Ada and I will put up the Christmas tree tomorrow. That's how traditional Germans do it—the tree doesn't go up until Christmas Eve."

With a heavy heart, Erika recalled happy childhood times with her parents, especially of Christmas in Oberschopfheim where she was born. Each year Erika's childhood task was to make a new crowning ornament for the tree, usually from paper or cloth. She worked on her creation for weeks. On Christmas Eve, never earlier, her father took her into the forest where she selected the tree. After her father cut it down and set it up near the fireplace, everyone did their part to decorate, her father lifting her so Erika could reach the upper branches. Lumpi, Erika's pet dachshund, always caused her mother consternation when the dog sought to use the tree for more practical purposes. After they lit the candles, the small family feasted on a traditional German Christmas Eve dinner of Weihnachtskarpfen—Christmas carp—prepared by her British mother who could not resist serving it with English figgy pudding. After dinner, her father always concocted some errand that required leaving the house, and the errand always required Erika's help. By the time they returned, the Christkind had magically visited. Her mother rang a bell, signaling that Erika and her father could enter and look at the gifts, which would not be opened until the next morning.

Erika remembered lying in bed with Lumpi on those Christmas Eve nights getting very little sleep in anticipation of the big morning ahead.

Chapter 29

Ryker's family

Arlington, Virginia
Next day—Christmas Eve, Sunday, 24 December 1950

At six o'clock this evening it was time for the eggnog party to begin. The café was closed, but all who had been invited were there. This included all of the Shield Maidens including three women Susan Wedeking had never met: a pair of sisters named Stephanie and Kathryn, and an exotic beauty named Amy Radu.

With Leroy Carr in Korea, Al Hodge had driven to Annapolis and picked up Kay Carr. Marienne Schenck and her husband were there, Harold having returned yesterday from his river shipment to Louisville.

The real shocker for Susan was watching Axel Ryker sit at a corner table with a woman and infant.

"Who's the woman and baby Ryker is sitting with," Susan asked Sheila.

"The woman is Rose Bristow, Ryker's wife. Rose is the daughter of Archibald Bristow, a shipping magnate and one of the richest men in America. Rose is an heiress, worth millions. By default that makes Ryker a millionaire, too. The child is their son, born last spring."

Susan watched in shock as the gruesome Ryker doted over his son and wife. She approached their table with a pitcher of eggnog.

"I put extra rum in this batch," Susan said. "Anyone interested? I was told that you are Axel's wife, Rose. My name is Susan."

Rose was no beauty queen. Thick eyeglasses and a hooked nose drew attention from other, more genteel features. But it was clear that the heiress had been refined at some of the best finishing schools in both the States and in Paris before the war where she had learned fluent French.

"Would you care to join us, Susan?" Rose asked.

"I'd love to, Rose. But I'm afraid I'm on eggnog duty right now."

"Then perhaps later."

"Yes, perhaps later," Susan replied.

"Axel, my darling. Show Susan our baby."

"I don't want to."

"Don't be rude, Axel. Here let me have him."

Ryker reluctantly handed the small bundle to Rose. Rose uncovered the face to reveal a 7-month-old boy with a cleft palate.

Ryker glared at Susan, but when she said, "He's beautiful." The anger seemed to evaporate from Ryker's face.

"We've talked to many doctors," Rose said. "Most want us to wait until he's a year old before surgery."

Ryker took his son back from his wife and gently kissed the boy's forehead.

Susan felt downcast as she turned her back and walked away. She knew the baby's physical defect could be corrected, but the innocent child would forever be the son of Axel Ryker.

Angelika, Erika, and Ada brought out the appetizers. Patty had been given the night off to be with her family. Instead of serving a formal carp dinner, which both Angelika and Erika knew most Americans might not find appealing, small pieces of the fish were cut up and rested on Ritz crackers with a special sauce that Bertha whipped up. Also offered were the cook's delicious German meatballs made from veal. Also, various cold cuts including ham, Braunschweiger, and Liverwurst were brought out. Erika was a Braunschweiger lover from way back and ate nearly half a roll by herself. Everything was set up on the bar where everyone could serve themselves.

For desserts, Bertha had turned that over to Ada. Platters of cookies sat on the bar: chocolate chip, ginger snaps, and raspberry thumbprints.

"Erika," Susan asked. "Did anyone get Ryker's baby a Christmas present?"

"No. We didn't think he'd show up, let alone bring his family. Don't worry about that, Susan. Ryker doesn't care about that sort of thing. That baby will probably get a college trust fund in his stocking tomorrow at the Bristow estate."

"Ryker doesn't care for himself, but I think you're wrong about what he wants for the baby. I'll be back as soon as I can." Susan got up and walked out of the café.

During the conversation with Susan, Erika had been sitting at a table with Al Hodge and Kay Carr.

"Erika, thanks for inviting me tonight," Kay said. "I won't be able to be here tomorrow for Christmas dinner. My sister and her family invited me as soon as Leroy left for overseas."

"I understand, Kay," Erika said. "You should be with family."

At ten o'clock came the big moment of the night. Susan had just returned. Erika shook the bell, signaling it was time to reveal the Christmas tree. Ada, Angelika, and Erika carefully removed the tarp covering it.

The presents were underneath. It had been agreed upon by the adults that presents would be for children only. That meant that Ada had hit the jackpot even though she couldn't open them until tomorrow morning. Yet, Ada came across one with the note written in German. She read it out loud, "To little Herr Ryker from the Christkind."

Rose started to cry. Axel Ryker looked around the room until he locked eyes with Susan Wedeking. She immediately looked away.

"Mutti," Ada said. "Can the baby open this now? You said Mr. Ryker cannot be here tomorrow."

Rose and Ryker had a grand Christmas Day feast to attend at the Bristow's elegant estate outside Philadelphia.

"Yes, my darling," Erika said. "Let the baby have it now."

Ada walked the present to the baby and handed it over gently.

"I'll have to help him with this, my dear," Rose told Ada.

Axel held the baby as Rose unwrapped the gift. Inside was a small, toy football.

"Where did you find that this late on Christmas Eve?" Sheila asked Susan.

"It wasn't easy," Susan answered. "A toy store already had its 'Closed' sign up but I saw employees inside so I made myself obnoxious by banging on the window until they finally let me in to stop the racket."

Sheila laughed.

At the table in the corner, Rose handed the tiny football to her husband. The baby tried to hold it but struggled with his small hands. Ryker held the toy for his son as if it were a $10,000 gold Swiss watch.

Heinrich Himmler's former top Gestapo henchman now allotted himself an additional duty. He would protect the café, it's civilian workers and Erika's daughter, and now, Susan Wedeking.

Chapter 30

A Gift from Zhanna

Arlington, Virginia
Next day—Christmas Day. Monday. 1950.

Last night, Erika took Ada to Midnight Mass at the Basilica of the National Shrine of the Immaculate Conception on Michigan Avenue in D.C.

Today, the private Christmas dinner for the mission crew and friends wouldn't begin until 2 p.m. Erika, Zhanna, Susan and Ada were there by 7 a.m. to help in the kitchen. Sheila and her husband had gifts to deliver to family. They would be there later. The three women took a cigarette break at one of the café tables at 10 a.m.

Ada had opened her presents that morning when they arrived. Zhanna had given the child a switchblade.

"A switchblade, Zhanna?" Erika asked incredulously.

"What's wrong with it?" Zhanna asked. "Is it defective?"

All Erika could do was shake her head. She confiscated the weapon.

Everyone who was there last night for the Christmas Eve party was coming with the exception of Kay Carr and the Rykers who all had other dinners they had committed to.

"Erika," Susan asked. "The women who were here last night—the Fischer sisters and Amy Radu. Who are they exactly? I didn't have much time to talk to them."

"Like Zhanna, Sheila, and myself, they are Shield Maidens. Sometimes we all work together, sometimes the CIA splits us up, depending how big a team is required for a particular assignment."

Susan nodded. "I see. All this has been an eye opener for me. Especially when you told me Ryker was married to an American heiress. How'd that happen?"

"It's a long story and complicated. I'll tell you about it sometime. But I'll say this, I think that small gift you gave Ryker's son last night was very endearing and might serve you well in the future."

"What do you mean?"

"Never mind."

◊ ◊ ◊

Christmas dinner was roast goose. Six small Cornish hens surrounded the bird of honor on the platter. Tables had been pushed together to give room to the bevy of side dishes.

"Bertha, you outdid yourself. What a feast," Erika said. Everyone picked up their wine glass and saluted the cook.

Chapter 31

Bloody Igor

Arlington, Virginia
Next day—Tuesday, 26 December 1950

A concern still had to be explored: what (or who) caused Svetlana to abruptly depart from the café Friday night.

Marienne had shadowed Svetlana home after she met with Zhanna at Woolworth's last week. They knew where the Brunnell's lived without Shiela being forced to access Pentagon personnel records. At noon today, Zhanna showed up at the Brunnell's home.

"Zhanna! What a surprise. Come in."

Zhanna stepped inside the small home.

"I have some coffee cake," Svetlana said. "I'll get it and put on a pot of coffee. I have one of those new electric percolators. They get coffee ready in half the time."

Svetlana returned from the kitchen carrying the cake. "Coffee will be ready in a few moments."

"It was nice of you and your husband to stop by the café Friday night," Zhanna said. "I was hoping to spend more time with you, but you left so soon."

"Yes . . . I . . . ah, forgot there was something I had to do."

"Really? What was that Svetlana?"

She didn't answer; instead, excusing herself to check on the coffee, returning with two cups on saucers.

"Who was at the café Friday night Svetlana?"

She paused and stared into her coffee. Finally, realizing the futility of avoiding the answer told Zhanna, "Bloody Igor."

[3 p.m. at the Lili Marlene]

"Svetlana left Friday night because she spotted Igor Gulin here at the café," Zhanna announced.

"Who's he?" Susan asked. They were all there: Erika, Zhanna, Sheila, Marienne, and Susan.

"During the war, he worked for the NKVD—the Soviet Secret Police—following just behind the front lines. His unit was charged with interrogating captured Germans. He was known as Bloody Igor because of the sadistic methods he used during interrogations. I never had any dealings with him but his reputation was well known. He was more or less the Russian's version of Axel Ryker."

"But apparently Svetlana had encounters with Gulin," Erika said.

"Yes," Zhanna replied. "He was assigned to her unit for three months in 1944."

"Well," Sheila said. "This at least tells us one thing we were wondering about. It's obvious that Lukov has turned this over to the Russian embassy—most likely for a lucrative finder's fee."

The other woman nodded.

"Zhanna, does Svetlana think Gulin recognized her?" Erika asked.

"I asked her that. She was wearing a floppy brimmed hat and never noticed Gulin make eye contact, so she doesn't think so. That's why she left so quickly."

[7 p.m.]

Dima Lukov, the head of the area's Russian crime family, and Igor Gulin met for dinner at a Greek restaurant in the Foggy Bottom neighborhood of Washington.

"Gulin," Lukov started out. "Since everything has been turned over to you and your people, I want that café to start paying their dues to my organization. They have two of our pinball machines and a jukebox and pay nothing for rental or give us our take. And they pay for no fire insurance. Those women are extorting my family."

It sounded funny and more than ironic when the mob boss complained about himself being extorted.

"You'll not change your agreement until things have played out with the Pentagon officials who frequent that café. Need I remind you of the generous compensation you received for your information? That should cover any lost revenue on your part for quite some time. When this assignment is over, then you can do whatever it is you do with these establishments."

"I have a lead to pursue," Gulin continued. "Friday night I spotted a comrade from the war at that café."

"Who is he?" Lukov asked.

"'He' is a 'she.' And I've found out her husband works at the Pentagon."

Chapter 32

James Brunnell

Washington, D.C.
Next day—Wednesday, 27 December 1950

Erika, Sheila, and Zhanna sat in Al Hodge's office at 9 a.m. Marienne had flown home to Pittsburgh with the understanding she would return if needed. Zhanna had filled in Hodge about Svetlana Urashova and her history with Bloody Igor. Hodge had the CIA file concerning Igor Gulin on his desk.

"You say that Svetlana believes Gulin didn't recognize her at the Lili Marlene?" Hodge asked Zhanna.

"That's what she feels."

"That's highly unlikely," Hodge said. "Gulin is now a professional operative who works out of the Soviet embassy under the title of a charge d'affaires.

"We have to assume he knows what he's doing and recognized Svetlana. This might provide us an opportunity."

[that afternoon]

In Hodge's E Street office now sat Colonel Howard Grainger and James Brunnell. Hodge had briefed both men about the latest developments.

"Mr. Hodge," Brunnell said. "Svetlana told me everything about her time in the Red Army. That's in the past. We want to move on with our lives."

"You are a military veteran, Mr. Brunnell," Grainger interrupted. "Are you telling us this leak at the Pentagon that is leading to Americans abroad being captured and likely tortured and killed doesn't concern you?"

"Of course it does!"

Hodge took back the conversation. "Then here's what I propose we do. Colonel Grainger will ensure that your clearance level is upgraded from Level 2 to Level 4. This will be temporary, you understand, but for the time being it will place you in access of certain types of information the Soviets would be interested in. Knowing you have a Ukrainian wife might entice the Pentagon mole to contact you. It's worth taking the shot."

"I want to help," Brunnell said. "But I don't want Svetlana involved."

"I can't guarantee that," Hodge replied. "However, if the Soviets believe you are cooperating with them, your wife will not be in any danger, Mr. Brunnell. That would be counterproductive on their part. Nevertheless, I'll place Zhanna Rogova in charge of keeping your wife safe."

[that evening]

It was another good night at the Lili Marlene. The fact that Grainger sent a few G-2 men each night briefed to watch for contacts by dubious strangers helped, but this was a small contingent—most nights only two or three G-2 men were sent. More might seem suspicious.

The main increase in business came from locals. Word had finally began circulating about a good new place on South Nash Avenue—a place offering good food and drink at reasonable prices. Also available were games of chance where wagering on dart games and pinball machines wasn't frowned upon.

That Angelika received free bartenders Susan and Axel Ryker didn't hurt the ledger book either. Her only paid employees were her cook Bertha, Zhanna, and Patty. When the college-student, Patty, couldn't be there or business became too much for her to handle then Erika and Sheila stepped in to help wait tables—more free labor.

All this meant was that things were looking up for Angelika (and for Erika's investment).

At eight o'clock, Erika asked Angelika to cover the bar for a few minutes while she met with the rest of the team upstairs.

Around the table sat Erika, Zhanna, Sheila, Susan, and Axel Ryker.

"Al Hodge called me into his office this afternoon," Erika said. "Susan, he had met with your Colonel Grainger before I was called in. Zhanna, Al also met with Svetlana's husband. Al told me that Grainger will upgrade Brunnell's clearance status from Level 2 to Level 4. He is hoping this might lure the Pentagon mole into contacting Brunnell, especially because of his wife's background. Grainger is going to begin sending Brunnell and Svetlana to the café on a regular basis. Give me your opinion of how Svetlana will handle this. You know her."

"Svetlana is well trained. I trained her myself," Zhanna said. "But she's different now. All she wants is a quiet life."

"Talk to her, Zhanna," Erika said. "This is important. Since the Russian mob turned this over to the Soviet embassy, we're not going to get anything from the mob. They're just puppets on the Soviet strings from here on out and won't be informed by the Soviets of what's going on. We have to do whatever we can to root out the mole by doing it from inside the Pentagon."

"I'm clearly behind in all this," Ryker grumped. "How do we know the Russian gangsters have enlisted the Soviet embassy?"

Zhanna said, "A man named Igor Gulin was at the café the night Svetlana left so quickly."

"Igor Gulin," Ryker said. "Are you referring to Bloody Igor?"

Everyone looked at Ryker who downed what was left of his Scotch.

"Axel, do you know him?" Susan asked.

"I know of him. We have never met."

"You didn't recognize Gulin in the café the other night," Erika asked.

"No, as I said. I never met him."

"Then that means he didn't recognize you," Erika commented. "That's good."

Sheila spoke up, directing her comments to Erika. "I have an easy way for Grainger to increase James Brunnell's level status without raising suspicion. Have Grainger transfer Brunnell to my Polish section. That would automatically take a clearance bump and I can work closely with him inside the Pentagon."

"Great idea, Sheila," Erika said. "I'll talk to Al tomorrow. Okay, we all should get back downstairs and relieve Angelika. If business keeps up like this, she's going to have to hire a second waitress. With Patty's school schedule, the number of hours she can work is limited."

◊◊◊

Back downstairs, Zhanna, Susan, and Ryker retook their positions at the long, busy bar. Angelika retreated back into the kitchen to help Bertha. Erika and Sheila helped Patty wait tables.

An hour before closing, a local who had obviously had at least three or four too many drinks waylaid Susan at the bar for a nightcap.

Slurring his words badly, he said, "Sister, give me a gin and tonic, and light on the tonic."

"I think you've had enough, Mister," Susan said. "I'll call a cab to take you home."

"Fuck that. What kind of place is this? A smart ass broad and Frankenstein's monster waiting bar." He obviously referred to herself and Axel Ryker who was at the other end of the bar where he could not hear the conversation. Zhanna had gone to the restroom.

"You just insulted a friend of mine," Susan said angrily. "Get your ass off that barstool and leave if you know what's good for you!"

The drunk slammed down his empty glass, cursed, but did as he was told. He left, only without the cab.

Ryker noticed the commotion and approached.

"Did you have a problem?" he asked.

"Just a customer who had a few too many. I convinced him to leave. All part of a bartender's life, right?"

Susan knew she had just saved the man from a probable broken arm if not worse at the hands of Axel Ryker.

Part 4

Chapter 33

Wrist wrestling

Arlington, Virginia
Next day—Thursday, 28 December 1950

This Thursday night meant something new at the Lili Marlene Café—a wrist wrestling competition.

Erika told Zhanna, Sheila, and Susan, "Ladies, nobody's going to beat Ryker so you can bet your ass and every dime you have on him." Erika even suggested to Patty that she bet all her tips.

A small table was cleared in the middle of the café and Ryker sat down across from a fat, burly man with a long beard and an anchor tattoo on his forearm. The man had to be 300 pounds if he were an ounce and his friends gathered around the table to bet on him. The hard-muscled Ryker weighed 270.

Susan acted as starter, making sure both men's right hands were locked properly and their left hand stayed on the table. They were not allowed to grip the edge of the table with their free hand.

When Susan felt assured the men were suitably positioned, she lifted her hands off theirs and yelled, "Go!"

The burly man immediately began pushing Ryker's hand down to the great cheering of his mates who had placed their money on him. When the back of Ryker's hand was within an inch of the table, Ryker nonchalantly took a sip of Jägermeister as if he were at a picnic, set the glass down, then powered the other man's hand back so hard it ripped a ligament in the man's elbow. The man shouted in pain as Ryker finished his drink.

That was the end of the brief competition. No other challenger spoke up. Erika collected the money from the table to distribute to the women according to how much they bet.

"Ryker, you just couldn't resist, could you?" Erika said. "Why did you have to do it like that? Now no one is going to challenge you. We could have cleaned up on this every Thursday night. You should have at least made it look like you were straining."

"I wanted to get it over with before fleas started jumping out of his beard," Ryker joked.

"Very funny," Erika said sarcastically. She then turned to the crowd. "Ladies and gentlemen," she said loudly. "We'll have this competition every Thursday night, but our bartender who won tonight says he's retiring from wrist wrestling so he won't be involved from now on. And don't forget, we have pinball machine and dart game wagering every night along with good food and drinks at reasonable prices. Tell your friends."

After Erika gave every woman their share, Sheila whispered, "I don't see Gulin in here."

"He's not," Erika answered softly. "But those two goons at the corner table work at the Soviet embassy. This afternoon, Al gave me a batch of photos of suspected Soviet embassy spies. You, Zhanna, Susan, and Ryker need to look them over before you leave tonight. The folder is upstairs."

Chapter 34

Zhanna and the beer bottle

Arlington, Virginia
Next day—Friday, 29 December 1950

Lieutenant Colonel Sheila Reid and James Brunnell sat in Al Hodge's office.

"Did everything go according to plan with the transfer?" Hodge asked.

"Yes," Sheila said. "James was transferred to my Polish section yesterday and bumped to Level 4 clearance."

Hodge looked at Brunnell. "Mr. Brunnell, you do realize this is a temporary assignment. When we've achieved our objective, you'll return to your former duties in data sorting at your previous clearance and pay level."

"I understand."

"Now we need to start getting you and your wife by the café," Hodge said.

Sheila spoke up. "Tonight and tomorrow night will be the only chances this week. Sunday is New Year's Eve but the café is closed and Angelika won't break that rule. It's a German thing. We're having our public end-of-the-year party tomorrow night—Saturday."

"Okay," said Hodge. "Mr. Brunnell. You and your wife drop by the café tonight and tomorrow. If someone you don't know approaches you, be friendly and act normal. You're not trained field agents and no one expects you to be—not us and not them."

"Should we sit by ourselves?" Brunnell asked.

"No. Avoiding people you know will look suspicious. If the Soviets decide to contact you, they'll find a way."

[that afternoon]
Susan Wedeking and Axel Ryker sat around the upstairs table. She had called for a security meeting. Zhanna tended bar.

"Axel, Al Hodge just called and told me Svetlana Urashova and her husband will start visiting the café tonight. Keep an eye out for any faces you recognized from the Soviet embassy folder Hodge gave us but remember our assignment. We're here to protect the café, Angelika, Bertha, and Patty. The Shield Maidens will handle the bait and hook angle of the mission."

"I understand my orders, Captain. I don't need a reminder."

"Need it or not, you just got one."

"How long is this assignment going to take?" Ryker asked gruffly.

"How should I know?" Susan said. "It will take as long as it takes."

"You Americans could learn from the Gestapo. We would have put an end to this by now."

"And how would you have done that? By arresting everyone in the Pentagon, strapping them to a chair, and torturing it out of them?"

Ryker shrugged. "By the way, my wife asked me to tell you that she's inviting you and the Shield Maidens to her father's estate Sunday night for his annual New Year's Eve party. The family's private plane will pick you up and bring you back. The attire is formal. I'll leave it to you to tell the other women."

[that evening]

Sheila had played pinball with a café customer and Erika played darts. Both won a small sum and donated their winnings to the bar's till. Now, Zhanna and Ryker manned the bar as Susan sat down at a table with Erika and Sheila.

Business was discussed first.

Erika asked, "Do any of you recognize anyone in here from the Soviet embassy photos Hodge gave us?"

Both Sheila and Susan said, "No."

"I don't either," Erika said. "Maybe they're taking a night off to avoid being conspicuous. That would be good procedure."

Susan changed the subject to something she had asked Erika before. "How in the world did Rose Bristow get hooked up with Axel Ryker?"

Erika explained. "I quit the CIA for about a year and went to work for the Department of State as a translator. Rose, who certainly doesn't need a job, volunteers as a French translator because of her father's contacts with the State Department. Rose and I were sent to a NATO conference in Belgium with other translators in '49 and she and I were assigned to share a room. She met Ryker in Brussels. Leroy Carr had sent Ryker there on CIA business to monitor the conference.

"To make a long story short, Rose told me she always considered herself homely and the only men who had expressed an interest in her were gold diggers only interested in her father's money. She said Ryker was the only man who showed her any interest who didn't know about her station in life as an heiress to a vast fortune. I tried to warn her away from Ryker but because of secrecy protocols I couldn't tell her about his past."

"So Rose doesn't know about her husband's past?" Susan asked.

"She does now, at least to some extent. I'm sure she doesn't know all the gory details but before they married, Ryker told her he was Gestapo during the war and that he now works for the CIA because they are protecting him from indictments in Germany and Austria. That's why he can't quit the CIA even though as Rose Bristow's husband he wouldn't have to work."

"Amazing," Susan said. "By the way, Axel told me that Rose has invited us all to her father's estate Sunday night for his New Year's Eve party. Have you ever been there?"

"I've been to the estate," Erika said. "Sheila hasn't.

"What's it like?" Sheila asked.

"Remember the Christmas party we attended at General O'Malley's estate in Bethesda? The Bristow estate outside Philadelphia makes his place look like Skid Row."

"Then I take it we're going," Susan stated.

"Yes," Erika answered. "If we disappoint Rose, Ryker will be pissed then we'll have to deal with his shit. Dealing with him when he's his customary insufferable self is hard enough."

"Alright," Susan said. "Axel told me it's formal attire and that the Bristow private plane will pick us up Sunday. I'll ask him about times and let you know. The bar is busy. I should get back to work."

When Susan left to return to the bar, Sheila said, "I don't know if it's possible to establish a rapport with a man like Axel Ryker, but do you think Susan has somehow done that?"

"It looks like it, Sheila. I think it has more to do with Rose than Ryker, but he likes pleasing his wife."

"It's a strange world we live in, Erika."

"Yes, it is, my friend. Do you ever miss the CIA?"

The red-haired Sheila responded, "I miss the camaraderie with the Shield Maidens. I don't miss being stabbed and shot at on a regular basis."

Both women grinned.

"What brought you back to the CIA, Erika? You had a cushy job for a while as a translator for the State Department."

Erika took a sip of her Asbach. "To be honest, Sheila. It was because of Zhanna. Leroy Carr was ready to can her. Where would she go and what would she do? She couldn't hold down a government job or even a job as a dishwasher for more than a few days. The Soviets would love to get their hands on her. She would have been totally vulnerable and without hope."

Sheila looked at her. "You just proved my point about my missing the friendship between all of us."

Their intimate conversation came to an end when they saw Svetlana Urashova and her husband enter. Svetlana spotted her six-foot-tall, jet-haired Russian friend and former mentor behind the bar and immediately walked up. There were not two side-by-side open seats at the bar, so the Brunnells stood and ordered drinks.

Zhanna told three men, "You guys please scoot down so my friend and her husband can sit together."

"I don't want to scoot down," one man said.

"I said 'please.' I asked you nicely," Zhanna said to the man.

"And I said I'm not moving. I heard your 'friend' talk and I've heard you talk. You both sound like a couple of Ivans. What is this, a commie bar?"

Zhanna grabbed the man's beer bottle and smashed it over his head. He dropped like a sandbag to the floor. Susan rushed over. "Axel. Damage control!"

Ryker circled around the bar, picked up the man, threw him over his shoulder and disappeared into the back. In the alley, he dumped the unconscious drunkard into a filthy trash bin where he would awake in the morning.

At the bar, Susan told the onlookers, "Nothing to be concerned about, folks. It was just a stunt. The man told our bartender he could withstand a beer bottle being broken over his head and paid her to do it to impress his friends. Looks like he was wrong. But he's okay. We'll take good care of him."

The men who had sat next to the drunk said nothing and moved down to give Svetlana and her husband two seats.

Chapter 35

Susan waits on a new customer

Arlington, Virginia
Next day—Saturday, 30 December 1950

Since the Lili Marlene would be closed tomorrow on New Year's Eve, tonight was the café's end-of-1950 party. The place was 8o percent full by 9 p.m.

Zhanna, Susan, and Ryker stayed busy behind the bar. Erika and Sheila sat at a table with Rose Bristow.

"Where's your baby, Rose?" Erika asked.

"He's back at the hotel. We brought our nanny with us from Philadelphia."

Sheila said, "Business has really picked up at your café, Erika. Congratulations."

"Thanks, Sheila. Like all places that serve alcohol, we get our occasional obnoxious drunk like the one Susan kicked out a few days ago and the one last night that Zhanna dealt with in her unique way. Yet overall, we have a good clientele—men and couples who are just out for an evening to relax, have a drink or two and a good meal. I'm happy for Angelika. She was very worried for a while."

"Do you see who I see?" Sheila asked Erika.

"Yep, over in the corner behind us."

Two men from Al's photo album sat drinking martinis.

Rose was confused. "Are they friends of yours?"

"Yes, just a couple of friends, Rose."

"We should invite them over to our table," the heiress suggested.

"Sheila and I are expecting a couple of different friends and we promised them we'd save them places at our table. The men back there will be fine, Rose. They have a table."

About ten minutes later, Svetlana and her husband walked in. "There they are now," Sheila said.

Svetlana again guided James toward the bar where Zhanna worked but Erika caught James's attention and waved the couple over to their table.

Svetlana carried a sturdy look about her but no one would ever confuse her with Zhanna. Svetlana was a good 5" shorter than her former trainer, had medium brown hair and light brown eyes as opposed to Zhanna's raven hair and dark, midnight eyes.

"I'm glad you could make it tonight," Erika said to the Brunnells. "You've met Sheila. This is Sheila's and my friend, Rose Bristow. Rose is from Philadelphia. Her husband is one of our bartenders."

"How do you do?" Rose said.

The Brunnells exchanged a handshake with Rose.

"James and Svetlana, what do you say we get you a drink then play some games," Erika suggested. "Rose and I will play pinball with Svetlana, and Sheila can take James to a dart board. How does 25 cents a game to the winner sound?—plus the pick-up from the onlookers who choose to wager.

Rose was especially enthused. She had spent most of her life being sheltered. Long stretches in finishing schools, and chaperoned trips abroad where she was never on her own. After the kidnapping and murder of the Lindbergh baby, her father hired a full-time bodyguard to take her to school, shopping, and any other places she wanted to go. She was never out of site of a protector in one way or another.

During her State Department trips overseas with Erika, she had finally been able to occasionally let her hair down. This gave her a passion for having fun in normal ways.

Erika suggested the split up for a reason. She knew Sheila would warn James Brunnell about the men at the corner table. Erika knew her job would be the easy one—simply entertain Rose and Svetlana.

◊ ◊ ◊

Axel Ryker had spotted the two Soviet embassy men. So had Susan, and Zhanna. Ryker didn't like it that his wife was here tonight. Susan knew what he was thinking. She placed her hand on his tree-trunk thick upper arm.

"Axel, relax," Susan said. "Erika won't let anything happen to Rose."

"I don't trust, Lehmann," Ryker confided.

"Why?"

"Past dealings."

"I'm telling you, Axel, I know for a fact Erika cares about Rose. If there is one thing you can count on, she protects her family and friends. We've seen that here at the café. That's why you and I are here."

Ryker jerked his arm away from her hand. "You better be right."

"That sounds like a threat," she said.

He looked at her with his lifeless eyes. "You have a lot to learn about me, Susan. I don't threaten, I make promises. Rose and my son are all I have to live for. If anything happens to Rose, I'll bring this damn café crashing down on all of you."

Susan retook his arm for a moment to calm him. This time he didn't pull away.

◊ ◊ ◊

At a dart board, Sheila informed James Brunnell about the two Soviet agents at the café.

"Don't turn around and look," she added quickly. "It's unlikely they will approach tonight. It's too early. They are here to surveil. And if we get lucky, they won't approach you at all. They'll have their Pentagon mole do it."

◊ ◊ ◊

Back at the bar, a man sat down at a barstool. He was a civilian, and after looking over the three bartenders, he chose a stool near the part of the bar covered by an attractive blonde bartender. Of the other two bartenders, the male barkeep looked like he shared genetic traits with Mary Shelley's nightmare. The jet-haired Amazon was attractive but looked frosty and inimical.

"Hi," he said to Susan. "I'll have Scotch on the rocks."

"We have Johnnie Walker Red and Laphroaig," Susan said.

"Walker is fine." He extended his hand. "My name is Stan Gregory. I heard about this place but this is my first time here."

"Then welcome to the Lili Marlene, Stan. My name is Susan. We hope you'll decide to become a regular. We have a great cook."

◊◊◊

At one of the two pinball machines, Erika, Rose, and Svetlana had pulled levers frantically while men stood around laying down bets. Although Rose wasn't doing well at the game unfamiliar to her, she kept adding dimes to the slot to continue playing. Svetlana did better but was only even at best. Erika's winnings offset Rose's losses and after an hour the women walked away with $22 in winnings.

"We won't donate this to the till," Erika said. "We'll use it for champagne at the end of the night. The profit will still go to the café."

Rose had thoroughly enjoyed herself. "This is a great place you have here, Erika. I know Axel is here only temporarily, but he and I will be regulars whenever we're in this area. What are your future plans for the café?"

"We want to remodel and update the restrooms," Erika said. "They need a lot of work. That's first on our list."

"That's wise," Rose said. "Many people judge a place on the quality of the restrooms. Have you talked to any contractors?"

"No. Not yet."

When midnight rolled around, Susan, Ryker, and Zhanna brought out three cases of sparkling wine. It couldn't legally be called Champagne because it came from California, not the Champagne region of France. But unlike real French Champagne, this was affordable for the Lili Marlene customers.

A toast was raised for the one day remaining in 1950. Since wishing someone a Happy New Year before the new year actually arrived was considered bad luck in Germany, Erika and Angelika raised their glasses and said, "Guten Rutsch!" It meant 'good slide' in German and was the traditional toast Germans made before the changing of the year was official.

Chapter 36

Siberian caviar

Outside Philadelphia, Pennsylvania
Next day—New Year's Eve, 1950

The Bristow's private, twin-engine Lockheed Lodestar took on its passengers at 6 p.m. for the 55-minute flight to Philadelphia. Snow had been predicted but so far only a few sparks had flirted with the earth. The 12-passenger Lodestar took to the air on time.

Onboard with Rose and her husband were their son and his nanny, Erika, Zhanna, Sheila, and Susan. Ryker and Rose would change into formal attire when they reached the estate. The Shield Maidens and Susan were already suitable dressed and manicured.

Less than an hour after take-off, the Lodestar dropped out of the clouds west of Philadelphia and sat down on the Bristow's private runway complete with a hangar where the plane could be stored and serviced.

Three shiny sedans and meticulously attired chauffeurs waited patiently. The group loaded into the cars and started their 40-minute drive to the mansion—the cars' journey taking nearly as long as the flight from Washington.

Along the way, the chauffeurs offered up information on some of the estate's sites they passed. One was a horse barn with acres of fenced in Kentucky bluegrass for the horses to gallop. The drivers informed their passengers that this was the home to three thoroughbreds that had raced in the Triple Crown over the years and were now out to stud. The drivers added that Mr. Bristow owned other fine horses.

Even though it was now well past dark, everything of interest was lit. They passed an enormous lake with several docks and lake houses. Erika knew Ryker and Rose lived in one of these elegant lake houses.

Finally, they reached the mansion. Even though it hadn't snowed since the plane left D.C., the chauffeurs hustled out and held umbrellas for the ladies.

The servants at the Bristow estate were a happy lot and most had been with the family for a long time. Archibald Bristow, Rose's shipping magnate father, paid the servants twice what most wealthy families paid servants, and he treated them very well, always looking out for their welfare. If a servant or one of their family members needed medical attention, Archibald paid for it. When the Bristows had an opening for a maid, kitchen help, chauffeur, or valet, the lines of those applying for a job at the Bristow estate at the Philadelphia agency Rose's mother used were extremely long. The family's authentic English butler, Neville (his surname), had been hired during one of Archibald's trips to London and had now worked for Rose's father for nearly thirty years. Neville was wealthy in his own right. In the early 1930s, Archibald had given Neville some shares of already valuable stock in his railroad shipping corporation for a birthday present. Even during the Great Depression, necessities needed to be shipped and stocks in railroads were one of the few investments that gained in worth during the 1930s. Then the war, with the increased need to ship war matériel and millions of soldiers, sailors, and Marines across the country from one point to the next, caused the stocks' value to rocket even higher. The butler could have retired a rich man years ago but remained with the family. Archibald and his faithful butler/old friend shared a delightful secret. The butler was wealthier than many members of Philadelphia's polite society whom he often waited on at one of Mrs. Bristow's fancy soirées held at their mansion.

The man who answered the door was just that man—Neville. Rose stepped in first.

The pure white, Italian marble floor of the colossal great room looked spitshined and the lamps and other accoutrements polished bright. What looked like expensive paintings and tapestries covered much of the stone walls. A strong fire danced in the massive marble fireplace that had been imported from a medieval castle in Bulgaria. A string quartet set up near the back of the grand room quietly played classics from Bach, Beethoven, Edvard Grieg, and Tchaikovsky.

Rose's Shield Maiden guests wore formal gowns—something unusual for them, especially for Zhanna Rogova. They all stood in contrast, both in gowns and manner. There was the blonde Erika with the sturdy, athletic build and stabbing hazel eyes that seemed to stare into one's soul—the eyes of a sleek jaguar ready to strike. Because of a knife wound on her left arm and a gunshot wound on her upper right arm, she wore a sleeved, gray and white taffeta gown. Then there was the nearly six-foot tall, jet-haired Russian with her ever-present neck scarf and spellbinding, sable Grim Reaper eyes that invited one to stare into *her* soul if one could summon the courage. The red-haired Sheila Reid also had a dreadful scar to cover—a stab wound to her shoulder. She accomplished this with a neck-high emerald-green satin gown. The blonde Army captain, Susan Wedeking, choose a pale yellow and white taffeta gown. All of them had their hair done today at the salon inside the Mayflower Hotel.

"Neville," Rose said. "Axel and I have to change into more appropriate wardrobe. Will you please make sure our friends are taken care of until we return?"

"It will be my pleasure, Mrs. Rose," the rich butler answered. He wore a traditional, 6-button tuxedo with tails as would be expected for an English butler at a formal affair.

Neville recognized Erika but said nothing to her and treated all of the women the same—with the utmost courtesy. He snapped his fingers and a waiter with golden goblets of French Champagne seemed to appear immediately, followed in step by a waitress carrying a tray of expensive hors d'oeuvres including foie gras and Siberian caviar on ultra-thin unsalted rye crackers. Zhanna dived into the Russian caviar.

It was about this time that Bernice Bristow, Rose's mother, spotted Erika and left the guests she mingled with.

"I'm so happy you could make it, Erika," Bernice said. "Rose told me she invited you and some friends."

"Thank you, Mrs. Bristow. This is Zhanna, Sheila, and Susan."

Bernice Bristow was the essence of congeniality. "You all look beautiful in your gowns. And I must say I love your hair—all of you."

"Mrs. Bristow," Erika said. "I don't think I've seen your husband."

"Sometimes I'd like to tar and feather that man," she said with exasperation. "He should be out here with his guests but he'd rather remain holed up in his study like some old, hibernating bear. By the way, when Rose and Axel get changed and come back down, Archibald hopes you will all join him in his study."

Everyone went about mingling for the next half hour. Many of the guests the women met could have easily been listed in a Times Magazine list of East Coast movers-and-shakers. At one point they spent ten minutes talking to Philadelphia mayor Bernard Samuel and his wife.

Finally, Rose and Axel descended the long, winding, marble staircase. Rose looked lovely in her shiny silver Parisian gown. Ryker looked like someone had stuffed a rhinoceros into a penguin suit. Nonetheless, because his tuxedo was custom-made by the best tailor in Philadelphia it fit well.

"Rose," Erika said. "Your mother told us your father was in his study and wants to talk to us."

"Yes, father mentioned that to me yesterday when I told him you were all coming. I'll take you back."

Archibald Bristow's study was two rooms away from the Grand Hall. They passed through a sitting room that contained a white Bechstein grand piano before entering the study. Bristow was a self-made millionaire having fought his way out of the Longshoreman docks and couldn't stand to be around people who put on airs like the socialites his wife invited to her fancy soirées. The Bristow's had a son. Steven was two years older than Rose. He was Bernice's favorite and right now in Switzerland skiing with old college chums, but Rose was without question the patriarch's darling.

Archibald stood when everyone entered the room. Rose kissed her father. He asked everyone to take a seat. The study was nicely appointed but not garish. The finely hand-sculpted mahogany parkay ceiling presented the highlight. The walls and floor were made from other exotic darkly stained woods. No expensive works of art hung from the walls. A small bar was set up along a corner fireplace in need of a stoke.

"May I have the kitchen prepare something for your guests, sir?" Neville asked.

"No thank you, Neville. We won't be long here then everyone can return to the ballroom for food. We'll pour our own drinks."

"Very good sir," Neville stoked the fire and made his retreat.

"A good man, Neville," Archibald said. "He's been with me since the early '20s."

"I adore him," Rose added.

"Rose, I've met Erika," said the distinguished looking, silver-haired captain of industry. "Who else do we have here?"

"This is Sheila Reid, she's a U.S. Army lieutenant colonel assigned to the Pentagon. This is Captain Susan Wedeking, also currently working out of the Pentagon." Rose knew she could tell her father these things. He was well connected in government circles and even held occasional conversations with Harry Truman.

Archibald cordially addressed both women.

"Father, this is Zhanna Rogova. She's a friend of Erika's."

Archibald knew what that meant—another CIA agent.

Zhanna interrupted. "Did you say we can serve ourselves? This Champagne is giving me gas. I'd hate to start farting on your fancy sofa."

Archibald laughed. This woman was his type of person.

"By all means, Zhanna," Bristow said. "Help yourself."

She rose, walked to the small bar, and poured herself a double shot of vodka.

"You have a rare batch of Ketel One," Zhanna said. "You really must be loaded."

"Help yourself to all you want," Archibald said. Apparently, the grand estate hadn't impressed the tall Russian. It took the expensive liquor to get Zhanna's attention.

Zhanna brought the glass and the entire bottle with her as she sat back down beside Erika.

Archibald Bristow opened a cigar humidor that sat on a nearby coffee table, offered Ryker one of the expensive Cubans and took one for himself. The Shield Maidens would have also taken one, but since Bristow had already shut the humidor they said nothing. Zhanna had brought cigars. They would smoke them on the plane during the flight back to Washington.

Archibald Bristow finally got down to business. "I've known for some time that my son-in-law works for the CIA. I had a telephone conversation with your Mr. Hodge yesterday. He filled me in on the details he thought I should know that concern Rose. I don't worry about

Rose when she's with Axel. I know he'll protect her. It's the periods of times when Rose and my grandson are alone at the Mayflower Hotel or out shopping that concern me. What can we do about this? We either find an acceptable solution or I must insist Rose and the baby return here to the estate until all this ends."

Erika thought to herself, *That would be the best solution.* But before she could speak up, Ryker said, "I have an agreement with Mr. Hodge. He assured me Rose and my son could be in Washington during this assignment. I expect him to keep his word. I will supply a bodyguard for Rose and our son when they are not with me."

"Axel," Erika said. "The Fischer sisters just left for an assignment in Amsterdam."

Sheila interjected. "Yes, but Amy Radu is available."

"Who is this Amy Radu?" Archibald Bristow asked.

Erika answered, "She's a Gypsy from Romania, Mr. Bristow. The newest member of the Shield Maiden team."

"And what qualifies her to guard my daughter and grandson?" Bristow asked.

Erika knew that Archibald Bristow had harry Truman's ear and Level 2 clearance. She couldn't tell him anything about current CIA business but she was free to tell him of the Maidens' background.

"Amy escaped from Sobibor Concentration Camp in '43 and spent the rest of the war fighting the Germans with the Polish resistance. Sheila can tell you more about that. Then after the war she was trained by the Israeli Mossad as an assassin."

"Before I sign off on any of this," Bristow said. "I want to meet your Miss Radu. I will go to Washington. Please ask Mr. Hodge to set up this meeting. I will take her to dinner—just the two of us so we can talk privately. Now, we better rejoin our guests before Bernice sends in the posse."

"It's about time," Zhanna said. "I'm hungry."

Archibald smiled again at the no-holds-barred Russian. He thought for a moment before saying, "I've changed my mind. I want Zhanna assigned to guard my daughter and grandson. If that leaves you short at the café bar then this Radu woman you mentioned can fill in there."

"Mr. Bristow," Erika said. "With all due respect, I ask that you leave these decisions to the CIA."

"And your request is denied, Erika, at least when it comes to the safety of my family. Rose tells me none of your bartenders are legally licensed to apply that trade. All of you will have those licenses this week—just send me a list of names through Rose. My daughter also tells me your public restrooms are in need of a significant upgrade. One of my friends in construction who I regularly employ will be at your café this Tuesday. His name is Jerry Drucker. Be at your café to greet him and his crew at eight o'clock that morning. I asked Jerry to bring a big enough crew so the work can be completed in one day and to send me the bill for his services. Your café's remodel will cost you nothing."

The great man stood up. "Now, let's go out to the ballroom and get our hungry Miss Zhanna some food, shall we?"

Chapter 37

Archibald gets his request

Washington, D.C.
Next day—Monday, 01 January 1951

Last night at the Bristow estate, everyone raised their glasses at midnight to signal the end of the first half of the 20th century, an era that has seen the two most devasting world wars in history. Everyone's hoped that the 2nd half of the century would see much more stability and peace.

This morning, Erika sat in Al Hodge's CIA office on E Street.

"Al, Archibald Bristow wants Zhanna assigned as his daughter's bodyguard. I suggested Amy."

"If Bristow wants Zhanna, he gets Zhanna," Al said. "I'm not going to enter into a pecking contest with Archibald Bristow over such a minor matter. If there is one thing eight years in the OSS and CIA has thought me, Erika, it's that one must pick his battles with the bigshots."

"It will be a blow to our plan losing Zhanna as a café guard."

"Amy Radu was trained as a Kidron assassin for the Israeli Mossad. My guess is that she can help Susan Wedeking protect a small café. You already have Axel Ryker. What more do you want?"

"Where is Amy and when can she be here?"

"Georgia. She's at Fort Benning taking some classes in logistics. I can have her here tomorrow. Anything else, Fräulein Nosey?"

[that evening]
In the storeroom upstairs at the Lili Marlene, Erika sat with Ryker, Susan, Zhanna, and Sheila.

"I had a meeting with Al this morning. He's not going to bump heads with Archibald Bristow on this bodyguard matter. Amy will be here sometime tomorrow. She'll be part of Susan's café security crew. Zhanna, you'll be in charge of protecting Rose and her baby."

Ryker seemed greatly relieved. "Thank the gods I don't have to hand over the well-being of my wife and son to a Gypsy/Jew."

Amy Radu was her Gypsy name but she was only half Roma. Her Jewish name was Bat-Ami d'Oz. This had gotten her into the Israeli Mossad.

"Ryker," Erika said. "How many times have I told you about your attitude? You work for the United State now, not Nazi Germany."

Ryker shrugged.

Zhanna had her objections. "I know nothing about taking care of a baby."

"You don't have to take care of the baby," Erika said. "Rose and her nanny will change diapers, feed and bathe the baby, dress him, and all of that."

"Why doesn't Rose take her baby and go back to her castle in Philadelphia?" Zhanna asked. "That would fix this problem."

Everyone knew the answer to that question. Rose wanted to be near her husband.

"I have an idea," Sheila said. "We'll bring in a crib and set it up here in this upstairs room with some toys for the baby to play with. When Rose and the baby are here, Ryker is in charge of their protection. When they are not here, Zhanna is in charge."

Everyone looked at Ryker. He nodded his agreement.

Erika added, "And I can bring Ada here to play with the baby. She'd love that."

"Just a second," Susan interposed. "If the Soviets make a move against the café, aren't we concerned with having these children around?"

Erika glared at her with her wolfish eyes. "Do you think I would put my daughter in danger? Or Ryker's son? The Soviets consider this place a milk cow. We have one assignment—to uncover the Pentagon mole. If we accomplish that, there are many avenues where Hodge and the CIA can direct blame and guard us from any fallout. My daughter and Axel's son are safer here than anywhere else. Here they have all of us looking out for them."

Chapter 38

The crew shows up

Arlington, Virginia
Next day—Tuesday, 02 January 1951

Jerry Drucker and his men were on time, knocking on the closed café door at eight o'clock sharp.

Susan answered the door. "Yes?"

"Lady, Archibald Bristow sent us here. We're supposed to see what we can do to upgrade your restrooms. Mr. Bristow told me to send him the bill. Now, show us the restrooms then stay out of our way."

The tough Army captain decided right away she liked these blunt union construction workers.

"Follow me," Susan said. She first led them to the ladies' room and then to the men's room.

"Sammy!" Drucker yelled to a man standing somewhere behind him. "These places are stink holes. Call the office and tell them to send four more men. Mr. Bristow wants this taken care of in one day."

When Erika arrived at the café that afternoon the cacophony of electric skill saws, drills, Sawsalls, and pounding hammers assaulted her senses. She hadn't forgotten this was the day of the restroom remodels but never assumed it would be this loud. The lunchtime crowd had basically come in and gone right back out after hearing the clamor. Susan handed out rain checks for a free sandwich if redeemed within two weeks.

[that evening]

Jerry Drucker and his earsplitting men had finally finished their job and had packed up and left around 5:50 p.m.

Now the restrooms at the Lili Marlene sported not only new walls, floors, and ceilings, but also new vanity cabinets, mirrors, sinks, toilets, and urinals. The new countertops were black marble.

"Rose, have you seen our new restrooms? Courtesy of you and your father?" Erika asked as they sat at a table near the bar.

"No. I've not yet seen them, Erika. I hope you're pleased."

"They look like smaller versions of restrooms one might see at the Paris Ritz."

Rose laughed as she readjusted her son's blanket.

"My father never does anything uninspiring or half-rate, Erika."

"Rose, we have set up a crib upstairs for your baby. You can use that crib anytime you like. Your baby will always be safe here at the Lili Marlene."

"I believe that. Thank you, Erika."

Chapter 39

Inclement weather

Arlington, Virginia
Next day—Wednesday, 03 January 1951

A blizzard had descended overnight on the Washington area. A foot of snow had already fallen with no sign of a let up. The wind howled like a wolfpack. Many urban streets were closed. Radio announcers advised residents to stay home.

Despite all of this, the Lili Marlene Café was open for business, although customers were few and mostly limited to those close enough to trudge through the snow on foot.

The café phone rang and Erika picked up.

"Erika, this is Amy. My plane was diverted to Raleigh because of the weather in D.C. I'll have to spend the night here. Hopefully I'll see you tomorrow."

"You have the address of the café in Arlington, right?"

"I was there for Christmas dinner, Erika."

"I know that. I was just wondering if you have the street address for the taxi driver."

"Yes."

"Okay. Come by the café before you report to E Street."

"Alright." Amy hung up the phone and so did Erika.

Chapter 40

Bat-Ami d'Oz

Arlington, Virginia
Next day—Thursday, 04 January 1951

The taxi carrying Bat-Ami d'Oz *aka* Amy Radu struggled negotiating the snow packed streets of Arlington but finally arrived in front of the Lili Marlene Café in the late afternoon.

When the striking Romanian beauty entered, she saw Zhanna Rogova and Susan Wedeking who she had met at Christmas standing behind the bar. Erika and Sheila Reid sat at a table. Amy took off her coat and hat and hung them on a coat tree then sat down with Erika and Sheila.

"Glad you made it today, Amy," Erika said. "Was it tough getting here?"

"I wouldn't say it was easy. Since you wanted to see me before I report to Al, I took a bus from the airport and then a taxi once I got to Arlington. How's business?"

"It started out real slow but has picked up," Erika replied. "Until last night when the storm hit."

"They're working on the streets," Sheila said. "By tomorrow it should be a lot easier getting around."

"Tell me more about Susan," Amy said. "We met at your Christmas party but she and I didn't get a chance to speak much. What's her role in all this?"

"This is a joint operation between the CIA and G-2. Susan isn't G-2, she's an Military Police captain, but she reports to a G-2 colonel at the Pentagon. She's tough and fits in well on an assignment like this. Let's go to the bar."

Erika, Sheila, and Amy took seats at the bar. Suddenly, Axel Ryker walked out from the back carrying a box of liquor to restock the bar. He spotted Amy.

"She did decide to come after all," Ryker said as he looked at Amy. "I thought you might have gone back to the Promised Land or hopped on a Gypsy caravan."

"Ryker," Amy said. "I see you haven't changed. You're still the obnoxious asshole you've always been."

◊ ◊ ◊

Later, Erika and Sheila took Amy upstairs.

"Okay, fill me in on exactly what it is I'll be doing," Amy said.

"You're taking over at the bar for Zhanna who is now in charge of protecting Ryker's wife and their baby. Rose's father has a lot of influence with Washington and he requested this."

"Zhanna will still tend bar," Erika continued. "She's only responsible for Rose and the child when they are out and about and Ryker can't be with them. That's the reason for the crib. When Rose and the baby are here or at the Mayflower where they all stay, Ryker is in charge of protecting his family. When do you see Al?" Erika asked.

"Tomorrow morning," Amy answered.

"He'll brief you on our mission. We're trying to flush out a mole at the Pentagon."

Chapter 41

Wienerschnitzel

Arlington, Virginia
Next day—Friday, 05 January 1951

It had been two days since the blizzard. The scraping and sanding trucks had been hard at work and the reappearance today of the sun had lent a hand. Traffic was almost back to normal. The Lili Marlene was hoping for a good Friday crowd.

Amy was behind the bar with Zhanna and Susan. Everyone was now a licensed bartender, even Erika and Sheila. Archibald Bristow had pulled the strings. Rose and the baby were there and Ryker sat with them because he wasn't needed at the bar. Even if all the barstools were occupied, there was no need for four bartenders. Everyone was getting extra breaks tonight.

Svetlana and her husband had not been in for a couple of nights because of the storm. Colonel Grainger instructed James Brunnell to take his wife to the café tonight.

When the Brunnells walked in, they spotted Erika and Sheila and sat down at their table. The café tables were about half full with couples eating dinner. The bar stools were all occupied by men trying to get a better look at the new bartender—the exotic beauty, Amy Radu.

"Grainger told us to come by tonight," James said to the women at the table.

"Now that the streets have loosened up, it's a good idea," Sheila said.

"Are you hungry?" Erika asked. "Bertha's German special tonight is Wienerschnitzel. Technically, the dish originated in Vienna, but Germans quickly adopted it."

Before the Brunnells had a chance to answer, Igor Gulin and another man entered the café.

Svetlana's face turned ashen.

"He made his first mistake," Sheila said. "He arrived too quickly. Gulin just let us know that he has men following Svetlana."

"Stay calm, Svetlana," Erika said. "You're safe here. Ryker, Zhanna, and Susan all saw Gulin walk in. Al briefed Amy about Gulin this morning. Susan or Zhanna will discreetly point him out to her. Now, let's get you two something to eat. How does the Wienerschnitzel sound? It's delicious. It comes with a potato dumpling and green beans."

Zhanna took a temporary break and came to their table. She didn't sit down.

"Gulin followed them here," the Russian said, basically repeating what Sheila had just muttered. "Yes, we already figured that out, Zhanna," Erika said.

Zhanna continued, now speaking to the Brunnells, "Both of you should be home tomorrow. Gulin will probably call on you at your house. Since he has men following you he will move quickly. It's how the NKVD works. Before you leave tonight, we'll tell you what to say and what not to say."

Zhanna would be proved right about Igor Gulin moving quickly but not in the exact manner she had predicted. After the café closed, he had men outside waiting for Susan Wedeking. Before she reached her car, a hand covered her mouth and two other men dragged her into a waiting 4-door sedan and roughly deposited her in the back seat. It drove off into the night.

Chapter 42

Soup and bread

Washington, D.C.
Next day—Saturday, 06 January 1951

The Shield Maidens and Ryker met early this morning with Al Hodge.

"Susan Wedeking's car was still parked near the café when we arrived there this morning, Al," Erika said. "Gulin must have her. He was at the café last night with another man."

"Who was the other man? Do you know, Zhanna?" Hodge asked.

"No. I didn't recognize him," the Russian answered.

Amy asked, "Why would Gulin capture a captain when he could capture Sheila, a lieutenant colonel? Susan isn't privy to top-secret intel like Sheila."

"The mole must not know about Sheila," Al said. "If Zhanna didn't recognize him it's a good bet he doesn't know about her. We know the mole has to be G-2. Sheila's not G-2. Susan isn't either but she's working with that section and the mole must know that. The only good news is that means that maybe the cover of Erika's café has not been blown yet. The bad news is they will probably torture it out of Susan."

Ryker spoke up. "I request that I be put in charge of reacquiring the captain."

"Why?" Hodge asked.

Ryker didn't reply but Erika knew why. It was because of the present Susan went out on Christmas Eve to buy his son, who had no presents under the tree.

Erika knew Ryker would be relentless. "I think that's a good idea, Al. Zhanna, with her knowledge of NKVD procedures, can be a big help and all of us will do our part."

"Okay, Axel," Hodge said. "You're in charge of the rescue team. I'll get Marienne back here to shadow Gulin. I know all of you have been trained in shadowing, but Gulin has seen your faces and there's too high of a risk that you'll be recognized. Gulin is no fool. He'll have men following him looking for a tail. We want to protect your covers and the same of the café if we can."

[that afternoon]

The Maidens and Ryker sat upstairs at the Lili Marlene.

"Axel," Erika said. "You heard Al. You're in charge of rescuing Susan. Give us your plan."

"When is the 'Ghost' going to be here?" Ryker asked. *Ghost* was Marienne Schenck's CIA codename. "I can do nothing until I have a location."

"She'll be here tomorrow," Erika said.

"My plan is simple," Ryker said. "The Bristow airplane will be here tomorrow to pick up Rose and my son. Rogova and I can no longer guard them properly while we undertake the captain's rescue. I want my wife and son safe so I insisted Rose take our son home. When Susan is located, then we will rescue her. If they harm her, they will all die."

"That sounds like a good plan," Sheila said almost shockingly. Sheila had been captured and tortured on a previous Shield Maiden mission. Her left arm was still somewhat immobile from a deep stab wound to her left shoulder.

Both Zhanna and Amy, the trained assassins, agreed.

"There will be political fallout," Erika said. "But I also agree. We won't abandon Susan."

[that evening]

A hood had been placed over Susan Wedeking's head during the drive after her abduction so she had no idea where she was but knew it wasn't the Russian embassy. The drab, windowless room she was locked in had to be some type of safehouse. Two guards stood outside her door.

She hadn't seen Gulin today or the other man who abducted her. She had also not been fed since her capture last night. Finally, one of the guards delivered some vegetable soup and a piece of bread that had been torn from a loaf. She ate it then knocked on the door. A small window about 6" wide opened.

“I have to use the toilet,” she said to the gaurd.

The impatient guard said with a Russian accent, “Very well.” When he unlocked the door, Susan jumped him. She struggled but was losing the fight against the trained Russian guard who had been forced to wrestle men to the ground many times during his career. Another guard came to his comrade’s aid and hit Susan in the head with the butt of his rifle, knocking her unconscious.

Part 5

Chapter 43

Ghost

Arlington, Virginia
Next Day—Sunday, 07 January 1951

Marienne Schenck sat a table in the closed Lili Marlene Café with the Shield Maidens and Axel Ryker. Rose and the baby had been picked up by the Bristow plane earlier this morning and were already home in Philadelphia.

"Al told me on the phone that Susan has been abducted by this Igor Gulin character," Marienne stated. "Tell me more."

"Gulin came in the café shortly after Svetlana and her husband Friday night," Erika said. "It was obvious he had them followed. Why he captured Susan is a mystery. Zhanna told us he'd move fast but even she thought the move would be aimed at the Brunnells."

"Alright," Marienne said. "I know it's my job to find out where Susan is being held. Clearly, it's not at the Russian consulate. Capturing an American Army officer and holding her at the embassy would allow the U.S. to raid the embassy. One of the very few things that would allow that move. The Soviets don't want that. All their spy apparatus—maps, machines, radios, documents—would be exposed to American eyes."

"If Susan hasn't already been whisked out of the country," Sheila said, "they most likely have her in some type of safehouse."

"First thing," Marienne said, "let's talk about Susan. As you mentioned, Erika, abducting her when Gulin has all of you to choose from is a baffler."

Amy spoke up. "That has to mean that Gulin doesn't know we are CIA. His mole at the Pentagon probably saw Susan reporting to Grainger, then when Susan was spotted working in here, Gulin decided he wants to know why before he proceeds with the Brunnells."

"I agree," Ryker said. "That would be my procedure."

"And the NKVD's as well," Zhanna said. "I was a fool to not consider Susan had been I.D.'d by the Pentagon mole since she reported there nearly every day."

"It's not your fault, Zhanna," Erika said. "If it's anyone's fault it's Grainger's. He should have had extra precautions on hand such as not calling Susan into the Pentagon at all. They should have had their meetings somewhere else."

The Shield Maiden leader looked at the *Ghost*. "Marienne, use all your skills. Find Susan. When you do, we'll handle the rescue. Ryker's in charge of that element."

"I'll need an assistant on this one," Marienne said. "Give me Amy."

Erika looked at the Gypsy. "Amy, you and Marienne are first at bat."

[same time]

Susan had little else to do other than while away time. She had checked the small, windowless bedroom many times trying to discover a possible way out, but the room was as secure as a prison cell with two armed guards always standing sentinel outside her door. After her hijinks yesterday where she attacked one of the guards; now, when she requested the toilet a third guard was summoned.

She had a knot on her head, a headache, and was famished. The guards brought her one meal a day, usually in the late afternoon. Yesterday she was given another bowl of soup and some bread. She would find out that today's dinner would be an apple and a peanut butter sandwich on stale bread. Her drink was always water. At least she could stay hydrated.

Suddenly, she heard her door being unlocked. The two guards walked in. One aimed his rifle at her chest while the other handcuffed her to a chair. Then Igor Gulin walked in.

"I apologize for the shackles Captain Wedeking," Gulin said. "This was not my intent but my men told me about your antics yesterday and I feel they are necessary to keep your attention."

"What do you want from me?" Susan asked.

"A great deal, Captain. Why don't we start with the reason a United States Army Military Police captain is working with G-2?"

Susan burst out laughing. "G-2! I don't know what you're talking about. You've got the wrong person, you idiot."

Bloody Igor delivered a vicious slap to Susan's face, hard enough to knock her and the chair over. The guards righted her.

"I see," Gulin continued. "Then how about this one? Why are you working as a bartender at a half-rate tavern in your off-duty hours?"

"The woman who owns the place is a friend. Business has been up and down. I'm working for free for a time to help."

Gulin smirked. "The woman is a friend, you say. Dima Lukov told me her name is Erika. You've met Lukov. This Erika has to be a very bold woman to extort a deal out of Lukov. Who is this Erika, exactly?"

"She's just a woman trying to make her business run."

"Of course she is," Gulin said. "And what a coincidence that this woman, Erika, who promised Lukov that G-2 officers stop in her tavern happens to be your friend, even though you claim to have nothing to do with G-2."

"Uncuff her," Gulin told the guards. "I have business that will take up most of this day. Her interrogation will begin tomorrow morning."

He looked at Susan with a sinister grin. "Enjoy your day, Captain. I assure you that tomorrow will not be as pleasant."

After Gulin left the room and walked down the corridor he was joined by his top aide.

"Yuri," Gulin said. "I want to know who the woman is who owns the Lili Marlene Café you and I have visited on a couple of occasions. I also want to know the identities of the other women who work behind the bar as well as the large man with the facial scars. Make this your priority."

"Yes, Comrade Gulin."

[that afternoon]

Marienne gave Amy her instructions in the upstairs room of the empty café.

"We'll start monitoring the Soviet embassy tonight in three-hour shifts. One of us will stay awake while the other tries to get some sleep in the backseat. We'll take some blankets. If Gulin exits the embassy on foot, I will shadow him with my walkie-talkie and keep in touch with you so you can follow in the car out of sight. This time of year, it's easy to conceal a walkie-talkie under a heavy winter coat."

"If he leaves the embassy in a car, then we'll tail him in our car," Marienne added. "Any questions?"

"No," Amy said. "That sounds straightforward."

"Just remember, Amy, we can't afford a mistake. Susan's life, if she is still alive, counts on that."

"I realize that, Marienne," Amy said.

Chapter 44

Mae West

Arlington, Virginia
Next day—Monday, 08 January 1951

Marienne showed up at the Lili Marlene at noon and sat down with the team.

"I'm here to give my report and get something to eat. Amy's still watching the Soviet embassy. Our walkie-talkies have a radius of 45 miles so she can contact me if something develops. When I return, I'll send her here for a break and some chow."

"Then I guess that means nothing has developed so far?" Erika quizzed.

"That's right. We haven't seen Gulin enter or leave the embassy since we started surveillance. That's not good news. It probably means Gulin is being cautious and spending his nights somewhere else, a hotel, or maybe even where they're holding Susan."

"What do you recommend, Marienne?" Sheila asked. "You're the expert."

"If we can't acquire Gulin, then we have to switch our focus to an associate of his," Marienne replied. "Do any of you think you might recognize any man who was in the café with Gulin from the photos Al gave you? Check them out while I go relieve Amy. She'll be here for a meal. If you come up with something, she can contact me on the walkie-talkies and bring me the photo."

[about that time]
The splash of water thrown in her face by a guard jostled Susan from her fog. She was again bound to the chair and had been knocked unconscious by Bloody Igor's electric cattle prod.

"There is no need for this, Captain Wedeking," Gulin leered. "You can put an end to it. I'll ask you again. Who is this Erika woman and your other cohorts at that tavern?"

"It's not a tavern, it's a café, dumbass."

Gulin again turned on the cattle prod.

"Okay, okay," Susan said. "I'll tell you. Erika is not her name. She's really an actress. Her real name is Mae West."

Gulin burst out laughing. "Thank you, Captain. I always appreciate humor." Then he again shoved the electric prod into Susan's stomach.

[that afternoon]

The team sat upstairs. Nearby was the baby crib that had never been used.

From the Russian embassy photos supplied by Al Hodge, they had identified a man they had seen in the café with Igor Gulin. His name was Yuri Sobolev. Like Gulin, the Soviets listed Sobolev as an embassy charge d'affaires.

The team had told Amy of this when she came into the café for a break and something to eat. Marienne and Amy were now out looking for Sobolev.

Ryker, who had been put in charge of Susan's rescue and had experience with similar missions for Nazi Germany, laid out his plan.

"As Marienne suggested, we must assume they are keeping Susan at some sort of safehouse. The Soviets surely have one somewhere in the Washington area like the Americans have in Moscow. As soon as Marienne and the Gypsy can give us any information about Sobolev's whereabouts we will move in and capture this Russian. I will interrogate him and quickly find out where they are keeping Susan but moving in on the safehouse is more dangerous for the captain. Guards there will be under orders to shoot her if the hiding place is compromised. Safer for Susan would be after we capture Sobolev, we contact Gulin and offer a trade—their charge d'affaires for the American captain. I will get Gulin's phone number out of this Yuri. I can promise you that. Gulin will have to accept that deal. Sobolev can give the American CIA and G-2 more top-secret information than an American military policewoman can give them. The most important thing is that Marienne and the Gypsy can tell us a location for this Sobolev soon."

"I agree," Zhanna said. "Gulin has surely tortured Susan by now. Anyone captured by the NKVD either talks first and is then shot, or if they don't talk they suffer the same fate. And Ryker is right about the guards' duties will be to kill Susan first, even before they defend themselves or the safehouse. That's how the NKVD always worked when I was with them."

Erika broke in. "If Sobolev is staying at the embassy, Marienne will spot him coming or going. When we capture him, we cannot bring him here and put civilians at risk. I know of another place."

Chapter 45

A new target for Bloody Igor

Arlington, Virginia
Next day—Tuesday, 09 January 1951

Amy Radu walked into the Lili Marlene at 9 a.m., before the café opened for the day. Angelika was in the back preparing for business. Amy sat down with Erika and Zhanna. Sheila was at the Pentagon running her department.

"It's obvious that Igor Gulin is not staying at the Soviet embassy," Amy told the two women. "We haven't seen him during surveillance, which Marienne and I started Saturday night. However, we saw Yuri Sobolev return to the embassy late last night. As of the time I left to come here this morning, Sobolev had not left. Marienne is there now watching. She's not leaving until she spots Sobolev. I need to take her something to eat."

Finally, some positive news.

"I'll ask Bertha to fix a meal to takeout," Erika said. "I know there's nothing we can do until this guy leaves the embassy grounds, but is there any other way we can help besides just sending food?" Erika hated feeling helpless during these times—times of waiting around until something developed that could be acted on.

"There's nothing any of us can do until Sobolev leaves the safety of the embassy," Amy replied. "When he leaves, and after we've followed him to where he's going, Marienne says she'll have me call you."

◊ ◊ ◊

Susan had yet to be interrogated today. Yesterday's repeated shocks from the cattle prod had made her sick. She couldn't hold down any food but Gulin didn't want her dead—yet. He still believed he could get what he wanted out of her. If not, he had his right-hand man, Yuri, working to find out who the people were at the café. He had to protect the Pentagon G-2 mole at any cost.

[noon]

In Susan's absence, Al Hodge had instructed Erika to give Colonel Grainger his briefings. She insisted the rendezvous not take place within the Pentagon. In case the Soviets were monitoring the place, she didn't want to be seen entering or leaving in case her cover (and the rest of the CIA team's covers) had not yet been blown.

She and Grainger met at a small mom and pop restaurant in Washington. Grainger's wife was sitting with him when Erika entered.

"Agatha," Erika said as she slid into the other side of the booth. "It's nice to see you again." The two women had met at General O'Malley's Christmas party.

"It's wonderful to see you, as well, Erika. I know you and Harold have things to discuss. I was just leaving. I have some shopping to do before I meet with my bridge club ladies this afternoon."

She rose and left after kissing her husband on the cheek.

"Your wife is a gracious lady," Erika said.

"Yes, she is. Now, what do you have for me, Miss Lehmann. Anything new about the status of Captain Wedeking?"

"As I told you yesterday, we know Susan isn't being held at the Russian embassy. That would be too volatile for the Soviets, and Gulin hasn't been seen there since her capture. However, we have identified a man that was seen with Gulin at the Lili Marlene. His name is Yuri Sobolev and he's listed as a Russian consulate charge d'affaires by the Soviets. Sobolev *has* been seen coming and going from the embassy. We're surveilling the embassy 24 hours a day. The next time Sobolov leaves embassy grounds we will follow and capture him at the best opportunity. Our plan is to arrange a trade—Sobolev for Susan."

Grainger thought for a moment. A waitress came by. Erika wasn't hungry. "Just a cup of coffee, please."

When the waitress walked away, Grainger said, "The Russians will have to take that deal. Us having one of their embassy charge d'affaires in tow will hurt them more than them having an American MP officer will hurt us. Captain Wedeking can tell them nothing of G-2 operations other than the one she currently works on with your group."

"That's our thinking, Colonel."

"What does Mr. Hodge think of all this?" Grainger asked.

"He agrees it's the best, and really the only plan available to us."

"I know our agreement requires the G-2 to keep hands off, but if there is any way we can be of service, let me know." Grainger felt guilty about getting Susan Wedeking involved with these CIA people who impressed him as a gang of government-paid hooligans.

[Soviet Embassy—Washington, D.C.]

Yuri Sobolev had spent two days combing through endless stacks of photographs. Finally, Sobolev made a match this afternoon. He sat looking at the photo. It was of one of the women he had remembered seeing behind the bar at the café. The photo was of a Soviet Union former SMERSCH agent. A woman who had won a Hero of the Soviet Union medal.

He had to get this information to his boss. He picked up a secure telephone and dialed the safehouse. A guard answered and summoned Gulin, identifying the caller.

"Yes, Yuri," Gulin said. *"What is it?"*

"Comrade Gulin. I have identified one of the women at that restaurant where the woman we have in custody worked. I'm sure you remember the tall woman with short black hair behind the bar."

"I remember."

"That is Zhanna Rogova," Sobolev blurted out.

There was silence for a moment on Gulin's end of the line. He had heard of the exploits of Zhanna Rogova. *"How sure are you of this, Yuri?"*

"I'm positive, Comrade. The description we have matches perfectly—5'11½" tall, raven hair, and always wears a neck scarf in public to conceal a rope burn after being hanged by the SS in '44. I'm looking at her official SMERSCH photograph as we speak. The face is the woman at the restaurant."

"This is remarkably interesting, Yuri. Good work. It's time I have another conversation with our stubborn American captain."

"Shall I inform the deputy ambassador of this?" Sobolev asked. Gulin reported to the deputy ambassador who was in charge of clandestine activity for the consulate.

"Not yet," Gulin replied. *"I want to be absolutely sure it's Rogova or we'll look like fools. Dima Lukov should have recognized Rogova. He was in Moscow during the war. I'll get back to you tomorrow morning."*

Gulin hung up and walked directly to Susan's room. The guards opened the door and followed the large Russian in. Susan was awake but looked very pale and disheveled as she laid curled up on the bed. Gulin grabbed her hair, jerked her off the bed, and deposited her in the chair. She wanted to fight back but was too weak.

Gulin's cavalier attitude during their previous sessions was now gone.

"We have recognized one of your friends!" he sizzled. "Zhanna Rogova has been identified. What is her role in your ludicrous mission?"

Susan raised her chin off her chest and answered weakly, "I never heard of her."

Gulin hadn't brought his cattle prod. With a clinched fist he punched Susan in the face, spraying blood from her mouth and nose onto the unform of a guard standing next to her chair.

"We'll get nothing from this woman," Gulin told the guards. "After dark tonight we'll dispose of her."

Bloody Igor's focus was now directed at Zhanna Rogova. He knew if he could deliver the former SMERSCH agent with a price on her head to his superiors, he could write his own ticket after that.

Chapter 46

A night out

Washington, D.C.
Same day—Tuesday, 09 January 1951

Yuri Sobolev was pleased with himself. Earlier today he had identified Zhanna Rogova who the Soviets considered a traitor. He was scheduled to meet with Igor Gulin tomorrow, but for tonight he would treat himself to a night out.

◊ ◊ ◊

It was just after 9 p.m. when Marienne and Amy saw Sobolev walk to the Russian embassy gate, pass through the guards, and get into the back seat of a waiting chauffeur-driven black Mercedes. Marienne was behind the wheel of her CIA-issued Pontiac.

"We're in luck," she told Amy as she started the engine. "There's no way to spot a car tail at night if we make just a few maneuvers."

Sobolev's car headed east. Along the way, when Marienne thought they had followed the Mercedes for too long, she boldly passed Sobolev's car, put on her right turn signal and turned off on a side street. Quickly making a U-turn, she steered the Pontiac back onto the boulevard, always maintaining at least a 50-yard cushion behind the Mercedes.

Sobolev's car finally stopped in front of a rundown building in Ivy City, one of the most crime-ridden neighborhoods in D.C. He exited the car and went inside. His driver stayed with the car. The building had no signs in front. It was obviously not a bar or nightclub.

"Did you see the telephone booth two blocks back?" Marienne asked Amy.

"I saw it."

"Hustle down there and call the Lili Marlene. Tell Erika that Sobolev is in a building in the 1300 block of Okie Street Northeast. Tell her to look for my car. I'll park a block away. This is a bad area, Amy. Be careful. After your phone call, get back here quickly. If Sobolev leaves before the team gets here, we'll have to leave with him to resume the tail."

Amy exited the car and began a brisk, two-block march to the phone booth. Arriving, she closed the door behind her, put a nickel in the slot, and dialed the Lili Marlene. When she finished speaking to Erika, she hung up and began her walk back to the car. Suddenly, a man who had been watching her from the shadows of a dark alley stepped out behind her.

The former Mossad agent quickly spun around, pulled her handgun and aimed it at his face. He immediately backed up and returned to the shadows. Not a word was spoken.

When she got back to the car, she slid in and told Marienne, "They're on their way." She didn't bother mentioning the alley man. It wasn't important. "How long should it take them?"

Marienne answered, "They have to come across the bridge and pass through much of D.C. It will take them at least a half hour even if they get lucky with stoplights."

"One of us should guard the back of the building." Amy said, remembering her training days with the Mossad.

"No need," the experienced Marienne Schenk said. "Sobolev isn't going to hightail it out the back. If he suspected he was followed, his driver would not be out front. While you called Erika, I saw men coming and going. This is either a bordello or an illegal gambling house. Either way, Sobolev will be here for a while."

◊ ◊ ◊

Erika was behind the wheel. Zhanna was a terrible driver, rarely being able to drive more than a few blocks before she drove up on a curb or sideswiped a parked car. And Erika (unlike Ryker) was familiar with Washington streets. She raced through the nation's capital as quickly as she could without going too fast and running stoplights and stop signs. They couldn't afford the delay of a traffic stop by a police patrol car.

◊ ◊ ◊

Marienne was right on both counts. The building with no signs or markings on the outside was both a bordello and an illegal gambling establishment. Run by a married couple, the wife fulfilled her duties as the madam for the girls; her husband oversaw the gaming tables. Yuri Sobolev always started out with the girls before he ended his night at the tables.

◊ ◊ ◊

It was just after 10:30 p.m. when a car pulled up behind Marienne's. Erika got out and slid into the back seat of the Pontiac sedan. They were a block away from the building Sobolev had been seen entering, but close enough so the gloomy yellow streetlights allowed them to see his chauffeur-driven Mercedes parked on the street.

Marienne pointed out the Mercedes to Erika, then said, "Sobolev is in the four-story red brick building with the crumbling white stucco across the street from his car."

"Amy. Take care of the driver," Erika said. "Make it look like a robbery. The Russians won't believe that, but it will divert police attention, especially in this neighborhood. Then come back to this car. Ryker, Zhanna, and I will go inside."

Amy affixed a sound suppressor to the muzzle of her French-made MAC 50 semi-automatic handgun and got out of the car.

"Marienne," Erika said. "After Amy takes out the driver, pull up in front of the building, pick her up and take her to your room at the Mayflower. I'll call you when we have Sobolev secured."

"Alright," Marienne said. Erika got out of her car and returned to the CIA-issued Dodge where Zhanna and Ryker waited.

As Amy walked toward the Mercedes, she opened her coat and unbuttoned two buttons of her blouse to reveal some of her brassier. The driver was dozing when she got there and her knocks on his driver's side window startled him. His first thought was to reach for his gun, but when he saw the woman he relaxed. She had to be one of the women from the cat house. He rolled down his window.

"I am on duty, waiting for my rider," he said with a Russian accent. "I am not interested. Go away."

Amy pulled out her handgun and fired three sound-suppressed rounds into the man's chest, then opened his door and dug through the dead man's pants for his wallet. Marienne pulled her car up. Amy got in and the two women drove off as Erika, Ryker, and Zhanna entered the building.

Chapter 47

Olive

Washington, D.C.
Same night—Tuesday, 09 January 1951

In a private, closed-off vestibule just inside the door, a middle-aged woman sat in a chair. An enormous black man stood nearby. When Erika, Ryker, and Zhanna entered, the woman stood up and smiled.

"We're here to deliver an important message to one of your customers," Erika told them both. "It can't wait. His name is Yuri. He is a short man, 40-years-old with thinning hair and wears eyeglasses. He speaks with a Russian accent."

The woman's smile disappeared like a magician's assistant. "If you're not here as paying customers, get out," the woman said. Her red hair was obviously a wig, and an ill-fitting one at that.

Axel Ryker grabbed the enormous man's arm and twisted it behind his back until it snapped. The man shouted out in pain and dropped to the floor. As Zhanna began stomping him, Erika produced her handgun and placed the muzzle tight to the woman's forehead.

"Tell us where Yuri is," Erika demanded.

"Go to hell, bitch," the woman said. "We pay some scary people for protection. You're in big trouble."

Erika changed her aim and shot the woman in the knee. The woman screamed and fell back into her chair.

"You shot me!"

"It looks like I did. Now where's Yuri?" Erika aimed at her other knee.

"He's with a girl on the third floor!" she shouted in agony. "I don't know which room!"

Ryker eyed the telephone on a small corner table and ripped the cord from the wall. He went through the door that led into the building proper, followed by Zhanna and Erika. They entered a room that looked like it might have been a movie set for a Sultan's harem in a low-budget B film. Women of all colors lounged around in various stages of undress.

When they saw the monstrous image of Ryker, several screamed and ran through a door to a back room. The team followed the women which took them into one of the gambling rooms. This one with two craps tables surrounded by about six men to a table.

"Who are you?" shouted a scarecrow of a man with a pencil mustache and too much Wildroot in his greasy, dyed-black hair. "How did you get past Hazel and Boozer?"

"Shut up," Ryker thundered. "We'll ask the questions. We were told a customer named Yuri is on the third floor. Which room?"

Both Erika and Zhanna had guns drawn. Out of the corner of her eye, Erika noticed movement. A man was attempting to slowly take his pistol from a holster at the back of his pants. She turned quickly and shot the man through the forehead. He was dead before he hit the floor.

"Alright! Alright!" Greasy hair shouted. "Yuri is on the third floor."

"I asked what room number?" Ryker grunted.

"Room number? What do you think this is, the Ritz? Second door on the right. You better not have harmed my wife. I pay out of my ass for protection. You don't know who you're dealing with. That blonde bitch just killed a made man."

Zhanna asked, "Is Hazel, the woman you mentioned, your wife?"

"That's right. You speak with a Russian accent. Who the hell are you?"

Zhanna aimed her sound-suppressed Mosin-Nagant and fired a round through the man's kneecap. The same knee Hazel received the shot from Erika. "Now," Zhanna said. "You and your wife are again a matching pair."

Someone had to stay behind and watch the remaining men. Ryker chose Zhanna.

"Put your hands in the air," Ryker told the men. He turned to Zhanna. "We need not waste time searching the others; most probably have guns so if any drop their arms, shoot them." He walked over to the fallen body of the man Erika killed, took his handgun and gave it to Zhanna in case she needed a backup.

Erika and Ryker left the room. They walked up the stairs. The second floor was another area devoted to gambling—this one to high stakes poker.

When they reached the third floor, the door to the second room on the right was closed but unlocked. All of the girls' doors were kept unlocked in case a customer became a little too rough with the white prostitutes. Management's philosophy was that damaged property could not work until it healed. If a customer's delight included beating up the girls, that was limited to the black girls and the customer had to pay extra for that particular perversion.

When Ryker and Erika entered the room, it was obvious that Yuri Sobolev had paid the extra charge. He had apparently finished with his fun and was in the midst of getting dressed. He had on his pants, belt, and suspenders over a white, sleeveless T-shirt. He had not yet had time to don his shirt or shoes. A young black girl who looked to be in her mid-teens lie murmuring on the bed, having been whipped by Sobolov's belt.

Erika first instinct was to kill Sobolev on the spot, then she thought of Susan.

Ryker delivered a vicious punch to the Russian's jaw, knocking him unconscious.

"We have to take the girl with us, Axel," Erika said. "If we leave her behind, she'll be questioned and probably end up at the bottom of the Potomac."

"Very well. You help the girl." Ryker grabbed the front of Sobolev's belt in one hand and used it like a suitcase handle to pack the unconscious man out of the room. Erika helped the girl to her feet. She had a club foot which caused her to limp. Erika spotted a robe thrown over a chair and put it around the naked girl then she picked up the girl's special shoes designed for her infirmity.

"Axel, both my hands are full," Erika said. "I can't help you if there's trouble on the way out."

"It is of no worry, Sonderführer. All we have to do is collect Rogova. Shooting one more will convince them to let us take our leave."

They descended past the second floor. The door to the poker room was half closed and no one noticed them. Now on the main floor, Ryker walked to the back where Zhanna had been left to guard the men. Erika stayed in the shoddy harem room with the girl who was too weak to walk on her own. This room was now totally deserted, all the woman having scampered off to other places within the building when the trouble started.

"What's your name?" Erika asked the girl.

"Olive," she said sadly and weakly.

That's when Erika heard the report from Ryker's PPK come from the room behind them. With a sound-suppressor, it sounded more like a camel spitting than a gun shot.

"Stand up, Olive. We're getting you out of here."

Ryker and Zhanna appeared from the craps tables room. When they walked through the vestibule, Hazel, who Erika had kneecapped, was not there. Evidently someone had taken her to a hospital or she had simply dragged herself to a safer part of the building. The large bouncer with the broken arm courtesy of Axel Ryker still laid unconscious on the floor from the subsequent stomping by Zhanna Rogova, his arm still grotesquely bent. Zhanna stomped him a few more times for good measure on their way out.

Outside, Ryker roughly deposited the unconscious Yuri Sobolev in the trunk of Erika's Dodge where he used duct tape to bind his hands. He also put a strip over the man's mouth. As he did that, Erika and Zhanna helped Olive into the car. Erika took the wheel with Ryker beside her. Zhanna sat in the back next to Olive.

"Where . . . where are you taking me?" Olive asked Erika as they drove away. "I have to go back. I'll get into trouble."

"What kind of fool are you?" Erika snapped. "If we would have left you there you'd be dead before you ever saw another sunrise. Now shut up! We'll supply you with safe haven tonight then decide what to do with you tomorrow."

For Yuri Sobolev, the plan was to keep him in a fleabag hotel near the river tonight. Tomorrow, they would turn him over to Al Hodge for safekeeping until it came time for the exchange. But now they had the girl to consider. Erika decided she would call Marienne and Amy and have them watch over Olive at the Mayflower. Because of foreign dignitaries from Africa, Haiti, and other nations that Washington's finest hotel occasionally hosted, it had no policy prohibiting Negro guests.

◊ ◊ ◊

Olive was now safely at the Mayflower Hotel. Marienne and Amy tended her wounds with a first aid kit asked for from the bell captain. Next stop was the bedbug hotel located in Washington near the Potomac River docks. Erika had found this place and made sure there was a telephone in the room. She wanted to get the call to Gulin right away for Susan's sake.

The duct tape on Sobolev had been removed on the dark street and he was packed into the hotel as a drunkard—a common occurrence to the disheveled man behind the desk who was no stranger to the bottle himself. Once inside the room, Ryker threw cold water into Sobolev's face. It awoke him but left him little strength after the events of tonight. When questioned under threat from Heinrich Himmler's top Gestapo henchman, Sobolev gave up the phone number without toil.

The phone rang several times before it was finally picked up by a guard at the safehouse where Susan was being held.

"I want to talk to Igor Gulin," Erika told the man.

"Comrade Gulin is not here. Who is this?"

"I am the person who now holds Yuri Sobolev captive. Listen carefully. Tell Gulin he will stop all interrogations of Captain Wedeking immediately or we will question Sobolev using similar methods as the NKVD. Tell him I will call this number tomorrow morning at ten o'clock. He'll want to be there to answer. At that time I will want to hear Captain Wedeking's voice to make sure she is still alive. He can talk to Sobolev to also assure his mind. I will give Gulin instructions after that."

Erika hung up.

Chapter 48

The telephone call

Washington, D.C.
Next day—Wednesday, 10 January 1951

Sobolev had already been taken away. A CIA pick-up team arrived at the grungy hotel this morning and spirited the Russian away before daylight.

"Where did you take Sobolev," Erika asked Al Hodge. It was 9 a.m., one hour before she was slated to call Igor Gulin. She had been there since 7:30 that morning.

"Right here in Washington," Al answered from across his desk. "The Coast Guard brig. We want him handy for a quick exchange."

"What about that girl?" Hodge asked.

"Marienne and Amy are taking care of her," Erika replied. "She's underage and a high school dropout. We're going to have to find her a school and some foster parents."

"What about her real parents?" Hodge asked.

"She says they're both dead. I don't know if that's true. She might just have run away from a bad home situation. That's how these low-life pimps get their hooks into many of these girls."

Neither Hodge nor Erika spent any more time discussing Olive. Susan was their only concern.

Do you have any questions about the plan?" Hodge asked.

"No," Erika said. "You realize there will be casualties, Al. When Ryker sees Susan there is going to be no one who can call him off—orders or no orders."

"The Soviets have no one to blame for this but themselves. They captured an American Army officer on American soil in peacetime. That's an act of war according to the Geneva Convention or anyone's Convention. There is no grievance they can file. All they can do is deny everything. All we can do is make sure no innocent civilians get hurt. The clock is marching toward ten. Almost time to call Gulin. We need to get to the Coast Guard brig. Gulin will surely want to verify Sobolev is still alive."

◊ ◊ ◊

When the Russian safehouse telephone rang, Gulin was nearby and picked up.

"Yes."

"Igor Gulin?" It was a woman's voice.

"Yes, yes. Get on with it."

"We are willing to exchange Captain Wedeking for your charge d'affaires, Yuri Sobolev."

"Put Yuri on the telephone," Gulin demanded.

"Not unless you can do the same with your hostage."

After Erika's phone call to the safehouse last night, plans to dispose of Susan had to be delayed.

Erika heard Gulin issue orders to someone in the room, "Bring the woman here."

In a moment, Erika heard Susan's weak voice.

"Susan!" Erika exclaimed. *"We're going to get you out of there tonight. Keep your spirits up."*

Gulin jerked the receiver out of Susan's hand and told his men to take her back to her quarters."

"And now, Yuri," Gulin snorted.

"Comrade Gulin," Sobolev blurted out as soon as he had the telephone in hand. "I'm being held at the . . . ."

Before he finished, Erika yanked the phone from his hand and clubbed him with it. She then put it back to her ear.

"Listen carefully, Gulin," Erika said. *"The exchange will take place tonight at 11 p.m. on Theodore Roosevelt Island in the Potomac River. Do not arrive on the island before 10:30 p.m. On your boat will be Captain Wedeking and no more than five of your men. They may come armed. At the center of the island, a campfire will be lit. It will be easy to find. You will not see us but we'll be watching you. When we feel confident you have kept to the rules of the exchange, we will appear with Sobolev at the campfire. That's when we make the trade. You will return to your boat*

and to Washington. We will depart the island from the Arlington side. Any questions?"

"I have no questions for you, Erika, or whatever your name is. But I have a change of plans. You've gone to a lot of trouble to liberate an Army military police captain. You want her badly. I'm upping the stakes, as the Americans say. For your captain, I want Yuri *and* Zhanna Rogova. If this is unacceptable, let me know now. I will shoot your captain and you can shoot Yuri. This will save us both time and trouble."

Erika was backed into a corner and had to think fast.

"Very well," she said. *"The Russian means nothing to me. Agreed."*

Sobolev was taken back to his cell, then Erika told Hodge, "Change of plans, Al. Gulin wants Zhanna in addition to Sobolev."

Hodge thought for a moment. "Have your team report to my office as soon as possible. Leave Marienne with the girl back at the Mayflower."

Chapter 49

The island

Theodore Roosevelt Island
That night—Wednesday, 10 January 1951

The 85-acre Theodore Roosevelt Island rose out of the Potomac River about halfway between Washington, D.C. and Arlington, Virginia.

About an hour ago, a low-lying fog had moved upriver from the Chesapeake Bay and came to rest over the river and the island like a lazy ghost too weary to continue its journey.

Igor Gulin and five men boarded a rented deck boat. One of Gulin's men took the helm. Another passenger on the boat was Susan Wedeking, her hands cuffed behind her back. A strip of duct tape covered her mouth. The blood had been cleaned from her face, but nothing could be done about the swollen, purple jaw.

The island was only a ten-minute boat ride from the Washington shore. Gulin's helmsman cut the engine and allowed the boat to drift slowly to the island's bank. Another man grabbed a rope and jumped out into two feet of water. He pulled on the rope until the bow grounded in sand then tied it off to a nearby tree.

Wary of a trap, Gulin said to one of his men, "Vasily, find this campfire we were told about then report back. Keep your eyes open."

Armed with a shotgun and a handgun, the man began his trek through the forest while Gulin and the others waited near the boat.

Vasily's walk was only about fifteen minutes when he saw the glow of fire in the distance. Proceeding cautiously, he came out into a small clearing where a large fire danced and spitted hot embers skyward from a stone fire ring. He looked around and then walked around but saw and heard no one. He double-timed it back to the boat.

"The campfire is there as promised, Comrade Gulin, but I saw no one."

It's what Gulin expected. "Oleg," stay with the boat. To the others he said, "Let's go. Bring the prisoner. Vasily, lead the way."

The men and Susan had been gone about ten minutes. Oleg, the boat guard, stood on the shore smoking a cigarette. Suddenly a hand went over his mouth and a searing pain seemed to set his right kidney afire.

Amy Radu stood behind him. She withdrew the dagger and stabbed him again. When she was sure he was dead, she dragged the body the short distance from the island's bank into the trees where it wouldn't be seen by any passing boats in the morning.

◊ ◊ ◊

Gulin and his entourage finally reached the roaring campfire. No one was there and he grew impatient.

"Enough games!" he shouted. "Show yourselves or I'll shoot your captain, leave her body here, and we'll be one our way. I'll then find a restaurant for a late-night meal. Perhaps steak and eggs. If you want the exchange, I want to see Rogova and Yuri now!" Everyone of Gulin's men had rifles or shotguns drawn.

Axel Ryker was the first to appear from the gloom, like a gruesome graveyard specter.

"Reid," Ryker said to the fog and shadows behind him. "Bring them out."

In a moment, Sheila walked out between Yuri Sobolev and a tall, jet-haired woman wearing a neck scarf. Sobolev looked weak and could barely maintain his feet. That afternoon, Ryker had interrogated him.

"Ah," Gulin said. "The great sniper and assassin Zhanna Rogova. It will be my pleasure to see you hang. Unlike the SS during the war, we will finish the job. I promise you."

"Send the captain to me," Ryker said. "When she is on my side of the fire, I will give you your lap dog and Rogova."

Gulin had four experienced armed men with him. On the other side of the fire stood only the two people he was trading for and Ryker and a red-haired woman Gulin had seen at the Arlington café. Gulin was also armed so he held a 5-to-2 advantage.

"As you wish," Gulin said. He signaled his man in charge of Susan. The man roughly pushed her forward.

As soon as Ryker had his arms around Susan, he used his body to shield her but Gulin and his men never managed a shot. Erika shot Yuri in the temple and immediately rifle shots from a distance began ringing out. Two of Gulin's men dropped almost simultaneously from head shots from Zhanna Rogova's sniper rifle somewhere in the near distance—she would have stationed herself farther away if it were not for the fog. Gulin and his remaining two men scampered for cover into the trees as did the American team. Then the chase began. Gulin ordered his men back to the boat. Erika threw off her black wig and platform shoes that brought her closer to Zhanna's height. Wearing just socks, she took up the chase with Sheila and Ryker.

Zhanna emerged from the gloom with makeup severe. A wide black streak encased her eyes from temple to temple. Underneath her black lipstick were three black streaks running down her chin. It was the makeup she had used during the war when she was known to the Germans as the Black Witch. She made her way to the campfire to tend to Susan. She helped the weak captain to her feet and began leading her to the waiting bowrider on the Arlington side of the island.

Erika was faster than both Sheila and the musclebound Ryker. She gained ground on her man as he wildly fired off rounds behind him as he ran. When she caught up to him, she took him to the ground and slit his throat. Sheila winged another in the back of the leg, forcing him to the ground. As he fell forward, he impaled himself on a jagged tree branch. He took his final breath as Sheila stopped beside him.

Erika knew Gulin had no chance. If he managed to get back to the boat, Amy was waiting. If Ryker caught him, he'd suffer an even worse end, but both she and Sheila again took up the chase to close the gap.

Gulin did indeed beat Ryker back to his boat but Gulin looked around and didn't see his helmsman. He started to untie the boat but was stopped by a shot in the buttocks from Amy Radu whom he never saw.

Ryker finally emerged from the woods and stood over Gulin. Ryker could have snapped his neck quickly for a fast death. Instead, he slowly twisted Gulin's head around, hearing every horrid crunch until Bloody Igor's bugged eyes faced his back.

◊◊◊

Twenty minutes later, Erika, Ryker, Sheila, and Amy made it back to their bowrider on the other bank. Susan was already aboard, wrapped in a blanket. Zhanna and Al Hodge waited on the shore.

"Everything is finished, Al," Erika said. "Let's get out of here."

"How many casualties?" Hodge asked.

"Gulin and all his men. Seven including Yuri," Erika answered.

"As soon as I can get to a phone, I'll call Housekeeping," he said. "We need to scour the site before daybreak."

Everyone jumped onboard. Hodge backed the boat away from the bank, turned the wheel hard to starboard and skimmed away toward Arlington.

Chapter 50

A bouquet of daises

Washington, D.C.
Next day—Thursday, 11 January 1951

Erika, Ryker, Sheila, Zhanna, and Amy sat in Al Hodge's E Street office. Susan was in Water Reed Hospital.

"First things first," Hodge said. "The girl—Olive— didn't suffer any significant injuries. Marienne was able to give her the first aid needed. This morning, Marienne is driving her to a Catholic nun's convent in Paterson, New Jersey. The sisters will look after the girl until we can find more suitable arrangements. We'll try to help that girl, but she's going to have to be willing to help herself. She has to make up her mind that she wants out of that life. You'd be surprised how many have a chance to get out but eventually go back.

"After Marienne drops off the girl, she'll again return to Pittsburgh with the promise she'll return if we need her."

"Susan is a different matter," Hodge continued. "I spoke with her doctor at Reed about an hour ago. No broken bones, but Gulin's cattle prod did a number on her. She still can't keep any food down. They have to feed her through an IV. The doc says she'll be in there at least a few more days. Grainger and his wife are there with her now."

"A few more days. That's good news," Sheila said. "From the looks of her last night I thought it might be weeks before she got out of the hospital."

Erika nodded. "Yes, that's good news," then asked, "How did it go with Housekeeping last night, Al?"

"It looks like they got the island straightened up. The bodies are in bags in the Walter Reed morgue. As you know, that hospital is military. The bodies aren't going anywhere until we decide what to do with them. I had one of the men in Housekeeping return Gulin's boat to the rental outfit so the owner wouldn't file a stolen boat report. In the waterways around Washington, that always gets the Coast Guard involved.

"Okay, ladies and gentleman, this costly detour with Susan came out of the blue but it looks like it's taken care of, at least for now. We still have our primary objective in front of us—expose the Pentagon G-2 mole. The question now is: How much did Gulin tell his embassy superiors about all of you and the Lili Marlene?"

"Gulin told his superiors nothing," Ryker interjected. "I interrogated him yesterday afternoon before the exchange. He told the truth. I would know if he were lying. Susan should be able to verify. She was with Gulin for four days."

◊ ◊ ◊

Erika sent Amy to the Lili Marlene to keep an eye out for any trouble. Sheila had to report to her department at the Pentagon. That left Erika and Ryker to visit Susan at Walter Reed. Ryker looked awkward carrying the small bouquet of daisies.

They spoke to the floor nurse in charge who led them down the corridor to Susan's room.

The MP captain was awake and smiled weakly when she saw them. Ryker fumbled around with the flowers, not sure what to do with them. Erika took them off his hands.

"Axel," Erika said. "Why don't you go down to the gift store and buy a small vase."

Ryker nodded and left.

"I think he's embarrassed," Susan said softly. "But that was sweet of him."

'Sweet' was not an adjective Erika had ever heard linked with Axel Ryker.

"How are you doing, Susan? The doctor told Al Hodge you might get out of here in a few days."

Susan nodded. "As soon as I can keep some solid food down." She had IVs hooked up to the back of both hands. "I drank a small cup of broth this morning."

"That's a good start."

"What did you come here to ask me, Erika?"

"How much did Gulin find out about me, Sheila, and Amy? We know he learned about Zhanna."

"He learned about Zhanna through his man Yuri. I overheard them talking. He learned nothing about you, Sheila, and Amy. When he asked me about you, I told him you were Mae West." Susan's laugh quickly turned into a coughing fit which exhausted her even more.

Erika calmed her with a cold wet rag as Susan dropped off to sleep. Ryker walked in with a vase. Erika filled it half-full of water from the lavatory sink, dropped in the daisies and placed them on a table along a wall.

"Let's go, Axel. She needs rest."

[that evening]

Susan Wedeking had done her part to protect the women's identities, suffering greatly to do so. That meant the café was also protected. Igor Gulin's self-importance had kept him from divulging what he knew about Zhanna Rogova to his Soviet overlords until he brought her in and turned her over. It was the last mistake Bloody Igor would make.

To everyone's great relief, the Lili Marlene was safe. Erika knew there might come a time when she would again have to deal with Dima Lukov and his Russian mob concerning the game equipment and jukebox she had extorted from them, but that was a bridge to be crossed on another day.

Tonight, the crew of the Lili Marlene was in high spirits. Susan was going to be okay and business tonight was good. Zhanna, Ryker, and Amy were behind the bar. Erika and Sheila helped the waitress deliver food. Ada was again in the kitchen washing dishes.

The Thursday night wrist wrestling competition would begin in one hour. Since Erika had banned Ryker from the event, locals were again signing up.

Part 6

Chapter 51

Flashback
Brussels, Belgium
April 1949

Erika had warned Rose to stay away from Axel Ryker so the Bristow heiress suspected that Erika would come looking for her. That obviously meant she and Axel could not eat at the hotel restaurant. Not having time to change into a dinner gown, Rose suggested that Ryker ask the taxi driver for a recommendation for a pub or café further from the hotel.

Unfortunately, the driver took them to a bar run by a friend of his in a rather seedy neighborhood of Brussels.

Nevertheless, Rose took Ryker's arm and he led her inside.

Ryker could see immediately that the place was a dive. He approached the bartender.

"Call us a taxi. We're not eating in this rat hole."

The bartender spoke English.

"Calling my place a rat hole is a mistake, friend."

If Ryker had been alone, he likely would have grabbed the man's hand or wrist and crushed a bone or two, but he didn't want Rose to see that. And it proved unnecessary. It took only a glare from the enormous, scar-faced Ryker. The man stepped over to the telephone behind the bar and called for a taxi.

Thirty minutes later, Rose and Ryker sat in a restaurant called Le Piquet located on the western edge of the Brussels city limits. Here, everyone spoke only French so it would fall on Rose to communicate with the staff.

"Thank you for considering me at that last bar, Axel."

"I would never subject you to a place like that."

Rose had already glanced at the menu. She knew her date didn't speak French. "Axel, there is an entrée available, Agneu marocain. In English that is Moroccan Lamb. I have never had it here, of course, but

I've had it before in Paris. It's lamb with squash, red bell peppers, and onions spiced with garlic and fresh cilantro." Rose didn't want to give her date a hint to her riches; so far in her life the only men who showed her any interest were after her money. Ryker didn't know about her fortune and she wanted to keep it that way, so she added, "I was lucky enough to spend a semester at the Sorbonne in Paris when I was a student." This was true, although luck had nothing to do with it. Her parents had paid the exorbitant cost for her semester at the exclusive Parisian university.

"I've had lamb but never this one you mention," Ryker admitted awkwardly. "I would like to try it."

Ryker was doing his best, but he knew he was not smooth with women. Because of his daunting looks, the only women in his life had been those he paid for.

When the waiter appeared, Ryker ordered a beer, Rose the same. She had grown tired of champagne and fancy mixed drinks it seemed everyone preferred at the boring, upper-crust parties she had attended myriad times during her adult life as a Bristow. While the waiter was there, Rose ordered the meals in French.

"Axel, I don't consider myself an expert on accents, but as a linguist and interpreter I've heard many. I cannot place yours."

Ryker told the truth. "I am German but was born in a German community in Lithuania so I grew up speaking both German and Russian."

Rose nodded. That explained it.

"What did you do during the war?" Rose asked as she adjusted her eyeglasses. She considered herself homely and hated the spectacles she thought added to her plain appearance.

Ryker felt he should lie, but he knew if he were ever to find a woman who actually cared for him, she would have to know the truth.

"I was Gestapo." He was breaking every rule but didn't care. "I will now escort you back to your hotel, Rose." He started to stand up, sure she would want to be rid of him.

Rose touched his hand. "Please sit down, Axel. We haven't had our lamb yet."

Heinrich Himmler's most brutal henchman looked at the warm and caring feminine hand on his. He had never experienced this gentleness from a woman before.

Chapter 52

New orders for Amy

Back to Present
Arlington, Virginia
Tuesday, 16 January 1951

It had been five days since Susan's rescue. She was released from Walter Reed yesterday morning. Ryker and Rose were there to pick her up. Yes, Rose was back in town. Since the cafe was not in danger, Ryker had brought Rose and their son back to Washington to their deluxe suite at the Mayflower Hotel.

Now it was dinnertime and Erika sat with Susan and the Rykers at a table in the Lili Marlene. Susan was now eating, but tentatively. Erika watched her shove food around her plate, occasionally taking a small bite.

Susan had regained some color to her face but was still a bit pale. Her left jaw, swollen and empurpled by Gulin's full-fisted punch, looked better but the injury was still noticeable.

"Some guy by the name of Stan Gregory has dropped in a couple of times looking for you, Susan," Erika said. "We told him you took some time off to visit relatives in Indiana."

"We should run his background," Ryker added.

"Already did," Erika said. "Al says he's clean."

"Rose," Erika then said, "May I borrow your husband for a few minutes. We won't be gone long."

"Of course. I have the baby to keep me company."

Angelika took over at the bar. She was quickly learning important vocabulary for her job. She was nowhere near being fluent in English, but she could now take food and drink orders without using her cheat sheet.

Erika, Ryker, Zhanna, Susan, and Amy went upstairs.

"Sheila and I had a long briefing with Al this morning," Erika said after they had all taken a seat. "Sheila's not here because she's at Colonel Grainger's home filling him in. As you all know, our original assignment to unearth the Pentagon mole is still ongoing. We've had setbacks that have delayed our progress, but we should all thank Susan for not giving up us or the cafe."

"I agree," said Ryker. The others nodded at Susan.

"Does Al have any new ideas?" Amy asked.

"He's asking Grainger to make a list of phony names of overseas G-2 operatives—men and women who are not really field agents but work for G-2 in some capacity overseas. These people will be warned ahead of time and protected. Grainger's instructions will include being extremely careful who has access to that list at the Pentagon. If any action is taken overseas against any of these fake agents, we'll at least have some names of Pentagon people who accessed the list. One of them will be the mole."

"That means we're back to zero and another waiting game," Zhanna said. "What about Svetlana?"

"I know she's a friend of yours, Zhanna, and she was ready to help, but Gulin's dead and our plans for Svetlana's involvement was because of him," Erika said. "You can tell her and her husband that they're off the hook. She'll be relieved. You told us yourself that Svetlana is happy with her life. Invite her and her husband to dinner here at the café. You can tell them then. I'll pick up the bill. There's no reason you two can't remain friends."

Amy said, "So, like Zhanna mentioned, we're back to a waiting game. Sitting on our thumbs until something happens."

"None of us like it," Erika replied. "Keep your fingers crossed that things develop quickly."

"What do we do until then?" Amy asked.

"We help Angelika run the café," Erika answered. "Weekend business is now pretty good but weeknights are still hit or miss. We have to keep coming up with ideas to bring people in on weeknights. Since I canned Mr. Ryker here from the wrist wrestling competition, that's now drawing in some people on Thursday nights. What else can we do? I'm all ears for suggestions."

"Amy, you should dance," Susan said. "Zhanna told me about the Gypsy Flamenco you did at the Barcelona cantina on your last mission."

Everyone looked at Amy. She said, "Sorry, I'm retired from dancing. Besides, it takes an experienced Roma guitarist for accompaniment. An American guitarist won't have a clue about how to play Roma Flamenco."

"Axel," Erika said. "You have your assignment. Find Amy such a guitarist. Perhaps Rose can help you with that and with finding Amy the appropriate attire."

"Rose can do both," Ryker said. "She knows nearly everybody in the arts and people who deal in garments."

Amy objected. "Erika, I don't want to dance anymore."

Ryker interrupted. "You'll fulfill your orders, Gypsy."

"If you think I'm dancing for the Gestapo, you're crazy."

"Amy, you're not dancing for Ryker," Erika said. "You'll be dancing to help the café."

"It's only temporary, Amy," Erika continued. "When this assignment is over, Al will have you return to Fort Benning to finish those classes you're taking."

"A Roma Flamenco dancer at a German café," Amy objected. "You can't be serious."

"That's what America is, Amy," Erika said. "A melting pot. Many Greek restaurants in America have belly dancers because they bring in customers, even though belly dancers aren't Greek. They originally came from Syria and Egypt. Let's give it a try."

"You're not going to find a homemade dress like we always wore," the Gypsy added. "And an authentic Roma Flamenco dress, even if you manage to find one in a specialty store, is going to cost someone a lot of money."

"A business expense we can take off our taxes," Erika countered.

"And if you find a real Roma musician, those guys are a hot-headed lot," Amy added. "If he isn't getting the cheers he thinks he deserves, or people are being stingy with tips, he's liable to take a swing at someone."

Ryker growled out some laughter. "I like the guy already."

Chapter 53

Lukov comes calling

Washington, D.C.
Two days later—Thursday, 18 January 1951

Erika sat in Al Hodge's office.

"Grainger has made up the list of phony G-2 field agents working in Istanbul," Hodge said.

"Who's going to see that list?" she asked.

"Only a select few G-2 officers, none of whom know it's a phony list. It will be kept in a safe and access will be through a master sergeant. Only the master sergeant and Grainger will have the key and combination to the safe. The name of anyone accessing the file will be recorded."

Erika nodded. "Hopefully, something we can work on will develop soon."

[that evening—the Lili Marlene]

The showdown with Dima Lukov, the Russian crime boss, happened sooner than Erika expected. All the Shield Maidens were there along with Axel Ryker when Lukov and five of his men walked in and approached the bar.

"Why are you here?" Zhanna asked in Russian.

"I'm here to talk to your boss—the blonde woman named Erika."

"She's busy. Go away."

"She doesn't look busy," Lukov switched to English. "She's sitting at a table over in the corner talking to a red-haired woman and Frankenstein."

Erika didn't have to be summoned. They had all seen Lukov and his men enter the café. She walked behind the bar, joining Zhanna and Amy. Sheila and Ryker stood nearby.

Erika had to be careful what she said. They had gotten lucky because of Susan. Their covers were intact and she needed to keep it that way.

"What can I do for you, Mr. Lukov?"

"It's time that you start paying your dues on my equipment and protection insurance."

"What does Mr. Gulin have to say about that? I had an agreement with him."

"I don't care what he thinks," Lukov sneered. "He doesn't run my outfit."

This told Erika that Lukov had no idea that Gulin was dead.

"We're still building the business," Erika said. "I cannot afford such an expense."

"But you can afford restrooms that look like some you'd see in the Waldorf. I sent a man by here last night."

"Those were a gift from a friend. I will pay you a fair price for the dart boards, pinball machines and the jukebox. None of those things were new when your men delivered them so I will not pay new prices. Find a figure that is fair and the café will pay you. And we are not paying for your 'fire insurance.' If this café burns down, so will your houses. That's my offer. Take it or leave it. Zhanna and I are made members of the Smaldone crime family in Denver (this was true). Have you ever heard of them?"

"I've heard of the Smaldone's," Lukov said.

"Call Checkers Smaldone," Erika added. "He can be reached at his restaurant called Gaetano's in the Little Italy area of north Denver. He'll verify who we are."

Chapter 54

A friend from Denver

Denver, Colorado
Next day—Friday, 19 January 1951

"Checkers," a bartender said. "It's long distance from Washington, D.C. Some guy wants to talk to you. He sounds Russian."

Checkers Smaldone, the head of Denver's top organized crime family, sat at the always reserved table at the back of Gaetano's, the family's Italian restaurant. Alongside him sat his brother Chauncey and his cousin, Fat Paulie Villano.

"A Russian from Washington," Checkers said to Chauncey and Paulie. "What the fuck can this be about?"

The bartender brought the telephone that was strung from a long cable to the table.

"Talk," Checkers said into the receiver.

"Is this Checkers Smaldone?" the voice from D.C. asked.

"Maybe it is and maybe it isn't. Who the fuck are you?"

"My name is Dima Lukov. You and I are engaged in similar undertakings. My areas are Washington, northern Virginia, and southern Maryland."

"You're also a dumb fuck for telling me that on the phone. Now what do you want and make it snappy."

"I'm calling about a couple of women who claim to be with your family—an Erika Lehmann and Zhanna Rogova. Do you know these women?"

"I know them, so what?"

"I have been conducting business with these women and they refuse to pay."

"Pay for what?" Checkers asked.

"A jukebox and some gambling equipment for their restaurant."

"They have a restaurant? What's the name of it?"

"The Lili Marlene Café in Arlington."

"Now listen to me, Ivan, and listen good," Checkers said. "I will do some checking into this. Nothing is to happen to those women or their restaurant. If they get hit by a bus or fall off a cliff, I'll have the New Jersey and New York families come down on you like buzzards on roadkill. Give me a phone number where you can be reached. I'll get back to you. Until then, hands off, you got that Mack?"

[that afternoon—Arlington]

Zhanna picked up the bar telephone.

"Lili Marlene Café," she said.

Checkers recognized her Russian accent. *"Zhanna. This is Checkers. Is Erika there?"*

"She's upstairs."

"Well, let me talk to her, dammit."

In a moment, Erika was on the phone. "Checkers. It's nice hearing your voice. How are things in the Mile High City?"

"Cut the crap, Erika. I'm calling from a pay phone. Is it safe to talk?"

"It's safe."

"I got a call this morning from some turkey named Dima Lukov. Apparently, he has a problem with you. What's going on?"

"I now have a café here in Arlington."

"No shit. Tell me something I don't know. I got the name from Lukov and I just called you there."

"I had to get a jukebox and pinball machines from his outfit. They control that business for bars and arcades in this area."

"And he wants weekly payoffs," Checkers said. *"You should have known that going in, Erika. What's wrong with you?"*

"I did know, Checkers, but decided not to pay for that or his arson insurance. I offered to pay him a fair price to purchase the equipment."

"Why didn't you call me? I have friends in both the Jersey and New York families that owe me favors. I could have gotten you that stuff with no dues or payoffs."

"I didn't know that Checkers."

"I never heard of this Lukov. He must be small time. I'll do some checking on him with the East Coast families. I'll take care of this for you. Just next time call me first."

"Thank you, Checkers. Please send my love to Paulie and all the boys and your wife, Frances."

[that evening at the Lili Marlene]

Erika sat at the bar talking to Zhanna.

"You didn't mention how the call with Checkers went," Zhanna said.

"It went good," Erika said. "I was concerned I might have to tell Lukov we were with the government to get him off our backs. That would blow our cover. Checkers told me he'd take care of the problem with Lukov. In other words, a mob problem handled by the mob. It couldn't have worked out better. Checkers once told us that he will always be there for us and he kept his word. I miss Denver and Gaetano's and the poker games. Maybe after this mission is over we'll get some days off and we'll go out there for a few days, Zhanna."

Chapter 55

Un dans ţigănesc

Washington, D.C.
Next day—Saturday, 20 January 1951

"No developments so far on Grainger's phony list of G-2 field agents," Al Hodge said to Erika and Sheila Reid who sat across from him on the other side of his E Street office desk.

"Al," Erika said. "We started this mission two months ago. We've tried various things but still we have nothing." The irritation in her voice was obvious.

"Don't you think I'm just as frustrated, Lehmann," Al said. "I don't need a bad attitude from you right now. Your job is to obey orders, that's all."

The conversation was becoming heated so Sheila stepped in. "Al, how many G-2 officers have accessed Grainger's phony file so far?"

"Only a couple, and there's been no moves on those people in Istanbul."

"So again we have nothing to pursue," Erika said.

"All we can do is be patient, Erika," Sheila said before she turned to Hodge. "Al, I know James Brunnell was supposed to return to his job in procurement when he was no longer in the picture as a target for Gulin. But Brunnell has proven he has promise as an analyst. I'd like to keep him in my Polish Department while he undergoes training."

"That's not my call, Sheila. That has to be approved by the big guns at the Pentagon."

"I know," she replied. "I'm just giving you a heads up that I will be sending that request up the ladder."

[that evening—Lili Marlene Café]

Susan, her energy returned, was now back at work behind the bar. The only remnant of her time with Bloody Igor was her still slightly discolored left jaw. Stan Gregory was there sitting at the section of the bar that Susan worked. He didn't ask about her jaw, assuming if she wanted to explain she would. She didn't.

It was a special night at the Lili Marlene. Besides the entire team, Al Hodge was there. So was Rose Bristow but she had left the baby back at the hotel with the nanny and a bodyguard Ryker had hired himself.

Tonight would be the café's introduction of a unique act—a genuine Gypsy Flamenco dancer. Although Amy's act was going to be offered on a weeknight to try to bolster one of the slower nights, her first dance would be tonight on the busiest night of the week in the hope that the crowd would spread the word.

Typically, a Gypsy campfire or cantina dance would be accompanied by several clan musicians including a guitarist, a fiddler, a Djembe drummer, someone on a cimbalom as well as other instruments. Nevertheless, a dance could be presented with just an experienced Roma guitarist. Rose Bristow, with her far-flung contacts in the art world, had found such a man in New York City and promised to pay his hotel bill in Arlington. Like Amy, the guitarist was Romania, and during the two brief rehearsals they held upstairs at the café yesterday, the two communicated in their native tongue.

The café was about three-quarters full when Sheila asked for everyone's attention.

"Ladies and Gentlemen," Sheila spoke loudly. "Tonight, the Lili Marlene presents to you something special. This act will normally be offered on Wednesday nights. If you enjoy it we hope you'll tell your friends. We have with us tonight Amy Radu and her guitarist—Javal. Both are from different Gypsy clans originating in Romania and tonight they are here to show us all something many have never seen—an authentic Gypsy Flamenco. The name of this dance in Romanian is *Un dans ţigănesc."*

There passed a brief delay then Amy and her guitarist appeared from the kitchen door to a half-hearted smattering of applause. The dark-skinned guitarist who was probably in his late-30s certainly looked the part with dark clothes, greased black hair slicked straight back and an equally lubricated mustache. Some tables had been moved to allow Amy room to dance. The stunning Romanian wore a black tribal Flamenco skirt covered with hand-painted red roses, so many that the red overtook the black. Her midriff and naval were exposed by the short, off-the-shoulder red and brown peasant blouse. Shocking green eye shadow and red lipstick with a glittered face and shoulders added to her unique look.

The one-of-a-kind handmade dress was found at a specialty shop in Manhattan and indeed was expensive, but here again Rose jumped in and took care of the costs including alterations.

The guitarist began thumping on his guitar as if it were a drum. Amy stood holding the pleats of her wide and frilly skirt outward and staring at the floor. She finally took one step forward, signaling the musician. Holding the guitar butt on his knee and playing it upright as one would play a cello, he began strumming out a slow, Roma tune of lament and heartbreak as Amy stomped her feet in unison. No castanets were ever used in Gypsy Flamenco. The dancer's hands were used to manipulate the skirt.

Yet the sufferings of this group of people who had been ostracized and even brutally persecuted over the centuries would not be allowed to take over the mood. Amy yelled, "Ola!" and her guitarist immediately shifted to high gear into a lively lilt of hope for better times.

The striking beauty from Transylvania kept dancing but started flirting with some of the men in the crowd. She would gently tickle under a chin or lean over for a kiss then pull back when a man tried to oblige. One of the men she tickled under the chin was Al Hodge. He turned beet red and pulled back. Amy laughed. Sometimes she'd hike up her skirt to her underpants as she stomped her black platform heels in rhythm to the guitar music.

When the song finally reached its crescendo, the busy guitarist was perspiring profusely as Amy let down her hair bun pinned in place with a red rose, held out her skirt and twirled and twirled, her hair whipping about madly.

When the song ended, the half-hearted applause that had greeted them was now a boisterous chorus. Half the crowd was on its feet. The Gypsy guitarist saw an opportunity, jumped up, and began circulating through the crowd holding his hat out for tips.

A lot of money went into that hat tonight, and it just wasn't coins. Paper money was thrown in, as well.

Chapter 56

Hair curlers

Arlington, Virginia
Next day—Sunday, 21 January 1951

As always, the Lili Marlene was closed on Sunday. Angelika and Bertha had the day off. Al Hodge called a meeting of the team and it was decided to get together at the deserted café. Susan put on a large pot of coffee.

Colonel Howard Grainger walked in with Carr.

A couple of tables were pushed together and everyone sat down while Susan and Zhanna poured the coffee.

"It looked like the café had a good night last night," Hodge said.

"Our biggest night so far. Mainly thanks to Amy," Erika replied. We normally close at midnight, Last night we were still serving drinks at 1:30. Three or four people asked Amy for her autograph. Did you enjoy the dance, Al?"

"It was alright," Hodge said in his understated way.

"We might have a break in the case," he continued. "Yesterday, one of the fake G-2 agents in Istanbul swore he was being followed. This morning he disappeared."

Grainger took over. "This man's name was on the phony list that only three people have seen, so we have some names as suspects. We can assume one of them is the Pentagon mole. Two of the men are G-2 captains and the third a G-2 major." Grainger handed Erika a folder. "This contains their names, photographs, and background checks. On paper, all three look squeaky clean."

Hodge added, "One is a widower, one is divorced, and the other has never been married. Nothing stands in the way of their succumbing to the charms of the Shield Maidens."

"Colonel," Erika noted. "Al said only one of the false agents has been followed—the man who disappeared. Why not more?"

"Mr. Hodge and I discussed that," Grainger recounted. "The man was the first name to be included on the list. The other two names were added a few days later. That leads us to think the mole has not yet seen the additional names."

"Colonel Grainger," Erika said. "Can you suggest to these men that they stop in here at the Lili Marlene some evening? Perhaps tell them we're offering half-priced drinks and food discounts that night to service men in uniform. I know you can order them to attend, but that would look suspicious."

"I'll take care of it," Grainger said. "I'll invite them to join me. When you ladies have your hooks in them, I'll make an excuse why I have to leave."

After more conversation about details, Hodge and Grainger left. Erika opened the folder and divided up the three men pictured inside.

"Susan, you take this one," Erika said. "Amy, here's your guy. I'll take this one. Sheila is married and Zhanna speaks with a Russian accent, we'll leave them out of this because it's going to come to nothing anyway. I have my suspicions who the mole is, and it's none of these three men."

[late that evening]

Howard Grainger sat at his desk in his dark home study illuminated only by his desk lamp. A gentle rain tapped and ran down his window. Agatha was in bed. The Grainger's lived in an upscale neighborhood in Chevy Chase, Maryland, on the border of Washington, D.C. On his desk was a dram of Scotch and the files on the three new suspects. He knew all three men and if one proved to be the mole it would be devastating to him on both a personal and professional level.

He gazed through the reports for the umpteenth time before finishing his drink and putting the reports back into the wall safe concealed behind a hinged painting.

Flipping off the desk light, he finally went upstairs to bed.

About an hour passed before the desk light turned back on. Agatha Grainger, with curlers in her hair and wearing a house robe, swung open the painting and dialed open the safe. Laying the files on her husband's desk, she began photographing them with a Leica mini camera.

A rain-soaked Erika Lehmann and Zhanna Rogova watched through binoculars from the nearby woods on the other side of the street.

"Haven't these people ever heard of curtains?" Zhanna asked.

"The colonel is innocent," Erika replied. "No need for him to draw the curtains, and those are tied curtains. Agatha would have to untie them, close them, then before she left, open and tie them back. She's confident she's under no suspicion so that's risking too much time for what she has to do."

Chapter 57

A surprise for Al

Washington, D.C.
Next day—Monday, 22 January 1951

"Al. We know who the G-2 Pentagon mole is," Erika said. She and Zhanna sat across from his office desk at E Street.

"What do you mean?" Hodge said.

"The mole is Colonel Grainger's wife, Agatha."

"What?!"

Erika explained what she and Zhanna saw at the Grainger's home last night.

"What made you suspect her?" Hodge still didn't believe it.

"It was a hunch. At General O'Malley's Christmas party she seemed overly interested in me and Sheila. Then we discovered a link between her and Igor Gulin. They had an affair in 1946 after meeting at an embassy cocktail party. Ryker got that out of Yuri Sobolev when he interrogated him. I kept it low key until I saw what I saw last night. There was rain on the windows but there's no doubt she was accessing the safe and taking photos."

"So Ryker knows?"

"He knows about the affair. Zhanna and I have discussed last night with no one. We wanted to tell you first."

Hodge leaned back heavily in his chair, lit a cigarette, and thought for a long moment.

"This has to be handled with delicacy," he said. "The evidence we have is not enough. She can deny sneaking into the safe last night and Grainger will believe her. We have to catch her red-handed. I hope for all our sakes you're not wrong about this Erika."

"What about the three G-2 officers we're supposed to curry favor with?" Erika asked. "That now would be a big waste of our time."

"I can't call that off without a good reason to Grainger. Everything will proceed as planned."

Zhanna asked, "Did Grainger break any laws by taking those records home?"

"He's operational head of G-2," Carr replied. "Pentagon department heads are allowed to check out certain top-secret documents if they apply only to their section. Sheila can do that with her Polish section. Grainger probably didn't break any protocols but it was surely stupid of him if what you're telling me is true."

"If it weren't true, we wouldn't tell you," Erika said, irked.

"I apologize," Hodge said. "It's just such a shocker I can't get my mind around it just yet. Do nothing until I get a plan in place."

[that night—Lili Marlene]

The team had just returned from upstairs where Erika filled them in on Agatha Grainger and all the latest. The place was less than half-full so there was no need for three bartenders. Amy and Susan held down those duties as Ryker sat down at a table with Rose. Again, the baby was not there. Until all this was settled, Ryker felt better with the baby and his nanny and bodyguard remaining at the Mayflower.

Erika and Sheila sat together at another table.

"I wonder who this bodyguard is that Ryker hired for his son and Rose when they're not with him," Sheila probed. "I'd like to find out what sort of man Axel Ryker would trust to guard his family."

"We probably don't want to know," Erika said. "It might dig up old ghosts from the past."

A few minutes later, Colonel Grainger walked in with three men—the three men from his folder of suspects.

Erika sighed. "Grainger didn't waste any time. I'll see you later, Sheila. This is up to Amy, Susan, and me."

Chapter 58

Zhanna's plan

Washington, D.C.
Next day—Tuesday, 23 January 1951

Erika and Sheila met with Al Hodge at the Hamilton Diner in Arlington, a popular breakfast stop that had operated at the same location since the turn of the century. Leroy Carr and Al Hodge had had many breakfasts here stretching back to their days with the wartime OSS.

Zhanna, currently living with Erika, was babysitting Ada at the apartment. Erika would brief the team later.

"Grainger and his three men stopped into the café last night," Erika said as she dived into a hearty-sized helping of sausage and eggs, hash browns, and biscuits.

"How'd it go?" Hodge asked.

"Grainger left soon. The rest of the evening Susan, Amy, and I just played friendly. We all knew we weren't dealing with the mole so we played pinball, threw some darts, had a couple of drinks, and that was about it. They left together around eleven."

Sheila asked, "How are we going to break this to the colonel—about his wife, I mean?"

"We're not going to until we have rock-solid evidence," Hodge said as he took a sip of coffee.

Erika interjected. "What we need to find out is how Agatha is relaying the information to the Soviets. It has to be through some sort of dead drop. A transmitter or meeting someone at a park or restaurant would be way too dangerous for someone in her position as the wife of a top supervisor at G-2."

"She doesn't know Gulin is dead, is that right, Al?" asked Sheila.

"No one knows," he said. "The Russians are probably in Code Red by now. Gulin and his men have been missing for almost two weeks now. The bodies are still on ice at the Walter Reed morgue."

"I'm sure the bodies have been thoroughly searched."

"Of course, Sheila. Everything is at E Street."

"Do you remember finding anything with Gulin's handwriting on it?" Sheila asked.

Hodge thought for a moment. "Yes. But nothing of importance. A list of liquor and a few grocery items Gulin apparently planned to pick up."

"When we finish breakfast, we need to take a look at it," Sheila said.

◊ ◊ ◊

Sheila Reid sat gazing at Igor Gulin's handwritten list. Erika and Hodge both knew what she was thinking.

"Sheila," Erika said. "It's unlikely that Gulin would contact Agatha Grainger directly through a handwritten note. Too dangerous. More likely would be for Gulin to have someone else set up a dead drop over a pay phone, like his man Yuri Sobolev. But Sobolev is also dead."

"I realize that, Erika. Still, there has to be a way."

"Before we go jumping the gun, let's all mull this over," Hodge said. "We'll only get one chance at this."

When the women left, Hodge sank back in his chair. His first thought was to recall Marienne Schenck to shadow Agatha Grainger but felt that would be a waste of time at the present. With no orders coming in from Gulin, Agatha Grainger wouldn't be going anywhere but on mundane errands and shopping outings. It wasn't worth putting a tail on her for that.

A plan was needed.

[that evening—Lili Marlene]

A large poster of Amy wearing her Roma tribal outfit hung on the door to the café advertising that her next dance would be held tomorrow—Wednesday.

Erika had the entire team assembled upstairs and had briefed everyone about that day's meeting with Al Hodge.

"Gulin died nearly two weeks ago," Amy said. "If the colonel's wife invaded the home safe Sunday night, she must still be getting orders from somebody."

"Maybe," Erika said. "Or maybe she's just going about her assignment laid out to her months ago. G-2 agents have been disappearing oversees since November."

"I suggest we eliminate the mole," Zhanna said. "That's the obvious remedy to this problem."

"You probably have something there, Zhanna," Erika said. "However, that's not how Al wants this handled. He wants her caught red-handed. She's the wife of the head of G-2 foreign operations and well known around Washington. Simply canceling her will open a shitstorm and everyone will suspect the CIA did it."

"Not if we supply proof pointing to the Soviets as eliminating her," Zhanna countered. "Perhaps they considered her a double agent. Her supplying names of false G-2 field operatives in Istanbul could lead them to believe that. That is the way we would have handled this in SMERSCH."

Everyone looked at Zhanna. They all knew this was one of the rare times she made sense.

"Point taken, Zhanna," Erika said. "I'll have to run this by Al." She would do that but she knew Al Hodge, and knew he'd never approve it.

Chapter 59

A sagging hat

Arlington, Virginia
Next day—Wednesday, 24 January 1951

Amy Radu would dance tonight and the Lili Marlene was packed. Every barstool was taken and people without tables stood with drinks in hand along the outer walls. Every member of the team was working. Ryker, Susan, and Angelika manned the bar. Bertha and Ada handled things in the kitchen. Not only did Ada do the dishes, but she also helped Bertha prepare some of the food with Bertha instructing her. Patty was overwhelmed so Erika, Sheila, and even Rose Bristow waited tables.

Earlier today, Erika had run Zhanna's idea past Al Hodge. He nixed the plan immediately, as she knew he would. They would have to find another way.

When it was time for Amy, Sheila again introduced her and her guitarist. Both wore the same attire they wore Saturday night. The crowd, made up mostly of men who had gotten the word about the beautiful Gypsy dancer at a local café, cheered the seductive siren on the dance floor. When the dance ended, the guitarist again jumped up and circulated through the crowd holding out his hat. When he was done, his hat sagged from the weight of the coins and overflowed with paper money dropping out which he had to pick up. Amy would get 70 percent of the tips. He would keep 30 percent.

Including food and drink, tonight would even surpass Saturday night as the most profitable night since the Lili Marlene opened over two months ago.

Chapter 60

Zhanna worries about a bird

Washington. D.C.
Next day—Thursday, 25 January 1951

Hodge had summoned Erika, Sheila, and Zhanna to his CIA office.

"I had our forgers produce this note from Igor Gulin's handwriting on his grocery list. We have the best forgers in the country working for us. Not even the top handwriting experts who appear in courts could deny Gulin wrote this." He passed the note around to the three women.

Dearest, I have been recalled to Moscow for a time. I don't know how long it will be before I return. Our important work must continue. During my absence, your new contact will be a woman named Zhanna Rogova. I know you might have seen this woman when you visited the Lili Marlene Café with your husband. Rogova is a comrade who I planted there when we found out this café was going to be an informal place for G-2 officers to gather. Follow her instructions as you would follow mine. She will contact you. Hopefully, I will return soon. —Igor

"How are you going to get this note to her, Al," Erika asked.

"Just an old school bump. I've got a couple of guys who are the best bumpers in the world. One of them will bump into her in a store or on the street and drop it in her purse. She won't discover the note till later. Then she'll think my bumper was sent by Gulin. The Soviets use bumpers like we do."

"It might work," Erika commented.

"It might or might not," Hodge said. "I'm taking a gamble with the endearment 'dearest' but if these two had an affair I'm wagering it won't seem out of sorts. Anyway, we're going to try it this way. We're not going to bump off the wife of the head of G-2 foreign operations. We're going to collect evidence. Does everyone here understand that?"

Sheila nodded and Erika shrugged. Zhanna had been watching a sparrow perched on a tree limb outside Hodge's window.

"I bet that bird is freezing its ass off," she finally said.

Chapter 61

A rude man

Washington, D.C.
Next day—Friday, 26 January 1951

Agatha Grainger walked along M Street on her way to a millinery shop. She dropped her eyes for a moment as she looked into her purse for her pack of cigarettes. Suddenly a man bumped into her, forcing her to look up.

"Hey, lady. Why don't you watch where you're going?" he said gruffly.

"I'm sorry," she said as the man walked away. As soon as she apologized, she regretted doing it. He had been so rude he didn't deserve an apology.

She would discover the small envelop in her purse when she paid for her new Panama hat.

[two hours later]

As soon as Agatha returned home she knew the first thing she had to do was destroy Igor's note. She burned it in an ashtray then flushed the ashes down the toilet. About a half hour later, the telephone rang.

"Hello," she said.

A woman with a Russian accent said, *"Answer only with a 'yes' or a 'no.' Have you checked your purse?"*

"Yes."

"Listen carefully. Meet me tonight at eight o'clock at the Foxtail Tavern. It's on 34th Street Northwest in Georgetown, not far from the university. Sit at a table. I will recognize you."

The caller hung up.

◊ ◊ ◊

[that evening]

Agatha took a taxi and arrived at the Foxtail Tavern twenty minutes before the appointed time. As instructed, she sat down at a table and ordered a drink.

No one approached her, but ten minutes later a tall, jet-haired woman entered, looked around, and spotted her.

When Agatha accompanied her husband to the Lili Marlene that night, she hadn't paid much attention to the staff, but now she remembered this woman because of her height.

The woman walked to her table, took off her coat, and hung it over an empty chair. She didn't remove her neck scarf.

"Hello, Agatha," the woman said as she sat down. The waitress came over immediately and the woman ordered a double vodka.

Agatha Grainger recognized the Russian-accented voice from this afternoon's phone call.

"I'm Zhanna," the woman said and extended her hand. "I'm glad to be working with you. It's an honor for me that Mr. Gulin chose me as his proxy while he's away."

"Hello," Agatha said as she shook Zhanna's hand. "I have to admit, all this makes me nervous."

"No need to be nervous," Zhanna said. "Mr. Gulin made it quite clear that it is my job to protect you. What did you tell your husband about why you had to leave tonight?"

"I told him I was visiting a sick friend. I can't be gone long."

"Then we'll get down to business."

Zhanna had to negotiate around a problem. She didn't know where the dead drops were taking place. If she really worked for Gulin, he would have told her.

She told Agatha, "The first thing we need to do is set up a new location for your dead drops. There is a large potted plant in front of the pharmacy across the street. That's why I chose to meet here. Place your envelope behind the plant in the vase where it cannot be seen by a passer-by. When you are safely away, I will retrieve the envelope. Do you have any more information for us at this time?" Zhanna knew she did.

"I have two more names of G-2 spies in Istanbul. The names are on microfilm along with places of operation and other information."

"I hope you are keeping your camera in a secure location." Zhanna said it hoping the woman would make a mistake and tell her where she kept the Leica that Erika and she had seen Agatha using Sunday night.

"It's secure. When do I receive the next payment to my account in Havana?"

"We need that microfilm as soon as possible. Make the dead drop tomorrow night at nine o'clock. We will wire your money the next day."

[one hour later]

Zhanna was now back at the Lili Marlene.

"We have a problem," she told Erika. "The Grainger woman is doing this for money, not for any feelings for Gulin. We don't know how much money is involved and I couldn't ask her. I'd blow my cover. Gulin's stand-in would know that information."

"Yep," Erika said. "That's a problem. We'll go see Al first thing in the morning."

Chapter 62

Pirates

Washington, D.C.
Next day—Saturday, 27 January 1951

"She made a big mistake mentioning her account in Havana," Hodge said in his office to Erika and Zhanna. "Our people can find that account and it will go a long way with evidence."

"Yes, but how much do we pay her?" Zhanna asked. "I couldn't ask."

"We've seen these payments to traitors range anywhere from a thousand bucks to ten thousand or even more. It all depends on the quality of the information. When we find her account, we'll see the amounts of the latest deposits and use that for reference. But we still need to catch her red-handed. I'll have hidden photographers on hand tonight during the dead drop. Because it will be nighttime, they might not be able to get a clear photo of her face if she's wearing a brimmed hat, but we'll have photos of her clothes. She must have those clothes in her wardrobe at home. That will also add to the evidence, but the key is to find her Leica camera. No one needs a Leica mini camera that takes microfilm images the size of the head of a tack unless they're up to something sneaky."

Erika said, "I can gain entry to the Grainger home when no one is there and search for the camera."

"It might come to that," Hodge said. "I'll let you know. Let's first see how the dead drop goes tonight."

Hodge ended with, "All you Shield Maidens are a pain in the ass, but this has been good work, ladies."

"Thanks, Al," Erika said. "We feel the same about you, including the pain in the ass part. Stop by the Lili Marlene tonight. I'll buy you a drink while we wait for Zhanna to report."

"Why do I think your buying me a drink will end with me shelling out a lot of money like the night you invited me to dinner at that place and took me to the cleaners?"

"That's why I'm inviting you," Erika said. "Don't forget to bring enough money."

[that evening]

It was shortly after 10 p.m. when Zhanna walked into the Lili Marlene. The café was busy. Ryker, Amy, and Susan all worked the bar. Sheila was waiting for Zhanna and took her upstairs where Erika and Hodge sat at a table. A bottle of Asbach was half empty.

"What did I tell you earlier, Reid," Al said. "Lehmann bought me one Scotch for 75¢ then when it was my turn to buy she orders this $20 bottle of brandy.

Sheila smiled. "Imagine that."

"Okay, Rogova," Al said. "Sit down and fill us in."

Zhanna handed him an unopened envelope. "This is what the Grainger woman dropped off. The dead drop went smoothy, but she wore a dark brown Panama hat and keep her head down so I doubt your photographers got a picture of her face."

Hodge opened the envelope. Inside were two small squares of microfilm wrapped in wax paper.

"I'll have our photo department make enlargements of these to verify what we think is on them. We found her Havana account. It's under her maiden name—Agatha Burke. The last few deposits have been $5000. We'll wire that amount to her account. Havana banks are open on Sundays for deposits because of the big hauls of cash from the gambling casinos on Saturday nights. Before we proceed with anything else, I need to see the enlarged microfilm images and the photographs taken of Agatha Grainger tonight. I'll have all that on my desk tomorrow morning. Erika, after the café closes tonight, brief the rest of your team."

"Al, would you buy me a drink?" Zhanna asked. "I'd rather have vodka than brandy."

"You're all a bunch of pirates," Hodge said. "Go ahead and order your vodka, Rogova, but if my electricity gets turned off this month because I can't pay my bill I'll be coming to all of you for a loan."

Chapter 63

The knock comes

Washington, D.C.
Next day—Sunday, 28 January 1951

Al Hodge had had enough. He had gotten word earlier this morning that one of the names on Colonel Howard Grainger's list of faux G-2 agents in Istanbul had been found dead in his car—shot through the temple with a small caliber handgun. Even though the government men in Istanbul had volunteered to pose as bait and were aware of the dangers, this was beyond the pale. If the situation had been reversed and authorities of the United States arrested some Soviets they felt were operatives, they would have been released when it became apparent the men were not a threat and had done nothing wrong.

Erika, Sheila, and Zhanna had just reported to his office. The enlargements of the microfilm revealed the dead man's name. There were also photos from the dead drop. Zhanna had been right. A face could not be clearly seen.

"Change of plans, ladies. An American has been murdered in Istanbul—a man on Grainger's phony field agent list. We're not waiting any longer. It wasn't easy on a Sunday but I got a search warrant for the Grainger home. It's on its way here by courier. When we get it, all of us will be part of the search team. There will also be some FBI agents and Department of Justice people. We have to find that camera. Erika, get in touch with the rest of your team."

"How did the Soviets get the dead man's name?" Sheila asked. "We got the microfilm last night. The Soviets have never seen it."

"They didn't need to see it," Zhanna suddenly spoke up. "They got the name from the first phony agent who disappeared last week. Torture. We were very good at it."

◊ ◊ ◊

The Graingers had just finished a late Sunday morning breakfast. Howard started gathering his golf clubs for an afternoon on the links with some Pentagon colleagues when the knock came.

"I'll get it, Agatha."

When he opened the door, Al Hodge stood there with what seemed like a platoon of men and women behind him.

"Colonel Howard Grainger," Hodge said. "I have here a warrant to search your home issued by the Department of Justice through a circuit court judge." Hodge handed Grainger a copy. "Please have a seat on your couch. Is your wife here?"

"Hodge," Grainger glared. "What the hell is this all about? Are you mad?"

Al ignored him and stepped into the house, followed by the others. Agatha had heard the grumblings of her husband and walked out of the kitchen still wearing an apron. When she saw Zhanna she became light-headed and nearly fainted. An FBI man helped her to the couch and sat her down beside her husband where she regained her wits.

The group scattered out and began searching the house.

"I'm calling General O'Malley," Grainger said. He started to reach for the telephone that sat on the coffee table between the couch and the Windsor chair where Hodge sat.

"If you'll look at the signatures on the warrant," Hodge said. "You'll see the General's name as one of the officials who authorized the search application."

"What are you looking for, Hodge?" Grainger demanded firmly.

"Evidence. The Pentagon mole is sitting beside you."

"You've gone totally out of your damn mind. There will be repercussions for this, Hodge. Severe ones for you and the CIA."

Susan walked out of the bedroom carrying a coat and a Panama hat. She laid the articles of clothing on the coffee table. Hodge handed Grainger a photo.

"This photograph was taken last night at 9:03 p.m. during a dead drop on 34th Street Northwest in Georgetown. As you can see, these items are identical to the ones in the photograph. Was your wife home at that time?"

"Yes! She was here the entire night!" He didn't remember her stepping out to visit a sick friend until after he said it.

"Then let me show you this," Hodge said. He took from his briefcase a bank account statement from the National Bank of Havana. The account was listed under his wife's maiden name and contained $85,000.

Erika suddenly walked out of the kitchen and added the Leica spy camera to the other items of evidence.

"It was wrapped in tin foil and at the bottom of a can of corn starch."

Agatha suddenly blurted out, "I did this for you, my darling—for us. What do you owe the Army? You should have been promoted to general five years ago but kept being passed over for lesser men!"

Everyone heard the admission. The CIA held no arrest powers for civilians so an FBI special agent stepped forward.

"Agatha Grainger," he said. "You are under arrest for espionage against the United States."

She sobbed bitterly as her hands were cuffed behind her back.

Howard Grainger sat there helpless and speechless, not knowing what he would do first—pass out or vomit.

"Colonel," Hodge said as he stood up. "There are no charges against you at this time. Your wife will be held temporarily at the stockade at Fort Dix until the Justice Department decides to move her. I'm truly sorry about all of this, Colonel. Get your wife a good attorney and don't contact the CIA about any of this. We'll tell you nothing. You'll have to work with the FBI. This evidence is theirs now and the case is in the hands of the Department of Justice."

Part 7

Chapter 64

Adelaide would rather wash dishes

Washington, D.C.
Next day—Monday, 29 January 1951

"Agatha Grainger was checked into the Fort Dix stockade last night," Al Hodge said from behind his desk. It was mid-afternoon. All the Maidens, Ryker, and Susan were there. "I turned over all the evidence to the Justice Department and sent a report to the White House stating the case is now in the hands of the FBI. We'll keep records of everything for our own files, of course."

"What a mess," Susan said. "I've known Colonel Grainger since the war. I could see the devastation on his face yesterday when they handcuffed his wife."

"Yeah, it's certainly a tragedy," Hodge replied. "Especially for the families of the men who have disappeared or been killed because of his wife's treason. General O'Malley called me this morning. The colonel is resigning his post and retiring from the military. There's no evidence that he was complicit in any way so he should get his retirement. He'll need it to pay attorney fees for his wife. We froze the account in Havana. Grainger won't have access to the money. It will eventually be confiscated for evidence."

"What will happen to her?" Amy asked.

"The way it usually works is since at least one man was killed that we know of the Justice Department will ask for the death penalty. Then they'll work with her attorneys and offer her a deal. Maybe something like twenty years if she cooperates fully and tells the FBI everything she knows about Gulin's operation. She's fifty-years-old, so twenty years might in itself be a death penalty, but then again she might walk out of prison as an old woman someday."

"Susan," Hodge continued. "Since Agatha Grainger is at Fort Dix, you won't be going back there until the FBI moves her. That's just standard protocol in case you're called to testify. The Justice Department doesn't want any possible contact between a prisoner and a potential witness. You're not CIA and unlike Sheila, you weren't assigned to us. You worked this case for G-2 so I can't protect you from a subpoena like I can everyone else here. You'll stay in the Washington area until your debriefings are over and the Army military police decides where to send you.

"Amy, after debriefings I'm giving you two weeks leave then you'll return to Fort Benning to finish up your logistics training. Ryker, you too will have to remain in Washington for debriefings. Your wife can return to Philly or stay here. That's up to you two.

"Everyone else—Erika, Sheila, and Zhanna—you're stationed in this area so your debriefings are all we have to consider. With all that said, if there aren't any questions, you're all dismissed for now. Debriefings will begin on Wednesday. I'll let you know the times when everything is arranged by our debriefing people."

Zhanna was looking out of the window, trying to spot the bird.

Erika said, "Al, you did a great job as our handler. Stop by the café for a drink some night. We won't stick it to you this time. I promise."

"Yeah, right. I can already feel my wallet getting lighter. Get out of here Lehmann. But to all of you, congratulations. This was a tough case."

[that evening]

Because Rose enjoyed the café, Ryker decided he'd continue working there until his debriefings were over and he and Rose returned to Philadelphia. But he took tonight off. Monday was usually the slowest night at the Lili Marlene. He went out for dinner with Rose.

Sheila stayed at home with Ricky. They had had little time together the past two months.

So tonight is was Erika, Zhanna, and Susan at the café. Zhanna was the only one among the women who got paid by the café. Even though the pay wasn't much, it was a job, and it kept Al Hodge or Leroy Carr from sending her to work in some greasy spoon during mission down times.

Erika sat at the bar. She knew the café would soon be losing all the free help from her other team members. She had already talked to Angelika about hiring another waitress.

"Where's your daughter," Zhanna asked Erika.

"I left her home tonight with the teenaged babysitter who lives in our building. Ada likes her but she gave me a hard time," Erika smiled. "She'd rather be down here helping Bertha and doing dishes. How many kids would rather wash dishes than stay at home and listen to the radio?"

Susan smiled. "None that I know. How about Amy?"

"She said she'd probably drop by for a drink later," Erika responded.

Zhanna asked, "Erika, even though our assignment is finished, I get to keep my job here, right?"

"Yes, Zhanna. I already cleared that with Al. You can work here as long as the place stays open."

"How is the café doing on the books?" Susan asked.

"Angelika has shown a profit for the past three weeks. After expenses it's not a lot, but at least salaries and bills are being paid with a little left over to put in the bank at the end of the month."

"That's great," Susan replied.

"It's too bad we'll be losing Amy soon," Erika added. "But she told me she'd dance this Wednesday."

A man sat down at the other end of the bar and Zhanna left to take his drink order.

Susan said, "You never told me about Amy's background other than she was originally trained by the Israeli Mossad."

"Amy's background is not a happy one. Being half Roma and half Jewish, she and her family had two strikes against them with the Totenkopf-SS. Her family was rounded up in Transylvania and sent to the Sobibor extermination camp in Poland. There Amy watched her parents and younger brother and sister marched into the gas chambers. Because of her beauty, Amy was spared to service the SS. She was raped many times before finally killing a couple of guards and escaping the camp. She finished the war fighting with the Polish resistance hiding in the forests, even in the wintertime.

"Even though she was raised in a Gypsy caravan, being half Jewish gained her citizenship to Israel after that country was formed in 1948. She trained as an assassin for a sub-agency of the Mossad called Kidron."

"How did she end up with the CIA?"

"That's a long story. In a nutshell, the Mossad knew their biggest ally, the U.S., was protecting Axel Ryker. Amy disobeyed Mossad orders and tried to kill Ryker. After that, she couldn't return to the Mossad. Leroy Carr ended up recruiting her into the CIA. The Mossad had to go along."

"It's easy to see there's bad blood between Amy and Ryker," Susan said. "Now I know why."

Erika changed the subject. "So what are your plans, Susan? Long term, I mean. Are you a military lifer?"

"Probably. I've been in ten years now. In another ten I can retire with a decent pension and then do something else if I want to. What about you, Erika? How long are you going to stay in the shadowy world of the spy business?"

"I don't know," Erika answered. "Probably not too much longer. At least that's what I hope." She didn't tell Susan that she had already tried to get out. Like Susan, Erika had been doing what she did for ten years. The first five for Nazi Germany and the last five for the United States. She had long ago surpassed the average life expectancy for an active field agent.

Chapter 65

The way of the Roma

Arlington, Virginia
Two days later—Wednesday, 31 January 1951

Tonight, Amy would dance and the crowd started arriving early. An hour before she was scheduled to appear, all the tables were taken with customers ordering both food and drink. Every bar stool had someone sitting on them and again some people without a place to sit were standing. Ryker, Zhanna, and Susan manned the bar. Erika, Sheila, and Rose waited tables along with Patty. Ada worked happily in the kitchen with Angelika and Bertha.

"Rose. You don't have to do this," Erika told the heiress as they both entered the kitchen to pick up another order of food.

"I enjoy doing it, Erika. By the way, Axel and I would like to treat Susan to lunch tomorrow, but before I ask her, I wanted to make sure you can spare her for an hour or so."

Erika looked at her. "Sure."

"The gift she bought our son for Christmas was so nice of her. It made Axel so happy. We want to thank her."

The Shield Maiden leader who had worked with Ryker for years wondered what being around a happy Axel Ryker would be like. And Rose, who was worth millions, was appreciative. Erika remembered during the confrontation with Gulin's gang on the island how Ryker had shielded Susan with his body, willing to give his life for someone who bought his son a 25 cents toy football.

"Zhanna can easily handle the bar during lunchtime, Rose. And Angelika will be here. Take all the time you need."

After Erika took plates of cheeseburgers and French fries to three men at a table, it looked like everyone had been waited on for the time being so she went upstairs where Amy and her guitarist were preparing.

Amy was already dressed and was doing her makeup while the Roma musician tuned his guitar.

"Javal, probabil asta va fi ultima mea dansă," Erika heard her say to the man in Romanian, which Erika didn't understand except for the man's name—Javal. (Amy had just told Javal this would probably be her last night dancing.)

"De ce? Sfaturile au fost bune," he said. (Why? The tips have been good.)

"Voi continua curând. Este drumul nostru de romi, nu-i aşa?" (I'll be moving on soon. It's our Roma way, is it not?)

Erika noticed the man clearly wasn't happy.

"Is everything okay, Amy?" Erika asked.

"Everything is fine, Erika."

"I just want to thank you for what you've done for the café."

"If you're referring to the dancing, it's a little thing. I was hesitant at first, but I've enjoyed it. It reminds me of happy times with my family before the war when I was a teenager and carefree."

◊ ◊ ◊

Tonight, Amy performed two dances. The first a song of lament, the second of hope. After that she was called out for an encore and performed the lively 'Ciclul vieții'—The circle of life. The dance, like many Roma dances, ending with her twirling madly with her head thrown back and hair whipping.

Javal quickly circulated with his hat. Some of the men had brought cameras and asked Javal if they could get a photograph with Amy. He thought quickly. "That is one dollar," the guitarist told them.

Amy would pose for pictures for almost an hour before she could finally get away to go upstairs and change.

◊ ◊ ◊

About an hour after the dance, some people had left but many others remained. It looked like it'd be another late night at the Lili Marlene. About that time, Svetlana and her husband walked in, spotted Zhanna, and approached the bar. A few bar stools had been given up, so the Brunnells were able to sit.

"Zhanna," Svetlana said as she leaned over the bar to exchange the customary kissing of cheeks. "James and I came by earlier but we couldn't get near the place. People were waiting outside to get in and there wasn't any parking for blocks."

"We had a dancer tonight," Zhanna replied. "She's become popular here at the café. How are you, Svetlana? What can I get you and your husband to drink?"

"We're doing fine, Zhanna. I'll have a vodka martini."

James Brunnell ordered a Yuengling.

"Zhanna," Svetlana said before their bartender walked away to prepare the drinks. "James got word today that his permanent promotion to Lietenant Colonel Reid's Polish department was approved."

James interjected, "I have to undergo some training first."

"Yes, but it is official," Svetlana said to Zhanna. "And it comes with a nice raise in salary."

"That's good for you if that's what you want," Zhanna said.

Svetlana Urashova said, "You saved my life during the war and I hope we can continue to be friends, Zhanna. We can go shopping, or James can take us to dinner once in awhile—things like that."

"That would be nice, Svetlana. I'm glad you stopped in. Now, I'll get your drinks and run you a tab." Zhanna looked at James. "And don't forget my tip at the end of the night."

Chapter 66

A job offer

Washington, D.C.
Next day—Thursday, 01 February 1951

It was the second day of debriefings. These interrogations usually lasted from four to five hours each day and included polygraph tests during some segments. How many days the process took depended on the complexity of each mission. The mission just completed had been grueling, frustrating, and time consuming. Erika had been through an untold number of post-mission examinations, both with the German Abwehr and the CIA. She was sure that these sessions would take them into early next week.

Each team member met with a different inquisitor without other team members on hand, and at various times of the day.

Today, before her 10 a.m. time to start session two, Erika called on Al Hodge in his office.

"Al, what time is Susan's debriefing scheduled to start today?"

Hodge had to check his paperwork. "She's already started—8 a.m. was her report time."

"Then she should be done by lunchtime."

"Maybe. Maybe not. Why do you ask?"

"Axel and Rose want to take her to lunch today."

Hodge paused and glanced at her. "Why?"

"They want to thank Susan for buying their son a Christmas present."

He shrugged. "I don't see a problem with that."

Erika said, "I told Rose last night that Susan would be available. Just checking with you to make sure I didn't mess that up. Any more developments with the Grainger case?"

"It's not in our hands anymore, Erika. All I know is that Agatha is still at Fort Dix. The only news I can give you is that I called Marienne Schenck yesterday and thanked her for her help and told her to submit her expenses and I'd make sure the disbursement department sends that to her along with her pay."

"I called and thanked her, too, Al. I think it was on Tuesday."

Hodge remember something else. "Oh, the prostitute, Olive, is still at the nunnery in Paterson but our placement people think they have found her a foster home with a Negro family in Syracuse. Both the mother and father are teachers at a Negro high school there. The mother is a math teacher, and the father is a gym teacher and the head football coach. It will be a good place for Olive to turn her life around. At least she'll get the opportunity."

"That's great, Al. I'd like to be updated about her progress along the way."

"Fine. You can check with our placement people whenever you like. By the way. Leroy is scheduled to return from Korea next week then I'll be out of here. I'm already three weeks late reporting for the spring semester at Brown. The chancellor had to hire a retired professor to handle my classes until I return. Now, if that's it, you better report downstairs for your debriefing. It's almost ten."

"Just one more thing," she said. "Do you know the name of the man that Axel hired to guard his family? I'm just curious."

"Leave that one alone, Erika. I don't want you digging into that."

[noon]

To Susan's surprise, lunch would be held in the Ryker's deluxe suite at the Mayflower Hotel. It was the finest hotel in Washington and the Rykers occupied one of its largest suites with three bedrooms, a study, and an entertainment area large enough to host a sizeable party. Rose opened the door after Susan knocked. Susan hadn't been told where lunch would be held. Rose had only mentioned to call on them at their suite. Because of this uncertainty, Susan wasn't sure what attire would be suitable so she wore her Army uniform, which was acceptable at any restaurant.

"Susan," Rose said as she held her son. "Please come in."

Ryker was sitting on the couch. Already laid out on a large cherrywood table near the window that looked out on Connecticut

Avenue was an iced bottle of Chateau Margaux and a large assortment of expensive hors d'oeuvres including caviar, goose liver foie gras on unleavened sour dough crackers, escargot pate, and various imported blocks of cheeses. A bowl of wild-grown huckleberry jam from the mountains of Idaho sat beside more sour dough crackers near the cheeses.

A young woman who looked to be 25 or so emerged from the study alongside a handsome man who looked to be in his early 30s.

"Susan," Rose said. "This is our nanny, Matilda. And this is Klaus, an old friend of my husband."

Susan guessed Klaus to be about 6'2" tall. He could have posed on one of Josef Goebbels propaganda posters as the perfect Aryan superman.

"How do you do?" Susan said to them both.

The nanny curtsied and smiled politely. Klaus nodded and said with a German accent, "Madam, it is my honor."

"Klaus and Matilda will be eating downstairs in the hotel restaurant," Rose added.

After the nanny and bodyguard left, Rose said, "Help yourself to the hors d'oeuvres, Susan. Axel, why don't you pour Susan a glass of Champagne?"

Ryker rose from the sofa and poured both Susan and his wife a flute from the $300 bottle of vintage Chateau Margaux.

Rose said, "Susan, I hope you like rack of lamb. It takes time to prepare so I took the liberty of ordering us one earlier, before you arrived."

"That sounds wonderful, Rose," Susan said. "It also sounds like a lot of food for a lunch with what you already have here."

"What we don't eat, I'll ask room service to box up. You can take it to the ladies at the café."

As they waited for the entrée to be delivered, they drank the wine and sampled the hors d'oeuvres.

Axel Ryker, who had yet to say a word, lit a cigar. He finally spoke.

"Captain Wedeking. How would you feel about leaving the Army and working for my wife as her companion/bodyguard? Rose feels uncomfortable with Klaus filling that position. She'd feel more comfortable with a female performing that duty. I feel your training as a police officer and the courage you displayed while being captured makes you qualified."

Rose interjected, "Susan, I'm sure we can give you a raise from your current Army pay plus health care. Plus, you can live in one of the lake houses on my father's estate free of charge."

This was all quite a shocker for Susan.

"That's a gracious offer, Rose and Axel, but I'd feel badly if I took someone's job away from them."

"You would not be taking Klaus's job," Ryker said. "He has many other duties. I have to be away from the estate during missions. I hired Klaus to be in charge of security for all of the Bristows and the estate. I had to take him away from those other duties when Rose decided that she and our son would join me in Washington. Your duties would apply only to Rose and our son."

"I'm pretty well settled in with the military," Susan added. "But I do thank both of you for your confidence in me."

"Before a final 'no', please think it over," Rose pleaded. "Mother and I are vacationing in Monte Carlo next month for ten days. I'd love to have you with us—all expenses paid plus your salary, of course."

Chapter 67

Surprise visit from former associates

Arlington, Virginia
Next day—Friday, 02 February 1951

The café wasn't packed as it had been when Amy performed, but it enjoyed a good Friday night crowd. Erika, Sheila, and Susan sat together at a table.

Susan had just told them about the job offer from Axel and Rose.

"What does this 'Klaus' look like?" Erika asked.

Because of her police training, Susan was able to supply a detailed description. "Early 30s, about 6'2", a muscular 200 pounds, dusty-blond hair, blue eyes. Spoke with a German accent. A good-looking guy."

"No last name?" Erika asked.

"Rose introduced him only as Klaus. I was in his presence maybe forty seconds, forty-five tops. Asking for his last name in that situation would have been inappropriate."

Erika nodded.

"Are you going to take the job, Susan?" Sheila asked.

"I told them 'no' but Rose asked me to think it over. I know traveling with Rose to places like Monte Carlo sounds exciting on paper, but I think my course is set. I told Erika the other day that I have ten years left before I can take my military pension. I'll be 41 then and free to do something else, or if I watch my expenses I can just kick back and be a slob."

Sheila laughed. Erika was still thinking about Klaus. But when two men walked into the café her questions about the Bristow estate's head of security vanished as her jaw dropped. A man wearing a checkered hat, and a short, overweight man had just walked into the café.

Erika immediately rose from her chair and rushed over to hug both men.

◊ ◊ ◊

Ten minutes later, Erika sat alone upstairs with Eugene 'Checkers' Smaldone, the head of Denver's organized crime family, and Paul 'Fat Paulie' Villano, the family's chief enforcer.

"I can't believe you're here," Erika said.

"You called me and said you're having troubles," Checkers said. "I told you that you can count on my help. And Paulie and I wanted to check out your operation." How Checkers picked up that moniker was always an item of disparity among those who knew him. Some said that he loved playing the board game as a child. Others thought it was because of the checkered houndstooth hat he always wore.

"I saw Zhanna and that fucking jerk, Ryker, at the bar," Checkers continued. "Who are the women sitting with you at the table when we came in?"

"The red head is Sheila Reid. The blonde is Susan Wedeking. Both are friends."

Fat Paulie asked in his terrible grammar, "Hows about the broad behind the bar that looks like a Turk. I hates Turks."

"That's Amy Radu, Paulie. She's not from Turkey. She's from Romania."

"How far is that from Turkey?" Paulie asked.

"Quit showing how stupid you are," Checkers said to his top henchman. "Look it up on a map."

"Everyone who works here can be trusted," she said to both men.

"Be sure of that, Erika," Checkers said, "or you'll have more booze going out the backdoor than you'll have being sold. Employees ripping off hooch and sticky fingering the cash register has sunk a lot of bars and restaurants."

"I'm sure I'm in good shape in that regard, Checkers."

Ada knocked on the door and entered with menus. The Smaldone family had never met Erika's daughter, although they knew she had one.

"Checkers and Paulie," Erika said, "this is my daughter, Adelaide. We call her Ada."

"What the fuck!" Paulie exclaimed. "She looks like she just fell out of your butt, Erika."

Checkers admonished him. "Paulie! We have a child in the room. What's wrong with you?"

Paulie realized his mistake. He said to Ada, "Excuse my French, Little Miss. Here, sweetheart, take this." He handed her a ten-dollar bill. "Just call me Uncle Paulie. Thanks for the menus."

Erika said, "I appreciate that you're here. Let me order your dinners. They're on me. I can't count how many dinners you bought me at Gaetano's. We feature one German meal each day. Tonight it's Sauerbraten. I know you'll like it. It's a beef dish.

"Ada, tell Bertha we'll have three Sauerbraten specials. I'll come downstairs and bring them up when they're ready."

"Yes, Mutti," Ada said.

After Ada left the room, Checkers addressed business. "I contacted the top underboss in the Gambino family in New York. They don't like these Russians setting up shop at different places around the country any more than I do."

He continued. "The Russians are a small, loosely knit group now. We don't want it to go beyond that. The Gambinos have their own problems right now—mostly legal, so I told them we would take care of this ourselves. I'm having a sit-down tomorrow with this Lukov character who has been trying to strong-arm you."

"Thanks, Checkers. I told Lukov I would pay him a fair price for the dartboards, jukebox, and the pinball machines. They were used when they brought them here, not new. Let me know the amount."

Fat Paulie started laughing.

Chapter 68

Mary

Washington, D.C.
Next day—Saturday, 03 February 1951

Checkers Smaldone and Paul Villano met with Dima Lukov and one of his men for lunch at the Old Ebbitt Grill on 15th NW. The restaurant was accustomed to serving clientele that included presidents dating all the way back to Ulysses S. Grant, senators, congressman, Supreme Court justices, cabinet members and others of the most powerful figures in America. It now hosted at one of its tables four mobsters.

The steaks had been delivered and bites taken. Business had already been discussed concerning the Lili Marlene Café.

"Then you understand our agreement," Checkers said to Lukov.

"I understand what you want, but I don't agree," Lukov said. "With the Gambinos and the other New York and New Jersey families backing you, I have no choice but to put aside payoffs from my machines, but I want to be paid for my equipment."

Fat Paulie glared. "Your payoff is you get to keep operating in this area as long as you don't expand, and you get to keep breathing, you commie bastard. Take it or leave it."

Checkers ended it with, "If you or your men bother Erika or anyone at that café again, my friend Paul here and his crew will call on you and they won't arrive in a good mood." Checkers handed Lukov the food bill. "I appreciate the lunch. Don't forget to leave the waitress a good tip."

Checkers and Paulie handed Lukov another gangland insult by rising from the table and walking out in the middle of the meal.

[same time—Lili Marlene]

"Have you given Rose and Ryker your final decision about the job?" Erika asked Susan as they sat at the bar. Zhanna stood near them on the other side.

"I thanked Rose but told her I'm staying in the Army. I don't think being an escort for an heiress is for me. It was a nice offer, though."

"What about the man who is always coming by here to see you?" Zhanna asked.

"Stan Gregory," Susan said. "He asked me out to a movie. I told him I didn't know how much longer I'd be in this area, but I agreed to go to a movie with him."

Erika looked at the clock behind the bar.

"I have to leave for a couple of hours, girls. I'll be back. Checkers and Paulie are coming by tonight for poker."

◊ ◊ ◊

Erika found a game store that sold decks of cards and what were advertised as 'recreational' poker chips 'not to be used for monetary gambling.' Caveats clearly meant to extricate the manufacturer and seller from legal hassles.

She now sat in Al Hodge's office.

"Al, I want to know who this 'Klaus' is who works for Ryker protecting the Bristows."

"Erika, I told you to drop it."

"Come on, Al. You know I'll find out on my own if you don't tell me."

Hodge sat back in his chair and grumbled something under his breath.

"His name is Klaus Vogel. He was Liebstandarte-SS during the war, assigned as one of Hitler's personal bodyguards."

"My husband Kai—and Ada's father—was Liebstandarte."

"I know he was, Erika. But if you're wondering if Vogel ever met your husband, that question has already been asked of Vogel by Leroy. Klaus and Kai never met. When Vogel was with Hitler, Kai was one of Otto Skorzeny's commandos."

"What's Vogel's connection to Ryker? Axel was Gestapo."

"They met a few times at the Berghof when Himmler would come calling on Hitler. Apparently, some of Hitler's SS bodyguards and Himmler's Gestapo henchmen had lunch together a couple of times while they waited for Hitler and Himmler to finish their business in Hitler's study."

"I bet that was fun for Vogel. I ate lunch with the Gestapo once," Erika said. "The three men at my table had the temperaments of sewer rats."

Hodge continued. "Unlike Ryker, there are no war crime indictments on Vogel. He underwent the de-Nazification program in Hamburg and he's in this country legally, so Leroy gave his okay when Ryker approached him about it several months ago. Archibald Bristow, the family patriarch, doesn't know of Vogel's background with Hitler and you're to keep it that way."

"I would never tell Rose or any of the Bristows. What good would that do?"

"No good at all."

Erika stood up to leave. "Al, try to stop by the café tonight. Checkers Smaldone and Paul Villano are in town. They'll be there tonight. We're playing poker upstairs. Come by and have a drink."

"What in the hell are they doing here?"

"They found out I have a small restaurant. They had business in New York so on their way back to Denver they detoured down here and dropped by last night." It was mostly true. Erika simply took a bit of artistic license with her answer.

[that evening]

Al Hodge did decide to stop by the Lili Marlene but his reason wasn't to see the Denver mobsters who would not arrive until later. He had a woman with him and he brought her there for dinner. Hodge was a widower, his only wife having died from tuberculosis in the late-30s. The middle-aged Hodge had dated infrequently since then, the dates rarely lasting past the first one.

Erika came over to their table but did not sit down, not wanting to intrude.

"Hi, Al," she said.

"Mary, this is Erika, a colleague of mine at the State Department. Erika, this is Mary. She's a waitress at the Hamilton Diner."

"I knew I recognized you, Mary," Erika said. "Al and I have had business breakfasts at the Hamilton several times."

Mary was a pleasant-looking brunette who looked to be about the same age as Al. Her Navy husband had been killed at Pearl Harbor, leaving her with two young children to support. Her children were now teenagers.

"It's nice to meet you, Erika," she said. "I also remember you from the diner."

"Have you decided on what you want for dinner?" Erika asked.

"Not yet," Hodge said. "We haven't looked at the menu."

"I'll send Patty over for your drink orders, and she'll take your food orders when you're ready."

Erika excused herself then walked away, finding Patty waiting at the bar for a drink order.

"Patty," Erika said. "The man and woman at table four. Take good care of them. When they finish, give me their bill. I'll pay for it."

Chapter 69

Fat Paulie figures out his fortune

The Lili Marlene Café
Same evening—Saturday, 03 February 1951

Al Hodge and Mary finished their dinner and had left the café nearly an hour before Checkers and Paulie arrived. The free meal and drinks surprised Al. He had looked around, intending to thank Erika but he didn't find her. She was already upstairs with Amy preparing the room for the poker game.

The players tonight would be Checkers and Paulie, Erika, Zhanna, Amy, and Ryker. It was agreed upon by Sheila and Susan that as military officers, playing poker with mobsters was not something they should have on their resumes. Susan and Angelika would handle the bar. Sheila and Rose would help Patty wait tables.

Zhanna and Ryker had played poker with the Smaldones and their crews in Denver and knew how things worked. Amy had not, so Erika schooled her as they set up plates and utensils for the food.

"Amy, you know how to play poker, right?" Erika asked.

"Erika, I'm Roma. We learned about every game of chance there is when we parked our caravan outside a town and the townsmen would come to the camp at night for the dances, fortune telling, and gambling. Poker is similar in ways to a card game we call Tute. Yes, I know how to play poker."

"Okay, good," Erika said. "But the Smaldones don't play for nickels and dimes. Watch your money."

"I'm using my tip money from my dances. If I lose that, I'm just losing found money, but thanks for the warning."

Erika looked at Amy, saw the confidence in her eyes, and then smiled. "I must look pretty silly coaching a Roma how to gamble."

Amy grinned.

◊ ◊ ◊

Checkers and Fat Paulie walked in just before 9 p.m. Erika took them directly through the kitchen and upstairs.

A long table of food and bottles of alcohol were set up on a wooden table alongside a wall. The round table, which would be used for the game, sat in the middle of the room.

"We don't serve Gaetano's delicious Italian food here," Erika told the two men. "But we have an excellent German cook. She's made us several German favorites tonight. We've got German meatballs, and Weisswurst, which is a white sausage made from veal that is very popular in Munich, where I come from. Try the Weisswurst dipped in the sweet mustard. That's the way we eat in in Bavaria. Bertha also made some homemade Fleischsalat and Obatzda."

"Sounds like youse is talking Swahili, Erika," Fat Paulie said. "I don't know what any of that shit means but let me at it." Paulie poured himself a dram of Scotch and began loading a plate with food.

As they waited for Fat Paulie to finish his assault on the food table, Checkers told Erika, "I met with Lukov today. We came to an understanding. He won't be bothering you anymore."

"Thanks, Checkers. How much do I owe him for the equipment?"

"Nothing. He decided to donate it to help you get started."

Erika looked at him. "Checkers, you've always been good to me."

Paulie finally finished loading his plate and walked over. "Who's playing cards tonight?" he asked Erika.

"You know everyone except Amy Radu," she said.

"That Turk is playing? I told you I don't like Turks."

"She's not a Turk, Paulie. I told you yesterday she's Romanian. In fact, Amy is a Roma—what most people call Gypsies."

"A Gypsy," Paulie said. "No shit? I've never met a real Gypsy. Can she tell my fortune?"

Erika grinned. "I'm sure she can for a price. They don't tell fortunes for nothing, you know." The rest of the players filtered upstairs one by one. Most got food first. When Ryker walked in, Paulie said, "Hey, there's the big fucking jerk. How ya doin' you fucking jerk?"

Ryker walked over and put out his cigar in Paulie's drink. Paulie draw his handgun when Checkers stopped him.

"This is Erika's place, Paulie," the boss said. "You can't disrespect it."

"The fuck put out his cigar in my drink!"

"And you started it by busting balls," The Denver don retorted.

Erika brought Amy over, which at least distracted Paulie from Ryker.

"Checkers and Paulie, this is Amy Radu, one of our bartenders."

"You're sure a looker," Paulie said. "I thought youse were one of those damn Turks but Erika says youse is a Gypsy from Rochester."

"Romania," Amy corrected his malapropism. She had long ago given up telling people that Gypsies didn't particularly like that moniker, preferring Roma. But it was a losing battle and she knew most didn't use 'Gypsy' to offend.

"Erika, are we here to play poker or bullshit all night?" Checkers asked.

"Alright, let's get started," Erika told everyone. "White chips are $1; red chips $5; and blue chips $10. It's dealer's choice of games with standard rules. Dealing will alternate to the left with the cut to the right. Two-dollar ante. No wild cards."

As Erika handed out chips depending on how much money each player put up, Checkers asked, "So Zhanna, how have you been?"

"Fine. Can I have one of your cigars?"

Checkers handed one over and Zhanna lit up.

As far as the gamblers among the CIA team, Erika was good at it. Zhanna was terrible, usually taking only a few hands to lose her stake. Ryker could hold his own—sometimes winning, sometimes losing. How Amy handled herself was yet to be seen.

Everyone chose a card from the facedown, spread-out deck. Amy drew the Queen of Spades, the highest card drawn so the first deal went to her.

Everyone watched in amazement as she performed fancy shuffling maneuvers worthy of any professional croupier.

"Checkers," Paulie said as they watched Amy shuffle like a magician. "I think I already know my fortune from this Gypsy. I lose my balls tonight. That's my fortune."

Epilogue

Although Susan Wedeking turned down the job offer from Rose Bristow, the MP captain still got her trip to Monte Carlo. Susan had leave time built-up and Rose insisted she go with her and her mother as their guest. It was just the three of them plus the baby and the young nanny. Axel Ryker asked Susan to keep an eye on his family during the trip and Susan agreed. When Susan returned from overseas, her military police supervisors transferred her to Fort Knox, Kentucky.

◊ ◊ ◊

Sheila Reid returned to her duties at the Pentagon, and Amy Radu returned to Fort Benning to finish her classes. Amy told Al Hodge she would take the two-week leave that he had promised her when her classes were completed.

◊ ◊ ◊

Zhanna, happy to have a job at the Lili Marlene after all her previous failures at civilian jobs, worked contently, never begrudging her fellow Shield Maidens who held down important government jobs in between missions.

◊ ◊ ◊

Erika was saddened when everyone split up, but she was exhausted from the mission and welcomed the hiatus. She was glad she had bought the café for Angelika. It was a small place and Erika knew she'd never get rich from it by any means, but it was doing better as time moved on and it was a place she could bring and be with her daughter who Erika had been away from for most of the child's life. If the next mission took Erika out of the country, she could trust Angelika to get Ada to school, keep the child happily busy at the café when not at school, and Ada could stay with Angelika in the small apartment over the café at night.

◊ ◊ ◊

As far as the poker game with Checkers and Paulie, Amy cleared $480. Erika won a paltry $15. Everyone else lost in various amounts with Paulie being the biggest loser. The Smaldone family enforcer proved right in his prediction about his fortune at the hands of the Gypsy.

{Note: for more details about the history between Erika and the Smaldones, read *A New Valhalla* and *Upstairs at Gaetano's* by this author.}

The Erika Lehmann Spy Series

Book 1: ***Invitation to Valhalla***
Book 2: ***Blood of the Reich***
Book 3: ***Return to Valhalla***
Book 4: ***Fall from Valhalla***
Book 5: ***Operation Shield Maidens***
Book 6: ***Hope for Valhalla***
Book 7: ***Search for Valhalla***
Book 8: ***A New Valhalla***
Book 9: ***Shield Maidens Return***
Book 10: ***Valhalla Won***
Book 11: ***Cliffs of Valhalla***
Book 12: ***Smoketown Legend***
Book 13: ***Farewell Valhalla***
Book 14: ***Singing with Wolves***
Book 15: ***Upstairs at Gaetano's***
Book 16: ***Nighttime in Berlin***
Book 17: ***Dancing for the Gestapo***
Book 18: ***Intrigue at the Lili Marlene Café***
Book 19: ***American She-Wolf***
Book 20: ***Roma***
Book 21: ***Children of the Night***
Book 22: ***Evansville's Finest Hour***
Book 23: ***Black Witch***
Book 24: ***The Parlor***
Book 25: ***Lessons from Transylvania***
Book 26: ***Valentin's Secret***
Book 27: ***Beads of God***
Book 28: ***Chabine***
Book 29: ***Erika's Ghosts***
Book 30: ***Forging a Shield Maiden***

Other books by Mike Whicker:

Krozel (a novel)
Proper Suda (a novel)
Flowers for Hitler: The Extraordinary Life of Ilse Dorsch (a true-life biography)

***All books available on Amazon.com as print copies or Kindle e-books**

Author welcomes reader comments.
Email: **mikewhicker@hotmail.com**

Mike Whicker is also on Facebook

Historical Note

The Western Allies intelligence communities displayed no qualms about bringing Nazis into their clandestine societies after WW II.

During the Cold War, both the CIA and British MI6 made use of Nazis (some who were boldly unrepentant). Records show both organizations went out of their way to recruit Nazi agents if the Germans could offer experience or expertise in working against the Russians. The CIA not only maintained a close working relationship with Reinhard Gehlen, they helped him set up shop. During the war, Gehlen served as the German Army's intelligence chief for the Eastern Front. With protection from the United States after the war, Gehlen assembled a large intelligence organization staffed with numerous ex-Nazis and known war criminals—at least 100 of Gehlen's operatives were former SS/SD officers or Gestapo agents. Gehlen's organization eventually became the official West German intelligence agency—the BND.

Records from the National Security Archive of George Washington University show that at least five associates of the notorious Nazi Adolf Eichmann worked for the CIA and 23 other Nazis were approached by the CIA for recruitment.

The Russians weren't ones to be left behind. The East German Secret Police the Soviets established after the war was filled with former Gestapo, SS, and SD agents.

Acknowledgements

A grateful thanks to Susan Wedeking Gregory for all her help with proofreading, editing, and her always dependable good advice. And thanks to Josh and Erin Whicker for their pointed suggestions.

www.ingramcontent.com/pod-product-compliance
Lightning Source LLC
LaVergne TN
LVHW091041080826
845145LV00002B/580

* 9 7 8 1 7 3 5 6 0 9 8 2 9 *